# FATEFUL

Also by Claudia Gray

*Evernight*

*Stargazer*

*Hourglass*

*Afterlife*

CLAUDIA GRAY

HARPER TEEN

*An Imprint of* HarperCollins*Publishers*

HarperTeen is an imprint of HarperCollins Publishers.

Fateful

Copyright © 2011 by Amy Vincent

Library of Congress Cataloging-in-Publication Data
Gray, Claudia.
    Fateful / Claudia Gray. — 1st ed.
       p.    cm.
    Summary: When seventeen-year-old Tess Davies, a ladies' maid, meets handsome
Alec Marlow aboard the RMS *Titanic*, she quickly becomes entangled in the dark secrets
of his past, but her growing love puts her in mortal peril even before fate steps in.
    ISBN 978-0-06-200620-2 (trade bdg.) — ISBN 978-0-06-211419-8 (int'l ed.)
    1. Titanic (Steamship)—Juvenile fiction. [1. Titanic (Steamship)—Fiction.
2. Love—Fiction.  3. Secrets—Fiction.  4. Werewolves—Fiction.  5. Supernatural—
Fiction.]  I. Title.
PZ7.G77625Fat  2011                              2011009160
[Fic]—dc22                                         CIP
                                                      AC

Typography by Andrea Vandergrift
11 12 13 14 15  LP/BV  10 9 8 7 6 5 4 3 2 1
❖
First Edition

# ⊰ CHAPTER 1 ⊱

*APRIL 9, 1912*

*It's not too late to turn back*, I tell myself.

As a group of sailors leer at me, I cross my arms in front and wish my coat weren't so shabby. Though the spring days are warm now, the nights are cool, and the sea-sharpened wind cuts through thin cloth.

The streets of Southampton darken as the hour grows late, not that I can see the sun or anything so cheery with all these tall buildings surrounding me. My feet, accustomed to either the dirt roads of my home village or the polished floors of Moorcliffe, stumble on the cobblestones. I like to think of myself as a steady sort of girl, but the unfamiliarity of everyone and everything around me has put me off balance. The city seems dangerous, and dusk here seems more forbidding than midnight at home.

I could go back to the hotel suite, where my employers await. I could just say that the shop was closed, that I wasn't able to purchase the bootlaces. Miss Irene wouldn't mind a bit; she didn't want to send me out on my own in the first place.

But Lady Regina would be furious—even over something as trivial as my not being able to purchase extra bootlaces for the trip. Lady Regina's fury would spill over into Mrs. Horne's punishment. I'm afraid of being out in a city on my own, but I'm more afraid of getting sacked before I reach America.

So I square my shoulders and hurry along the road. My servant's dress, long and black, complete with white apron and puffy linen cap, marks me as lower class and insignificant. But it also says that I am employed by a household wealthy enough to have servants run the errands. Maybe that keeps me safe. The men around me know that I work for people of quality, and that if anything were to happen to me, those people might be upset and demand justice.

Luckily, these men don't know Lady Regina. Her only reaction to my death would be annoyance at having to find another maid who could fit in the same uniforms, so she wouldn't have to pay for new ones.

Something dark swoops overhead—a seagull, I think, and I lift one hand above my head to ward it off. I never saw a gull before this afternoon, and already I've come to despise the loud, greedy things.

But it's not a seagull. I don't get a very good look at it, fast as it goes by, but I see the sharp angles of the wings, the quick flutter. It's a bat, I think. Even worse. That reminds me of the gothic novels I've sneaked peeks at in the Lisle family library— *Frankenstein* and *Dracula* and *Udolpho*, all the scary ones that were so much fun to read in a warm, well-lit room but seem far too plausible when I'm alone as darkness falls.

I wouldn't have expected to see a bat flying through the streets of Southampton, but then, what do I know of the world beyond Moorcliffe and my home village? Only once before in my life have I ever been anywhere else—and that but for a day, just because Daisy needed me very badly.

And now I am planning a greater journey yet—

*You mustn't think of such things right now. You can worry about all that after you get on the ship.*

*After it's too late to turn back.*

Resolutely I continue on my path toward the shop. The sailors thin out a bit, though the streets still seem crowded to me. I know I've got to get used to it, because we're traveling to New York City, which I understand makes Southampton look like a small town.

All the same, it's a relief to turn off the main road and take what I hope is a shortcut toward the shop. This alleyway is so old and worn down by time that the stones dip into a V in the center, and my hobnail shoes make me clumsy as I continue on my way. Oh, for a pair of Miss Irene's dove-gray boots, of such soft leather they would never blister, and light on the feet instead of heavy—

The bat swoops overhead again, so close I think it's diving for my cap.

Though I feel a chill, I don't let my imagination run away with me; instead, I focus on the practicalities and clutch my cap to my head. If some fool bat steals part of my uniform, the Lisles will make me pay for a new one.

What time is it? No telling—I've never owned anything so fancy as a wristwatch, and there's no church tower clock to be seen here. Surely no shop will be open at this hour, but Lady Regina has it in her head that things are done differently in cities. I take heart as I turn a corner and see a group of men walking along—not ruffians like the sailors, but gentlemen in fine hats and coats. They won't bother me.

I hasten my steps so that I'll fall in only a few feet behind them. They seem to be heading toward the shop, if I've understood the directions the hotel concierge rather brusquely gave me. That gives me a little protection for the last bit of my journey. Breathing easier, I let my mind wander to tomorrow's voyage—my first-ever glimpse of the ocean, my first-ever time to leave England—

And, if I have my way, the last I shall ever see of my home country—

"You like to eavesdrop."

Caught off guard, I look up at the gentleman who has turned to face me. He, and all the others in his group, have stopped in their tracks. I drop a quick curtsy. "No, sir. I wasn't listening, sir. I beg your pardon, sir." That's the truth, too: One of the first things you learn, as a servant, is how to ignore conversations you don't care to hear. Otherwise you'd go half-mad with boredom.

In the twilight shadows, I can't quite make out his features— only the dark spade of his Vandyke beard against his too-pale skin, and the uncanny glint in his eyes. His expensive pocket watch, worth more than ten years' of my salary, dangles from a fob, oddly scratched for something so priceless. He tilts his head slightly as he studies me. "You beg, you say."

"Beg your pardon, sir," I repeat, and hurry past them without

4

waiting to be excused. Normally I'd never be so rude to gentlemen, but these are strangers, and probably they hoped to amuse themselves by making me grovel. I'm in a hurry, thank you very much.

I cast one worried glance behind me, expecting to see them either laughing at me or already on their way. Instead, they're all gone. As if they had vanished.

Unnerved, I try to remember what they said that they were so displeased I might have overheard—though I was paying them no mind, I can recall a few words and phrases now. "Valuable influence," they said. And "must be close by." A name: "Marlowe." And something about "let him know he's being watched."

That does sound a bit suspicious, but surely they know, whatever it is they're up to, there's nothing any servant girl could do to stop them.

I try to refocus on my errand. Where was I supposed to take that last turn? Is this the name of the street? I can find no signs. It can't be more than ten minutes until nightfall, and finding my way home after dark will be difficult.

Then I hear footsteps, heavy and distinct. Coming closer.

I look behind me but can see no one. The footsteps are coming from some other angle, one I can't see. So probably whoever is coming can't see me either and is headed in this direction by no more than coincidence. But it unnerves me for no reason I can name. I turn to continue on my way, then gasp as I realize I am no longer alone.

A man is standing with me in the alley—not one of the frightening group from a few moments ago, but a young man, perhaps only a few years older than I am. He has the rich chestnut curls of a poet and the broad shoulders of a farmhand. His eyes are those of a hunted criminal.

Was it his footsteps I heard? Impossible—they were from another direction. And he too is looking into the not-so-distant dark. His alarm is greater than my own.

"Come with me," he says.

"I beg your pardon, sir, but I can't." Does he take me for a streetwalker? How horrifying. And yet he looks well-bred in his handsome suit and gleaming shoes; surely he must recognize what my uniform means. "I've an errand to run—"

"Damn your errand." His voice is rough, his broad hand tense as it closes around my upper arm. "If you don't come with me now, you're dead."

Is he threatening me? It sounds like it, and feels like it too from the rough way he drags me along with him as he starts walking quickly through the alley back toward the main street. And yet I don't believe that's what is happening here. Whatever's happening is something I don't understand.

"Sir," I protest. "Let me go. I can find my way to the main road on my own."

"You'll be dead before you go ten steps without me." His hand is warm as it clasps my arm—more than warm, hot. As if he burned with fever. I can hear our pursuers coming closer. "Stay by my side and walk faster. And for the love of God, don't look back."

I wonder that he doesn't suggest we run, but I realize that it's all he can do to walk himself—he's almost staggering, and not in the way Layton Lisle does after he's downed two bottles of wine. It's as though the man is in pain. And yet his fingers dig into my flesh with an almost unnatural strength.

The steps behind us change. No longer do they sound like footsteps. Instead they're softer—and yet they click upon the cobblestones—

As I'm unable to wrest myself free from my captor, I defy him by looking back. And there I see the wolf.

The scream rips through my throat even as the dark wolf pounces, its enormous body seeming to black out the last light of the day. I'm pulled to the side just in time by the young man, who slams me against the wall of the nearest building and flattens his body against mine, his back to my front.

"What's happening?" I gasp. Wolves attacking in the middle of the city? And this—this enormous black creature, snarling as it paces back and forth—I had never imagined a wolf could be so large.

"Leave us," the young man says, as if the wolf could understand. "Leave us now!"

The wolf cocks its head—not like an inquisitive dog, but an almost human gesture. Its teeth are still bared, hot saliva dripping from its jaws. A deep growl rumbles through its chest, and its golden eyes seem to be locked on me, not the man guarding me.

"Go now!" The young man sounds desperate now, as well he might. I can feel the hard, quick rise and fall of his chest against me with every ragged breath, and his muscles are taut beneath my palms braced against his shoulders.

And yet somehow, it works. The wolf simply lopes away.

"What in the world was that?" I say as my rescuer slumps forward. "It looked to be a wolf."

"It was." He sounds exhausted.

"But why would a wolf—" Be here in Southampton, find his way to an inner alley instead of preying on people and animals he would have had to pass on the way, and give up when spoken to sharply? None of it makes any sense. But I know what I saw, and what this man did for me. "Thank you, sir. For your kind help."

When I look back at him, though, he doesn't look pleased. He looks crueler than the wolf ever did.

"Leave me," he says. His eyes have that uncanny glint to them again, though now he looks less hunted. More criminal. "If you don't leave me now, you're dead."

I can't tell if he's warning me or threatening me. Either way, I don't have to be told twice. I run out of the alleyway toward the shop, not looking back once until I reach the store's door. It is, of course, closed.

All the way back to the hotel, and all the way through Mrs. Horne's lecture on my tardiness and inadequacy as a ladies' maid, I am only half-present. In my mind, I'm still in the alleyway, repeating the events over and over, braving the fear I felt in an effort to make sense of it all.

I don't understand what happened to me in that alley, or what the wolf was doing, or the intentions of the man who seemed to save me and threaten me within the same minute. Even as I go to bed, I keep turning it over. It must have been some sort of freak occurrence, the wolf, and if the man who rescued me was behaving strangely—well, maybe he was a sailor after all. One better dressed than most, but just as given to drink.

But I can't shake the thought of it until I realize, all in an instant, that this is the last night I will ever spend in England.

That pulls me into the here and now as nothing else could. I tug my thin blanket more securely around myself and think of everything I'm leaving behind. My home village. Mum. The wheat fields where I used to play. Daisy and Matthew. Everything from my life before. The voyage before me seems more perilous and frightening than anything that happened in the alley.

Yet I know that this is the best chance I'll ever have to make a new life for myself. Quite possibly it's the only chance.

No, it's not too late for me to turn back. But I won't.

# ⊰ CHAPTER 2 ⊱

*APRIL 10, 1912*

It's a fine spring morning at the seaside—the sort of thing I've dreamt of my whole life. Novels describe the scene by saying that the air is fresh and the blue water dappled with sunlight. I've pictured it a thousand times, up in my dark attic. This morning, the very first thing I thought was, *At last I will see the ocean.*

But the ocean isn't blue, not this close to land; it's the same silt-brown color as the millpond, except with an eerie greenish cast to the waves. The harbor is no peaceful oasis for a young girl to stroll; instead it's more packed with people than the streets were last night—poor people, rich ones, fine lace up against coarse weave, and the smell of sweat thicker in the air than that of seawater. People shout at one another, some happy, others impatient or angry, but the fevered energy of the throng makes it hard to tell which is which. Crammed in the water are as many ships as could be made to fit, including our liner—the largest of them all. The ship is the only thing I see here that's actually beautiful. Stark black and white, with vibrant red smokestacks reaching into the sky. It's so enormous, so graceful, so perfect in its way that it's hard to think of it as anything built by human hands. It looks more like a mountain range.

At least, more like the way novels describe mountain ranges. I've never been to one of those either.

"Enough dawdling, Tess," says Lady Regina, who, as she is fond of reminding everyone, is the wife of my employer, the Viscount Lisle. "Or do you want to be left on the dock?"

"No, ma'am." Caught daydreaming again. I'm lucky Lady Regina doesn't light into me about it the way she usually does. Probably she has spied one of her society friends in this crowd and doesn't want to be seen dressing down a servant in public.

"Mother, you forget." Irene—the elder daughter of the family, precisely my age, with a face as wholesome as it is plain—gives me an uncertain smile. "You ought to call her 'Davies,' now that she's my ladies' maid. It's more respectful."

"I'll give Tess respect when she's earned it." Lady Regina looks down her long nose at me, as I hurry to catch up. I readjust my grip as I go; none of the hatboxes are that heavy on their own, but it's a bit much to handle four at once. Fashion has made hats large this year.

"Is that Peregrine Lewis?" says Layton, the lone son and heir of the Lisle family. He's long and lean, nearly bony, with sharp shoulders and elbows. He peers through the people around us and smiles so that his thin mustache curls. "Seeing his aunt off, I suppose. Polishing her trunks and begging for postcards. The way he licks her boots and fawns for her! It's vile."

"He won't inherit his fortune from his parents, so he must be attentive to the family he has." Irene glances up at her brother; her lace-gloved hands knotted together at her waist. She is always so shy, even when she's trying to defend another. "He hasn't had your advantages."

"Still, one must have some pride," Layton insists, oblivious as ever to the fact that he's following his mother like an obedient lapdog.

Next to me, Ned mutters, "Noodle."

This one word makes me bite my lip to hold in the laugh. It's a nickname Ned gave Layton below stairs, and it's stuck: Layton is just that skinny, that pale, and that limp. He was almost handsome during his university years; I used to have a bit of a crush, before I was old enough to know better. But the bloom of youth is fading for him much faster than it does for most.

"You're lucky to have a position at all, disrespectful as you are." Mrs. Horne, even grumpier than usual, glares at both of us as she shepherds her charge along—little Beatrice, Lady Regina's change-of-life baby. Only four years old, Beatrice is wearing a straw hat bedecked with ribbons that cost more money than I make in a year. "Both of you, look lively. It's an honor to be brought on a journey such as this, and like as not the most excitement you'll ever have in your lives. So attempt to do your work properly!"

*This won't be the most excitement I'll ever have*, I swear to myself. First of all, last night—whatever happened with the wolf and the handsome young man—well, I don't know what else you'd call it, but it was exciting.

More than that, though, I have plans for my future. Plans more thrilling than any life Horne's ever dreamed of.

But I mustn't smile. I imagine the old oil paintings that hang on the walls of Moorcliffe, those moldy ancestors in the fashions of another century, imprisoned by frames dripping with gilt. My face needs to be as serene as theirs. As unreadable. The Lisle family and Mrs. Horne must not suspect.

Ned and I do what Mrs. Horne says and hurry along in the family's wake, as much a part of their display of wealth and power as the clothes that they wear. He's Layton's valet, a job I wouldn't wish on my worst enemy, much less dear friendly Ned. He has a long, thin face, ginger hair, and ears like the handles on a milk jug, and yet he's charming despite his plain face. Thanks to the isolation of life at Moorcliffe, Ned's one of the few young men I know—one of the only ones I've ever known. But we've never had eyes for each other. Honestly, after so many years in service together, he feels more like a brother.

I've known Mrs. Horne as long as I've known Ned, so perhaps I ought to say that she feels more like a mother to me. She doesn't feel like anybody's mother, though. It's impossible to imagine anyone as dry and joyless as Mrs. Horne having given birth to anything, or doing what you have to do to get with child in the first place. (We call her Mrs., but it's an honorary title; you don't have to have a husband to be a Mrs., just really old, so Mrs. Horne counts.) She's the ladies' maid for Lady Regina, and essentially has the role of housekeeper at Moorcliffe. Nobody among the servants outranks her except the butler, who's too senile to matter much.

Most of the time, Mrs. Horne terrifies me. She has total power over my life—how much food I get to eat, how many hours I get to sleep, whether I stay in the house to work or get cast out to starve.

*But not anymore*, I think, and it's all I can do not to smile into her shriveled, smug face. *One week from now, everything will be different.*

As we get closer, walking becomes easier. We've made it through the passersby, the curiosity seekers; now, everyone is moving in the same direction, flowing onboard. The ship looms over us, taller than the church steeple, taller than anything I've ever seen. It seems larger and more majestic than the mud-colored ocean.

Lady Regina waves at one of her society friends, then says, too casually, "Horne, you ought to know that we've put the three of you in third class. I understand that the stewards will show you how best to reach us."

Ned and I can't resist looking at each other in dismay, and even Mrs. Horne's thin lips twist in a poor effort to hide her disappointment. When the Lisle family last took a sea voyage a decade ago, the servants stayed in first class with them—feather beds soft as clouds, they said, and more food than you'd ever seen on your own table in your life. We'd hoped for the same. Some people make their servants travel second class; third class is unheard of.

"We'll be penned down below with a lot of damned foreigners," Ned mutters. It does sound dreadful, but I remind myself how little it matters.

Layton waves at their friends—approaching now, no doubt fellow passengers. They will have several days on the ocean to talk to one another, but of course they must pay each other every compliment immediately. My arms ache, and I want nothing more than to lay the hatboxes on the ground while we wait. Irene wouldn't mind, but Mrs. Horne wouldn't have it. I call on the muscles I have from years of scrubbing floors to see me through.

Then Lady Regina says, "Tess, set those hatboxes down. Mrs. Horne can see to them."

Mrs. Horne looks put out, probably because she's now got to handle a small child *and* four hatboxes. I do what Lady Regina says straightaway and present myself for whatever task she has in mind—because it's not even worth asking if she saw I was tired. She wouldn't care. The only reason I get to lay one piece of work aside is to take up another.

Lady Regina snaps her fingers at one of the porters she hired to help, and he hands me a carved wooden box—heavier than all the hatboxes put together. What can they have in there? I manage to grip the small iron handles, though the twists of the metal press into my palms so sharply that they burn. "Yes, milady?" I say. The words come out breathy, as if I'd been running uphill; last night I was too unnerved by the strange incident with the wolf to sleep well, and my exhaustion is showing earlier than usual.

"This needs to be placed in our suite immediately," Lady Regina says. "I'm uncomfortable leaving it on the dock so long—there are rough characters about. The stewards onboard will show you the way. We've arranged for a safe in our cabin; that's where you're to put the box. Don't go leaving it on a table. Am I understood?"

"Yes, milady." I'm never meant to say anything else to her besides "yes" and "no."

Lady Regina stares down at me as though I have deviated from the rules in some way. She is a handsome woman, with vibrant beauty that didn't come down to her daughter—lustrous brown hair and an aquiline nose. Her wide-brimmed hat is thick with plumes and silk flowers, a striking contrast to my shabby black maid's dress and white linen cap.

"I don't like sending you to do this alone," she says sharply. "But I don't suppose you can manage as many boxes as Ned, and besides—you won't run off, will you?"

"No, milady."

Her full lips curl into a contemptuous smile. "I trust you're a better sort than your sister."

It feels like scalding water being poured over me, or perhaps like being thrown outside into a snowdrift on an especially cruel winter's day—something so shocking the body hardly knows how to take it in. My skin burns with rage, as though it's too tight for me, and my mouth goes dry. I'd like to rip that hat off Lady Regina's head. I'd like to rip her hair out with it.

I say, "Yes, milady."

As I go, I feel a strange wave of dread—as though I were back in that alleyway last night. Hardly likely to find a wolf stalking here, amid the ship's crowd. And yet I feel something prickling along my neck and back, the way I imagine a rabbit knows the cat is watching.

The weight of the box pulls at the joints of my arms, but it's worth it for a few moments of escape. Or so I tell myself. In truth, it's a little frightening to be on my own in a crowd like this—more people than I've ever seen in one place, all of them pushing and shoving. Also, I can't tell precisely where I'm supposed to go. There is an entry for first-class passengers, another for third class—going to different decks of the ship altogether. I look down at my burden. Which of us counts more: me or my employers' possession?

Then I feel it again, that prickle at the back of my neck. The hunter's eyes on its prey. I glance behind me, expecting to see— what? The wolf from the night before? The young man who rescued me, then told me to flee for the sake of my life? I see neither. In the crush, perhaps I can't see them, but then they wouldn't be able to see me either. But *someone's* watching. I know he's there, down deep within me, in the place that doesn't respond to thought or logic, just pure animal instinct.

Someone in this crowd of strangers is watching me.

Someone is hunting me.

"Lost your way, miss?" says a bluff sort of man, with red cheeks and sky-blue eyes. His voice makes me jump, but the interruption is welcome. He wears what I believe is an officer's uniform, so why he's speaking to the likes of me, I can't imagine. But his voice and face are kind, and I feel safer having somebody to talk to, no matter who it might be.

"I'm to deliver this to my employers' cabin," I say. "I'm in the service of the Viscount Lisle's family."

"Then it's first class for you."

"But I'm traveling in third class."

He frowns. "A bit cheap, aren't they?"

I ought to be prim and offended that he's slighted the family I work for. Instead, I have to stifle a giggle. "I know it must be . . .

unusual. But now I don't know how to board the ship."

"First class, I think. I remember the head steward talking about this now—they've arranged for you to have keys to help you get about. Unusual, yes, but nothing is too good for the family of a viscount." The touch of sarcasm in his voice is light enough to allow me to ignore the joke or enjoy it, as I prefer. I enjoy it. "The stewards will show you the way once you get aboard. Sure you don't want to get one of them to handle it? That looks heavy for you."

It's the nicest thing anybody has said to me in days, and I'm surprised to feel a small lump in my throat. But I know my duty; I know the potential repercussions. "Milady wants me to handle this personally. Thank you just the same, sir."

He touches his cap before striding away to whatever duty he put aside to help me. I hurry to the first-class gangplank, hoping that whoever was staring at me before is third class. Some foreigner, no doubt.

And maybe it was no more than my imagination playing tricks on me, bringing out the fear beneath my skin. I have reasons enough to be nervous. This voyage—these next few days—are going to change my life forever.

The first-class gangplank is more like a promenade; people take their time, seeing and being seen in the sunshine. Ladies turn that way and this so that their wide-brimmed hats will be seen to their best advantage, and they hold parasols of finely worked lace that cast scrolling shadows below. Gentlemen's canes and shoes shine. It might be a fashion parade, were it not for the few servants in the mix panting under our burdens. We move so slowly that I dare to put the box down for a few seconds.

As my tired muscles relax, I slip one hand into the pocket of my dress. There I clasp a small felt purse, one I sewed myself out of scraps. I had to do the work late at night, and they only allow us one candle in the attic, so it's hardly my finest accomplishment as a seamstress. But nobody sees this purse besides me.

The felt is heavy in my hand. Through the fabric, I can feel the weight of coins, the slip of wadded notes. For the past year and a half, I've saved every bit of money I could. I even kept a pound note I found on the stair the morning after a dinner party—a real risk, one that could've got me sacked if anybody had found out. Nobody did.

I've saved enough to live on for a couple of months. That's not very long, but it's more than I've ever had together in my whole life, even though I've been in service since I left school at thirteen. It's going to be enough.

Enough so that, when this ship reaches the United States, I can walk off it, slip away from Lady Regina and Mrs. Horne, and never, ever come back.

We shuffle forward on the gangplank, and I take the box up again. It feels even heavier than before, but I can bear it. Freedom is only a few days away.

*All I have to do is make it through this one trip*, I think, as I step off the gangplank and finally board the RMS *Titanic*.

# ⊰ CHAPTER 3 ⊱

MY LORD, THIS SHIP IS BEAUTIFUL.

The path for the first-class passengers to enter the ship begins near their dining hall, and the staircase leading down to it is more magnificent than anything found in Moorcliffe. Gleaming carved wood, stairs arching down in two graceful curves, a cast-iron clock finely molded: This is something I would expect to see in a great manor house, not a ship. Even the creamy beige carpet beneath my feet is thicker and softer than any Aubusson rug.

Or am I naive? As I begin this journey from the life I have always known, I am acutely aware of the limits of my experience. So who am I to judge this ship or its grandeur? Perhaps this is very ordinary, and I reveal myself as an ignorant country girl by marveling at it.

But no. I turn my attention to the wealthy people around me, and although they are too refined to voice their amazement, I can read it in their eyes. A good servant learns how to study faces, to glean hints of her employers' moods from the slightest change in expression—but no such subtleties are necessary here. They laugh in delight, smile at one another in satisfaction, and allow their hands to trail sensually along the fine wood carving. The *Titanic* is as spectacular to them as it is to me. No one here is immune to its splendor—

Wait. Someone is. Two someones, in point of fact.

Just inside the doorway, unobserved by most of those walking past, are two gentlemen. Both are remarkably tall and broad-shouldered. One is a little older, perhaps nearing his thirtieth year. He wears a Vandyke beard as black as iron . . . rather like that of the man who briefly accosted me in the street, though my glimpse of him was too swift to be sure of any true likeness. The other—

Him, too, I only saw briefly, but I would never forget his face. The other is the young man from last night.

He is younger than I'd realized. My elder perhaps by only four or five years—twenty-two, then? And now that we are in light—both the brilliant sunshine and the glow from the *Titanic*'s elegant frosted-glass lamps—I am free to really look at him. To drink him in.

His jaw is strong and sharply angled, throwing his high cheek-bones into relief. His mouth is well-shaped, with full lips any girl would desire. Shoulders broad, waist narrow, a hint of real muscle beneath. I remember how firm his body was when he pressed me against the wall. His wildly curly hair—in that deep chestnut color, with fine glints of red that bring out the dark brown of his eyes—I cannot decide if it is his one flaw or his best feature. Untamable, I would guess. He doesn't clip it short as most gentlemen would

21

in a similar situation. Instead he lets the curls flow freely, as I've heard artists and bohemians do. This is no bohemian, though, nor any sailor, as I briefly suspected; the well-cut suit he wears speaks of his wealth and privilege.

My steps slow. The box is suddenly no longer heavy in my hands, or at least I don't feel the ache of it. I can't get over the shock of seeing him again, seeing him *here*, or of the powerful effect he has on me.

It feels as though he must notice me—as though whatever strange force brought us together last night would call to him as powerfully as it calls to me—and yet he doesn't turn. He and his fellow traveler are distracted. They lean in closely to each other, as though they do not wish their conversation to be overheard. His body is twisted slightly away from that of the man with the Vandyke beard, as though he wished to walk in another direction. But they talk so intently. Are they arguing or conspiring? I can't tell. And usually I am good at reading people—

The tense moment between them snaps as his companion, the one with the beard, looks up at me—as though he were the one tied to me, not his friend. His icy blue eyes sweep over me, only for a split second, but it is enough to send a chill through the marrow of my bones.

He looks as if he knows me. As if he hates me. And there is something eerily familiar in his gaze. Is that the man from last night after all?

Quickly I turn away. Surely his animosity is no more than a rich man's irritation. He has caught me eavesdropping on their conversation—intruding on my betters. If he complains to a purser or, worse, to Lady Regina, my life won't be worth leading over the next five days.

And yet I feel the stare on my back again. It is as real as the clothes on my back. It is cold, and it is evil, and it follows me even as I walk toward the nearest steward to make my escape.

The Lisles' suite is located on A deck, which I can tell from the steward's expression is especially grand. The first-class passengers are all escorted to their cabins, but the steward expects me to find my own way. He doesn't offer to take the box from me, or find anyone else to take it—why should he?—and so I set it at my feet as we conduct our business. I am given the key to their rooms and the safe's combination without question; I cannot be a useful servant without having access to anything my employers could possibly desire.

Then he takes out another key. "This lets you go from third class to first class." His face is sour. "We're not meant to be handing these things out to everyone. United States regulations say we have to keep those doors shut, and if we find you haven't, we'll confiscate that key posthaste, and the viscount's lady will just have to do without her servants for a while."

This steward has clearly never met Lady Regina; she'd wither him on the spot with a mere glare. But I'm meant to be cowed and serious, so I nod as I drop the key into my pocket and stoop to pick up the box. "Yes, sir. I'll be careful, sir."

He nods and waves me off, already eager to turn his attention to people far more worth his time. The rest of the way, I'm on my own.

I cast one glance behind me to make sure the bearded man with the cold blue eyes isn't watching any longer. He's nowhere to be seen. And yet I still feel the hunter's gaze. With a shiver, I hurry toward the lift, eager to get farther from him.

Even the hallways of the *Titanic* are luxurious. The carpet, now red with a floral pattern, is soft beneath my aching feet, and the white paint is gleaming and new. After the clamor of the dock, the silence is startling. Although others down the corridor are entering their first-class accommodations, nobody is especially close. It feels briefly as though I have the ship to myself.

What would I do, if I were on this vessel all alone for five days? All alone except for the crew, of course; I'd scarcely get very far without them. I could slide down those majestic banisters on the grand staircase. I could sit by myself in the sumptuous dining hall and snap my fingers, demanding course after course of the sort of rich food I usually only get if Cook has burnt it too badly for the Lisles to eat. And what would I wear? With only the crew to look at me—no one to boss me, no one to judge—there would be no more need for this shabby uniform. I imagine taking off my white bonnet and letting it float down from the deck railings into the ocean below. The sharks can eat it, for all I care.

So pleasant is it to daydream, unhampered, that I do not notice the man coming close to me until he is almost at my side.

It's *him*. Not my chestnut-haired man—the older one with the Vandyke beard. I know now that he is indeed the same one who accosted me the night before. Nor is this merely awkward coincidence—his gaze focuses on me, and his jaw is set.

"So, you like to listen to other people's conversations." His voice is a deep bass rumble, and the words are accented in a way that is unfamiliar to me—Russian, perhaps? The Lisles entertain foreign nobility too rarely for me to be certain. "Last night, and again this morning! That is a good way to hear many interesting things, but very bad manners. Very bad manners indeed."

It's almost a relief to think he's nothing other than an obnoxious man who dislikes eavesdroppers. This close, I can see that he, too, is a handsome man—or would be but for the unnatural chill in his pale blue eyes. "I beg your pardon, sir. I overheard nothing, sir. Please, I beg your forgiveness." *Don't tell, don't tell.*

"You overheard nothing? Again? And yet you were paying such close attention this time."

"The room was very loud, sir. Beg your pardon, sir." Sometimes, if you make a slip like this (whether real or imagined), all the aristocrats want you to do is eat dirt for a bit, humble yourself until they feel suitably powerful, and there's an end of it. But the more I apologize to this one, the angrier he seems to get. The energy around him is increasingly dark, and I feel even more profoundly unsettled than I did before. At least I have already reached the Lisles' cabin—all I have to do is calm him down long enough for me to get to the other side of that door.

His eyes travel down to the box I hold. "What a heavy burden you carry."

"It's all right, sir."

"The crest of the Lisle estate—am I correct?"

It's not so unusual that one member of the nobility would

25

recognize the heraldry of another. "Yes, sir."

"I thought so." He steps closer to me—too close—and I can tell that his natural scent has a hint of wood smoke about it. His smile is small and tight within the black spade of his beard. There's something odd about his teeth. "You must be very tired. Will you not allow me to help you?"

He speaks almost kindly, which is more frightening than before. Though I cannot say what it is about this man that distresses me so, I trust my instincts and step away. "No, sir. Thank you, sir."

"That won't do at all." Now anger simmers beneath the surface of his words. One of his black-gloved hands grips an iron handle, and I pull the box back in the split second before he would have snatched it away.

I stumble backward until the cabin door presses against my shoulders. I want to shout for help, but I see no one else, and—I am a servant girl. This is a gentleman. In any dispute between us, he will be believed, and I will not. But why would a gentleman be attempting to commit robbery?

His grin widens. "It would be just like a nasty, thieving maid to try to rob her employers at such a time. Give them an inch—isn't that the expression in English? Service in the great house takes you out of your humble home and your settled ways. Your proper position in society. So you turn into a conniving little thief."

"Sir, you are mistaken." It's such a foolish thing to say, but I cannot think of anything else. Even now, I must not offend him. "I've stolen nothing. This is my employers' box, and I must put it away, sir. Please excuse me."

"What would they think if they opened their safe and the box were not there?"

I must assert myself, but how? I'd like to kick him in the shins, but there are no words for the trouble I would be in if I assaulted a gentleman. "Sir, that will not occur. I believe I must now fetch a steward."

"I do not think he will arrive in time to rescue the little servant girl," he croons. The bastard is having fun. "Give me the box, girl. Or I shall deeply enjoy taking it from you."

He lifts his black-gloved hand and strokes one finger down the side of my face. When his eyes bore into mine, fear slices into me—not mere nervousness, but real terror.

These were the eyes that followed me on the dock. Even before I saw him with the young man from last night, he had seen me.

This is the hunter. And he is still hunting me. He has caught me.

*Give him the box*, I think. *Give him the box, and tell them it was stolen, and even if they don't believe you, they won't put you in jail. Or will they? Is that all I'll ever see of America—a jail cell?*

But scared as I am, I can't give up so easily. Lord, but I hate a bully. "No, sir," I say, and I lift my chin, daring him to do his worst.

He takes the dare.

His hands grab my shoulders and yank me forward so that I'm off balance and his face is close to mine. His breath smells like he recently ate undercooked meat. Then he shoves me back against the door, hard enough that it slams painfully against my head. For one moment, I smell blood.

He hisses, "What scares you the most?"

"Get off me!" I try to shove him back, but the heavy box in my hands makes that difficult.

"Being sacked and turned out to starve?" Although he's still gripping my shoulders tightly, his thumbs make circles as they press into my flesh—a caress meant to bruise. "Being hurt? Someone you love being hurt? Whatever it is, I can make it happen."

I don't know what to say to him. I don't know what to do. I just know that I hate him. So I spit in his face.

The saliva dribbles onto his beard, and the ice-blue eyes suddenly blaze like fire. My fear deepens as I realize that this really wasn't the worst he could do—he's about to do that now—

Then a voice calls, "Stop this."

We turn to see him—the other, the younger man, the one who saved me last night and is saving me now. I sag against the door in relief, and the bearded man's face distorts, as though his displeasure were melting him like wax. "Leave us, Alec."

Alec does nothing of the sort. "This is neither the time nor the place for your games, Mikhail. Leave the poor girl alone."

The hunter—Mikhail—responds, "Someday you'll learn that it is never a bad time to enjoy our birthright." But he lets go of my shoulders. Something passes between them then: some kind of shared knowledge I cannot guess at.

Are they friends, then? How can that be possible? Mikhail terrifies me, but Alec—his effect on me is something altogether different. Should I be as afraid of Alec as I am of Mikhail? Beauty is no guarantee of goodness; Lady Regina is proof enough of that. I don't know, and want nothing so much as for this to be over.

Mikhail gives me another look that makes my stomach clench, then tips his hat to me—a mockery of manners, or of me. Then he walks away.

And yet I know this is anything but over.

Alec's eyes study me in turn, but his look is different. At least my reaction is different. When Mikhail stared at me, I went cold; Alec's attention warms my blood, flushes my cheeks. Yet I can't tell if he is looking at me with desire or contempt or—I can't guess. I can't fathom the depth of his intense gaze.

He says to me, roughly, "You should watch yourself."

I cannot tell if it is a warning, or a threat. And yet I know— beyond any doubt—I have been rescued.

Before I can speak, Alec walks away, very quickly, as though he were a criminal escaping from the scene. At first I stare after him in shock, unable to understand what happened here—and what might have happened, had Alec not arrived.

Then I feel the key pressing against my sweaty palm, hard against the box, and curse myself for a fool. I hurry inside the cabin and lock the door behind me, safe—for now.

# ⊰ CHAPTER 4 ⊱

AS MY HEARTBEAT SLOWS AND MY BREATHING returns to normal, I try to understand what happened in the hallway, but I can't.

I'm absolutely certain that Mikhail was the one spying on me as I came aboard the ship. Also I know that, had Alec not arrived when he did, the situation would have become much worse. But I can guess no more.

Mikhail wants this box—the one now sitting on the floor of the cabin. No doubt it contains immense riches; I am sure that Lady Regina's best jewelry, and the few baubles Irene owns, are enclosed within. More than that, too: It's no secret, downstairs at Moorcliffe, that the Lisle family is not so wealthy as it once was. Rumor has it that this trip is largely about finding some rich industrial heiress for Layton to wed on the charms of his title—his personality obviously wouldn't do the trick on its own. No doubt the Lisles would rather marry off Irene, leaving their son and heir to choose a wife from the nobility, but Irene's charms are too modest for her to make an illustrious match. So Layton will take as his bride the daughter of some Philadelphia man who builds railway track, or perhaps a Boston girl inheriting the wealth earned by mail-order goods.

In short, the Lisle family wants to impress the kind of people they usually spit on. They can't do that if they're not traveling in style. So the box contains many of the priceless ancestral valuables the Viscount Lisle's family has held for the past four hundred years—and now intends to sell.

Reason enough for theft. But Mikhail is traveling first class on the *Titanic*. Mrs. Horne says tickets cost thousands of pounds, a sum I can hardly imagine seeing in a lifetime, much less spending on a single trip to America. Why would anyone able to pay that sort of money for a voyage need to steal anything? He must be enormously wealthy, almost certainly more than the Lisles.

And the way he looked at me—the cold-blooded stare that chilled my bones—is that because he thinks I overheard something I shouldn't have last night, or today? Already I realize that our encounter the evening before was more than coincidence; Mikhail was near because he was already tracking the Lisles. I wasn't his original target.

But perhaps I am his target now.

I shake off that chill as I quickly put the box into the suite's iron safe. Surely I'm only being silly. If Mikhail isn't a thief, then he's merely the kind of rich man who thinks servant girls are his to do with as he will—to threaten, to tease, to bed, and to discard. That's hardly unusual among wealthy gentlemen. After years of dodging Layton's randy friends from Cambridge, I shouldn't find that attitude surprising. Once I vanish belowdecks, to my third-class accommodations, Mikhail will turn his attentions to some unhappy stewardess aboard ship, and I can continue about my business.

Although I do not entirely believe this sensible explanation, I force myself to accept it.

The safe's door swings shut with a resounding clang, and I sit back heavily on the cabin's sumptuous bed. As I do, my thoughts drift toward an altogether more pleasant subject.

My mind wants to dwell on Alec. Only on Alec. Even knowing his name makes me feel closer to him somehow. And now he's saved me from danger twice. If only I had thought to thank him! I imagine my fingers winding into his thick chestnut curls, my mouth open as he leans close—

The daydream makes my cheeks flush and my heart thump too fast. I'm no doubt being foolish, like any other servant girl who has finally had the chance to be alone with an attractive man. The household doesn't allow any of us girls much chance to be with men of our own class—we're not meant to fall in love and get married, only to drudge on and on in service until we dry up and go gray and our teeth fall out. And here I am acting like an idiot over a man who's shown no interest in me, save keeping me from harm like any decent human being would.

Especially given that he protected me today, but threatened me last night. He may not be as serious a danger to me as Mikhail, but that doesn't mean Alec doesn't present dangers of his own.

The feather mattress is soft—so much softer than the lumpy

flock pallet I've slept on for the past four years. And this cream-colored coverlet: The fabric isn't silk, but it's so sleek to the touch it might as well be. This bedroom is as grand and elegant as any of the Lisle family rooms back at Moorcliffe. More even than that.

For a moment I imagine myself a fine lady, traveling in style aboard the *Titanic*. I imagine that I am wearing a beautiful negligee of Viennese lace instead of my drab black servant's dress. I lie back on the soft, soft mattress and wish that I could close my eyes and give in to sleep.

Then I wish I could open my eyes and see Alec lying next to me.

Don't be stupid, I tell myself. You don't know his last name. You don't know if he's good or bad or in the fathomless distance between the two. You don't know anything about him, except that he keeps bad company, is brusque and strange, and is rich enough to sail first class—which means he'd be after only one thing with a maidservant.

But as I lie on the soft bed, feeling the silky fabric next to my skin, giving in to that one thing seems tempting enough—

Abruptly I sit upright and push myself off the bed. There's already some cool water in the china jug on the nightstand; I use a bit to splash my face and shock me back to my senses. Enough time for daydreams and romance and whatever else might follow after I reach New York City. For now, it's best if I stick to the hard reality of the tasks ahead.

First class was almost silent; third class is anything but.

"*Permesso, permesso,*" says a swarthy man I think must be Italian, as he pushes his way through the crowd, followed by his wife and no fewer than five children, all of whom are chattering at once. Men and women of every age and size and shape and nationality are shoving into one another in an eager search for their cabins. It doesn't smell like wood polish and cedar down here on F deck; it smells like honest sweat and mothballs.

I'd expected to be repulsed by this bedlam, but instead, it energizes me. Though this is a strange crowd, it's a happy one. I realize that, for the first time in my life, I'm surrounded by people who share my goal of starting over in America. Because the big trunks they're hefting, the bundles of clothes the women hold close—those aren't supplies for a sea voyage. They're the foundation of a new life.

Besides, even the third-class accommodations are impressive on this ship. While it's not as sumptuous as first class by any means, the floors here are polished wood, and the walls freshly painted bright white. The brass fittings gleam, and a poster informs us that our tea will include vegetable soup, meat, bread, cheese, and a sweet. As much as that! I bet tonight I won't feel hungry even once. This is far better than the damp, chilly attic room I left behind at Moorcliffe, or the bread and butter we had to make do with most nights.

At last I see the number of my room. The steward said I wasn't rooming with Mrs. Horne, which is a small mercy. I dare to hope that I've got the room to myself; they say maiden voyages of ships never sell every ticket, because most people want to wait until the kinks have been worked out on a journey or two. After years of sharing my bed with one or two other servant girls, having a bedroom to myself seems like the height of luxury.

I open the door. No such luck.

White, cast-iron bunk beds stand on either side of the room. On one of the lower bunks sits a girl, perhaps a year or two older than I am. Although I'm not actually surprised to see someone, I am surprised to see that they've put me in the same room as a foreigner.

I don't even have to ask if she's a foreigner. I just know. Her skin is a deep tan, her thick hair such a perfect black that it almost has a bluish gleam, and her brilliantly embroidered skirt and shawl aren't the kind of thing I've ever seen anyone in England wear.

But I've always heard that foreigners were dirty, and this girl isn't. As strange as her clothes are, they're clean, and actually rather pretty. And I've always heard the "English rose" described as the ultimate standard of beauty: delicate frame, pale skin, pink cheeks, and fair curls. I've always rather liked that description, because it applies to me—at least it would, if I ever got to wash up properly and wear something nice. And yet this girl, dark and statuesque as she is, is far lovelier than I am.

Even more surprising: She's not hopping up to greet me, begging my pardon, or welcoming me to the room. In fact, she seems more displeased to be sharing a room than I was. Even though I'm English—as though all the world didn't look up to England!

"Who are you, then?" she demands. Her accent is thick, but her English is good.

I put my hands on my hips. "I'm Tess. And who are you?"

"Myriam Nahas. Why are you on this ship?" It sounds almost

35

like she's asking how I dare to be here.

"I'm ladies' maid to the Honorable Irene Lisle, daughter of the Viscount Lisle, who is traveling with her mother and brother to do the season in New York." I say it as grandly as I can. Their titles ought to give me some credit here, at least. They don't. Myriam couldn't look less impressed. So I snap back, "Why are *you* on this ship?"

"I've left Lebanon to join my brother and his wife in New York City." Pride shines from her, and yet I can also see how tired she is; she has already traveled all the way from Lebanon, and she still has an ocean to cross. "He has a garment business there that is doing well. I can help sew for him. Perhaps that doesn't sound very fine to the likes of you, but it suits me."

It sounds fine enough. I'm jealous, in fact. Myriam is aboard this ship for the same reason I am—to emigrate to the United States—but unlike me, she has family and a job waiting for her.

Maybe that's what annoys me about her. Or maybe it's that she isn't being deferential and obedient, like I would have expected from a foreign girl. Most likely it's just that she seems to be annoyed by me first, for whatever reason. But our eyes are narrowed as we stare at each other, and I sense a power struggle in the making.

"I have taken one of the bottom bunks," Myriam adds. "They shift around less with the moving of the ship."

"Then I'll take one as well."

"Others will be in this room with us. They, too, will want bottom bunks."

"They'll be out of luck, won't they?"

Her eyes narrow. "They will attempt to persuade one of us to move, and it will not be me."

I sit down deliberately on the other lower bunk. "I don't intend to settle for less just to make you more comfortable."

"Nor I."

"Listen here. I'm an Englishwoman, and this is an English ship." That ought to settle her.

Instead, Myriam folds her arms and lifts her chin, and despite my annoyance with her, I can't help but notice the perfection of her profile. "You are a servant," she sneers. "I answer to no one but myself."

Anger flushes my cheeks, and I open my mouth to tell her what I think of impudent foreigners—but then the door to our cabin opens again, revealing our other two roommates. The first lady is ancient, seventy-five if she's a day; the second is older. They totter in, carrying little more than carpetbags, with their snowy-white hair atop their heads in braids. I don't recognize the language they're speaking, but a badge on one of their cases has a flag that I think is Norway's. Their wrinkled faces crease into smiles of welcome, and whatever they're saying to us sounds friendly.

And there is absolutely no way either of them can take a top bunk.

I clamber up to one of the top bunks instantly, and turn to snap at Myriam to do the same—but she already has. We stare at each other, shocked to realize that, despite our sour tempers, neither of us is actually that bad. It's almost funny. If we knew each other any better, I think we'd laugh.

Instead, I flop back onto my bunk. It's not as soft as the ones in first class, but it's better than back home. Comfortable as anything. I imagine it as a magic carpet, whisking me away to another, better world.

"Do they tell stories about magic carpets in Lebanon?" I ask Myriam as we walk down the corridor on F deck.

"I believe you are a few centuries behind the times," she says, but not unkindly.

Though I still think she's rather rude, and she still seems to have her back up where I'm concerned, we'll get on well enough for a few days' journey. As I don't need to return to the Lisles until shortly before the ship gets underway, I decided to take a walk belowdecks, and she's joined me. Hopefully I can talk to her about emigrating to America; she's the first person I ever met who has the same goal as I do.

Of course, I don't intend to admit that's my goal. Nobody can know until we reach New York City. But I might find out some things anyway.

Although there's still plenty of bustle in the corridors, that has slowed down somewhat as everyone has found their bunks and is getting themselves settled. Amid the hubbub of the corridors, I see a ship's officer, which surprises me—I'd have thought that only stewards would come down to steerage. Even better, I recognize him; it's the friendly man who helped me on the dock.

He remembers me too. "I see you've got yourself sorted out."

"Very well, thank you, sir."

Then he glances at Myriam, no more than a simple look—and

just like that, he's caught. Her beauty holds him fast, as if he were a fly and she were honey. Myriam likes the look of him too, I can tell. But she doesn't simper or act silly in a rush to make conversation, the way I have the few times I've been able to talk with young men in the village pub. She simply smiles back at him, slow and warm, completely unhurried. This is obviously a much better way to handle it. I must remember this for later.

The officer pulls his hat off his head, as though we were gentlewomen. "George Greene, ship's seventh officer, at your service."

"Myriam Nahas." She inclines her head only slightly. Her eyes never waver from his.

"Tess Davies," I say, just so neither of them forgets I'm standing here. "It's a lovely ship."

"Finest in the White Star fleet. Finest in the world, if you ask me." George gestures toward the doors at the far end of the corridor, the ones blocked off that we're not supposed to enter. "Would you like a bit of a tour? Haven't time for much, but I could show you ladies around the lower decks. More down here than meets the eye." When Myriam hesitates before answering, he quickly adds, "We have first-class amenities down here, so that will be useful to you, Miss Davies. Knowing how to get between different classes of the ship, I mean, since you'll be running about so much."

It's nice to be called "Miss Davies," as if I were a proper lady. And I don't think he's just trying to impress Myriam, either, at least not with that; real kindness and politeness shine from George's blue eyes.

"It would be very interesting to see more of the ship," Myriam says, as though George's company hasn't anything to do with her decision to come along.

George, anxious to please, leads us through F deck, showing us the third-class dining hall first. Long wooden tables reach from side to side of the enormous room. This, too, is bright and cheerful—better than the servants' table downstairs at Moorcliffe by far. "And there are decks outside for you, too," he says. "You won't be cooped up all journey, like you would on most ships. *Titanic* has a lovely deck just for third-class passengers, so you can have a bit of fresh air."

Myriam folds her arms. "Such special treatment to people who just had to be combed and picked over as if we were dogs."

They combed the third-class passengers? Looking for lice, I realize. How insulting. Thank goodness George told me to enter through the first-class passageway.

The poor man can't apologize fast enough. "Begging your pardon, Miss Nahas. It's crude and unconscionable treatment, and you can be sure it's not White Star policy. It's those American laws. You wouldn't believe the nonsense with quarantines and all they stick us with."

"Well. If it's all the fault of the Americans." Myriam tosses her hair, slightly—but not entirely—appeased. "Of course, I'll be an American soon."

How will poor George get out of this one? I can't help a small smile as I look at him. But the good man rallies quickly. "Then I suppose they'll improve in a hurry, won't they, miss?"

Instead of replying, Myriam smiles. I feel rather unnecessary, but I keep tagging along, more for mischief's sake.

After that, he looks around a bit to make sure we won't be

witnessed, then takes us to a heavy door that brings us to the first-class section of this deck. "Can't lead you through—more of those American regulations—but you can pass by here if you need to, Miss Davies."

"Won't I disturb the first-class passengers in their cabins?"

"No staterooms down here," George says in a tone of voice that makes it clear no rich people would ride down this low, where you can feel the movement of the ship. "But special amenities for them. Like the Turkish bath." I laugh, disbelieving. I half thought those only existed in old novels about exotic foreign lands. "Steam room and all," he says. "Nice as any you'd find in Istanbul."

"Have you been to Istanbul?" Myriam looks doubtful.

"Only once, Miss Nahas, and that too briefly. But I'm told by those in the know that the fittings here are the finest. Porcelain tiles, feathered fans, lounging chairs, you name it."

"How well-traveled you are." Myriam's much more impressed by George than by the baths, and he actually seems to glow as he realizes it. I try not to roll my eyes.

"What else is through there?" I say, honestly wanting to know. Lord only knows whether Lady Regina or Layton will demand any of the services provided in this area.

George grins. "Want to play a game of squash?"

"Squash! On an ocean liner?" I start to laugh, and Myriam joins in; it's both disbelief and delight. The *Titanic* is like its own floating world.

"Anything the heart could desire," George swears. "And you don't have to worry about the waves upsetting your game. See how steady she sails? We might as well be skimming over smooth glass."

My laughter stops. "We're already at sea?"

"Set out more than a quarter hour ago."

"I'm late!" Good Lord, the Lisles will have been expecting me for nearly half an hour now. "I've got to go. Oh, blast, how do I reach the upper decks? Wait, no, I've got it."

"Never fear," he says as I use my key to open the locks that keep me out of first class. "You'll be there in a flash."

"Thank you!" I call behind me as I run into the first-class area of the ship. The door clangs shut. No doubt George and Myriam are perfectly happy to be left alone. Much happier than Lady Regina will be when I show up late again.

As I step into the lift, and the grated door shuts behind me, I see someone standing in the corridor—the dark figure of a man.

And in that first moment, I *know* it's Mikhail.

The lift rises, erasing my old view, and I slump back against the wall to gather my breath. The lift operator, a boy a few years younger than I am, doesn't appear to notice anything in particular. He'd have noticed a first-class passenger down there, wouldn't he? He would have held the lift for him.

So it must have been my imagination. Mikhail wouldn't have followed me down here.

He wouldn't still be hunting me.

I try very hard to believe it.

# ❧ CHAPTER 5 ❧

THE MIDAFTERNOON SUN GILDS THE DECKS OF
the ship as if it were a golden ornament instead of anything real.
I would swear that the *Titanic* glides above the surface of the
ocean, because this is as smooth and idyllic as flying is in dreams.
And the ocean now looks as I always imagined it: depthless, dark
blue, crowned with foamy waves—

"Tess!" barks Lady Regina. "Don't fall behind."

So much for daydreams.

I walk a few steps behind Lady Regina, Layton, and Irene, carrying the ladies' shawls should they need them. Apparently travel at
sea can sometimes be cold, though this afternoon is anything but.
The ship is heading toward Cherbourg to pick up the final passengers. So if the ladies will stay on deck until then, I can actually
glimpse a bit of the coastline of France.

I try to think of such things: pretty metaphors about the ship,
or the excitement of seeing another country for the first time in
my life. If I think about those things, then I don't have to think

about Mikhail. I'm in first class now, his part of the ship. He could walk by at any instant, and then I will have to know, for certain, whether it's just my imagination or whether—whether he's truly hunting me.

Then maybe I could tell someone, though I'm not sure who could help me. George Greene seems a kindly man, but he'd still believe a gentleman's word above that of a servant, I'm sure. Ned, perhaps? But what could Ned do about it?

No, I'm alone in this.

Irene's ivory-colored dress fits her well, thanks to my sewing, and the blue ribbons that gather the neck and sleeves flutter nicely in the breeze. I do wish Lady Regina had taken my advice about her daughter's hat, though. It is wide-brimmed and high-crowned, the latest in fashion, but it overwhelms Irene's slight frame. As fond as I am of her, I can't help but think that she looks a bit like a mushroom. The enormous hat wobbles on her head while she animatedly talks about some excitement on deck as the *Titanic* left port, an incident I missed while Myriam and I were down below.

"They say we came within four feet of colliding with the tugboat," Irene insists. "A man on deck declared that was a bad omen. He says he will disembark at Cherbourg."

"Superstitious nonsense," sniffs Lady Regina. "Ahhh, look there. The Countess of Rothes. Well worth the knowing."

Irene's sigh is so soft that Lady Regina can pretend to ignore it. But Layton snaps, "She's hardly any older than you, but she's done a fair bit better for herself, wouldn't you say? You might want to learn from her example."

"I hope the countess married for love, not for money," Irene says.

"She married well," Layton says. "She kept an eye out. You might try doing the same, Irene, instead of hiding up in your library all the time."

Sometimes I hide in the library with her; more often I go on my own. Irene promised me at Christmastime that I might borrow what books I wished, Sherlock Holmes or anything else, and if anybody in her family ever noticed them missing, she'd swear she'd insisted that I read the volume in question. It was kind of her, though we both knew there was little chance of anybody else in her family noticing a missing book. Between the three of them, I doubt they've ever read anything more complex than *Burke's Peerage*.

"Humph. I believe those would be the Strauses." Lady Regina's nose crinkles as if she's smelled something bad. "Enormously wealthy Americans. They own some store in New York City—Macy's, they call it. I suppose that is so nobody will realize it is owned by Jews."

I sneak another peek at the Strauses; I've never seen any Jewish people before, and I'm curious. They don't look any different from anyone else. In fact, they look like a rather nice elderly couple, walking along the deck arm in arm. Lady Regina holds her head high as they pass, refusing to acknowledge them, and Layton follows suit. Irene's cheeks turn pink at their blatant rudeness. Happily, the Strauses don't even notice. They are deep in conversation with each other, obviously affectionate in a way the Viscount Lisle and Lady Regina haven't been in years, if they ever were.

Lady Regina nudges Irene. "Now *there* are some Americans far more worthy of our acquaintance. Howard Marlowe of Marlowe Steel—quite a large concern. One of the new titans of industry in the United States. And that must be his son, Alexander. A very eligible bachelor . . . and, it seems, extremely handsome as well."

I stop peering over my shoulder at the Strauses so I can see this handsome man for myself—and my feet suddenly seem fixed to the deck. I can't move, can't breathe. Because Alexander Marlowe is Alec.

Our eyes meet. His gaze is dark and devouring. Something blazes within him as he looks at me, but I can't tell if it's anger or desire. My breath catches in my throat.

"Mr. Marlowe!" Lady Regina trills, stepping forward with her hand outstretched. This is remarkable behavior toward a man she's never met, particularly one who isn't a member of the nobility. "I am Viscount Lisle's wife, Lady Regina. So pleased to make your acquaintance."

"The pleasure is mine, madam." Howard Marlowe is as tall as his son, though Alec's thick curls must have come from his mother—the father is as bald as an egg. "This is my son, Alec. He's been studying in Paris these past two years. It will be good to see Chicago again, won't it, son?"

"It will." Alec turns from me, and for the first time I see a smile on his face—small and rueful, and yet a smile all the same. Somehow when he's smiling, he's even more beautiful. "I've missed being home."

I seize on each fact as though it were another precious coin

46

to add to my stash. His name is Alexander Marlowe. He is from Chicago. His father is a steel magnate. Although this last fact makes it even more obvious that Alec can never, ever be mine, it is something else I can know about him. Knowledge is the only thing about Alec I can ever possess.

Mr. Marlowe, his father, is all politeness to Lady Regina—but he doesn't humble himself the way so many people do. Obviously he doesn't care for titles; he knows what he's worth. "And may I have the compliment of being introduced to your children?"

"My son, the Honorable Layton Lisle. My daughter, the Honorable Irene Lisle," Lady Regina says, stepping back as though she were presenting some sort of show pony instead of her own child. Irene is always shy with strangers, but she manages to nod and smile. That would do, but Lady Regina continues, "Irene has just completed her London season, and we are eager to show her more of the world."

"Always a fine idea," Mr. Marlowe says.

"And we were just talking of Chicago!" I glance down at the deck, not only to keep myself from staring openly at Alec, but to prevent myself from laughing at Lady Regina's obvious lie. "How we would love to visit that fine city."

"Any good shooting there, what?" Layton looks nearly pleasant for a moment as he thinks of one of the few things he enjoys doing, namely blowing the heads off some ducks to make himself feel manlier. "Chicago's rather on the wild frontier, I take it."

Alec doesn't respond with any of the jokes or invitations that most upper-class young men would; instead, he looks almost grave.

"I don't go in for shooting. And Chicago is no longer the western frontier."

Mr. Marlowe shoots his son a look, perhaps a warning against rudeness, though Alec spoke reasonably enough. "Chicago is a true world city now. Even you must have heard of the Columbian Exposition! We have museums, theater, all the refinements you could wish."

Normally I would expect Lady Regina to snort with contempt at the idea of anything in America being refined, but she's all sunshine and light now. "You make Chicago sound most thrilling, Mr. Marlowe. If we do travel there next month, I trust we may call on you and dear Alec to introduce us to society?"

"But of course, madam. It would be my honor." Mr. Marlowe's smile is more stiff now, and who can blame him? Lady Regina is essentially forcing a friendship on them—and any fool can tell why. Between this and her unsubtle mention of Irene's already having had her debut, Lady Regina's all but announcing that she'd like Alec to consider Irene as a bride.

It stings like a thousand cuts. It stings because Lady Regina is being rude and obvious. It stings because Irene is now so exposed, so awkward, and all she wants is some nice quiet man who would actually value her goodness more than her fortune. Above all, it stings because it reminds me that Alec will belong to some rich woman somewhere, and never, ever to me.

But I'm the one he's looking at with those dark eyes.

And I'm the one he speaks to.

"You—had no more difficulties aboard?" Alec says.

My cheeks flush with warmth. "No, sir. Thank you, sir."

Lady Regina glares at me, as though she hopes her stare has the power to melt me where I stand. "Tess? Were you bothering Mr. Marlowe?"

"Not at all, ma'am." Alec steps forward slightly, placing himself between Lady Regina and me. Is he defending me from her, or showing me how easily he can separate me from others? The thrill I feel when I'm near him is equal parts attraction and fear; I don't know which emotion is true and which is an illusion. Maybe they're both justified. "She was carrying a burden much too heavy for her earlier today. She required some help to reach her suite. Your suite, I mean."

He didn't tell them Mikhail was threatening me. Which of us is he protecting—me, or Mikhail?

"Tess often pretends to need more help than she requires. I hope you weren't taken in." Lady Regina laughs lightly. "It's always the way, with servants. They shirk their tasks the moment you're not looking."

She's trying to shame me, but I'm not ashamed. I know the truth—and so does Alec. He already knows so much about me . . . more, perhaps, than I care for him to know. It doesn't make me feel any safer.

Despite her shyness, Irene pipes up, trying to change the subject. "Mr. Marlowe, have you seen John Jacob Astor? Is he really on board?"

"Indeed he is," Mr. Marlowe says, obviously pleased with the change of subject. "With his new wife—who's not much older than you."

Lady Regina can't resist gossip, and soon the entire party is walking forward again, the parents and Layton chitchatting easily, and Irene trailing in her mother's wake. Alec remains a few steps back—not beside me, but closer to me than to anyone else. It's as though I can feel his presence next to me, the deep, slightly uncomfortable warmth of standing too close to a fire.

As the others round the corner of the boat deck toward the stern, Alec turns to me. He's so close to me now that I can feel his warm breath on my cheek.

His voice is rough as he says, "You told them nothing."

"No."

"About me or about Mikhail."

"No. I swear."

Alec's eyes bore into mine as he leans even closer and whispers, "If you value your life, keep your silence. That's the only thing that will save you. Do you hear me, Tess?"

"Yes."

Then he walks forward again, as smoothly as though he had never spoken to me at all. Alec even smiles when his father waves him forward to stroll by his side. I don't know what to think, but I follow behind, once again the obedient servant.

Was Alec trying to protect me, telling me that Mikhail would strike at me if I spoke to anyone about him? Or was it a threat?

Either way, he's just confirmed what I've been trying to deny all afternoon. I'm in danger.

"How could you be so impertinent, Tess?" Lady Regina tosses her hat down on the sofa in the Lisles' suite. "Putting yourself forward like that. Trying to monopolize Alexander Marlowe's attention."

"Mother, he spoke to Tess first," Irene tries to point out, but Lady Regina ignores her.

The lecture goes on for some time, but I hardly notice. It's all I can do to stand there and nod on cue; my mind is consumed by Alec's threat. Or his warning—I still don't know what it was. I can't stop thinking of Mikhail's cold eyes.

I tell myself that I've lived up to my end of the bargain. I've told no one. Alec said that would protect me, and why would he lie? Keeping quiet and telling nobody my true story has kept me safe up until now. This is just one more thing to stay quiet about.

Lady Regina doesn't stop venting her anger at me until late, and then I've got to prepare Irene for dinner. As I help her into her cornflower-blue evening dress, Irene can't stop apologizing for her mother. "She's only nervous," Irene says, as if that cow were ever nervous about anything. "Mother's been preoccupied with— with a lot of things lately. It makes her cross. Please don't take it personally."

"You're not supposed to apologize to me for anything," I say as I sweep her lank hair up in jeweled combs, which will at least give her some glitter. It helps that she's finally old enough for us to put her hair up; that lets me hide how straight her hair is. "I'm your servant. I know my place."

"Your place doesn't have to mean being treated badly." Irene sighs as she looks at her reflection in the mirror. "Oh, what's the use?"

"You look nice tonight. You just have to brighten up a bit. Smile. Confidence is half the battle, miss."

And she does look better than usual this evening—the color suits her, as do the dress's simple lines. At any other time, I'd be proud of my handiwork. It's my job, as ladies' maid, to see that Irene is shown off to her best advantage. When her mother gets out of my way, and stops forcing Irene to wear ruffles that drown her slight frame and pale, "pure" colors that wash out her complexion, Irene is—well, no ravishing beauty, but at least pretty. I may have been made a ladies' maid too young and with no experience, but I've learned quickly.

Tonight, though, I can't revel vicariously in this triumph. It seems as if I can hear nothing but the blood rushing in my ears, and the memory of Alec's whisper.

*Keep your silence.*

"Well, that's not so bad," drawls Layton as he strolls into her room. Irene frowns—she likes her privacy, but her brother respects that as little as he does anything or anyone else. "At least you won't be an embarrassment tonight."

Behind his shoulder, I can see Ned, whose freckled face is flushed with anger. He hates it when Layton picks on Irene. But he says only, "Will that be all, sir?"

"Quite all." Layton is, indeed, impeccably turned out; his tuxedo is so well pressed and brushed that it seems to have been polished. "You are dismissed for the evening."

"You too, Tess," Irene says, with a small smile.

But then, from the next room, I hear Lady Regina call, "Tess,

52

you stay here. Horne is busy with me. Get Beatrice to bed, would you?"

My stomach is empty with hunger and fear, but there's nothing to be done. Whatever I'm ordered to do, I must do. "Yes, milady."

By the time little Beatrice is washed and asleep, and Lady Regina's finally done with me, I'm not afraid any longer. Although I still feel wobbly every time I think about Mikhail's threat, or about Alec, hunger has taken over. It seems as though I can face up to anything if I can just eat.

But by the time I arrive back in third class, it's well after tea time. What time is the second meal service over? I hurry down the long white corridor that I think leads toward the dining hall, and run into Myriam—who, rather interestingly, is accompanied by George.

"Haven't you got a ship to manage?" I say before I can stop myself.

George turns out to look adorable when he's flustered—at least to Myriam, who smiles sidelong at him. "Off duty this past hour, miss. Thought Miss Nahas and I might take a stroll on the third-class deck."

"Of course you're welcome to join us." Myriam gives me a smoldering look that clearly means, *Interfere with this and you die in the night.*

She doesn't need to worry; I have better plans. "Thanks for the invitation, but I need to get something to eat. Tea hasn't ended, has it? I know I'm too late for the first shift, but—" I read the truth in their dismayed faces. "Oh, no."

George straightens his uniform jacket. "Listen here. Go to the kitchens—the staff will still be clearing up. If you give them my name, they'll be able to set you up with a plate. Plenty of leftovers, never fear."

Maybe he said it just to get on Myriam's good side, but I don't think so. Honestly, I don't care. "Seventh Officer George Greene," I repeat, to make sure I've got it right. "Thank you!"

"Have a good night!" Myriam calls after me. She might actually mean it.

I hurry down the hallway, pushing past a few other after-dinner stragglers. But already I'm doubting myself. I don't remember this turn at all, and the corridors feel like a maze. I'm not used to finding my way around new places, since I only just left the house I've worked in for the past four years and the village where I'd spent my whole life before that.

Glancing over my shoulder, I look for Myriam and George, but they're already out of sight. Nobody else around me speaks English or looks likely to; two of the men closest to me even appear to be from China. So much for asking for directions.

So I head back the way I came, to the doorway that leads to the first-class areas of this deck. Maybe I can reorient myself and get turned back toward the dining hall.

As I reach the doorway, my stomach rumbles, and I hope I won't be lost much longer—and the doorway opens.

Mikhail steps through.

My body seems to freeze in shock. *He's hunting me after all*, I

54

think—but that's not right. He looks as surprised to see me as I am to see him.

Only for a moment. Then Mikhail's face steels as he clamps his hand around my upper arm, hard enough to hurt. "You'd be a fool to scream."

"Let me go."

He pulls me back through the door—how does *he* have a key?—and I try to resist, but he's stronger. Although I want to scream, I keep reminding myself of what Alec said: *Keep your silence.*

Now that we're alone in the quieter first-class corridor, Mikhail leans close to me, pinning me against the corridor wall, clearly meaning to loom over me. But I'm too tall for that. It doesn't faze him. "How interesting to see you again."

"I've told no one about—about before," I say. "I don't plan to."

"Perhaps." His eyes are so cold. I can feel that shiver pass through me again; it's hard being so close to his hunter's stare. He frames my body with his arms. "When I first saw you, I thought you were simply a temptation. A deviation from my mission." *The box*, I think through my panic. *He was stalking me that first night because he was already after the Lisles.* Mikhail leans even closer to me, so that I can smell the strange, animal scent of his skin. "Or perhaps a means of whiling away an hour or so before I took care of my business with the Lisles."

I can't tell if that hour is the one he wants me to spend in his bed or in my grave.

And then I'm so scared I'm not scared anymore. I'm furious. I shove Mikhail back, not caring whether I'll get into trouble or whether I hurt him. "If you try to steal from me again, I'll tell a ship's officer. Now leave me alone."

As soon as the words leave my mouth, I know I've made a terrible mistake. Not shoving him, not even threatening to tell. Mikhail's expression changed the moment I said *steal from me*. The moment I revealed that I knew whatever he really wants is inside the Lisles' safe.

He lunges at me, gripping my arm in one hand and covering my mouth with the other. My back slams against the wall so hard it knocks the breath out of me. If I thought he was strong before, I didn't understand the half of it; Mikhail can hold me in place, as though I were helpless. His strength is beyond anything I've ever known. Almost inhuman.

"That's a very sensible plan," he hisses as I struggle to inhale. "But I can't have my work here disrupted by a mere woman. So why don't I make absolutely sure you'll never tell?"

I go crazy. I claw at him, try to push him back, wrench my neck to the side so hard it hurts. But even when I manage to scream, I know nobody will come. The first-class section of the deck is deserted except for us at this time of night; the third-class passengers probably can't hear through the door, and if they can, they won't have the key to get through.

Mikhail grabs my hair, which hurts so much tears spring to my eyes. He's dragging me down the corridor, and I keep trying to clutch something, anything to hold on to, but it's useless. We reach a doorway, and he flings it open. Just before he shoves me though, I see the sign: This is the Turkish bath.

I fall through darkness, through heat, as I tumble onto my hands and knees upon a floor of moist green and white tiles. The steam of the bath still clouds the air, as though I'd been tossed into the fog. I can't see, can't breathe. The main light is from the hallway, and it outlines Mikhail's body as he walks inside after me and slams the door behind him.

I expect to be beaten, or raped, or killed.

I do not expect the wolf.

# ⚜ CHAPTER 6 ⚜

FIRST I SEE THE EYES.

They're green-gold. Flat and reflective. It's so dark I can hardly make out any shapes, at least not yet, but whatever light is in this room gleams in this animal gaze.

I gasp. Hot, vapor-heavy air burns my lungs and makes me cough as I push myself away from those eyes. But I hit something—someone. Mikhail. He's standing right behind me.

Mikhail's laughter echoes in the tile room. I scramble away from him, toward the corner, but the eyes follow me. As my own eyes adjust to the darkness, the beast's enormous shape appears amid the swirling steam. Pointed ears, wide shoulders, muscled legs, thick red fur.

*Wolf*, I think, just at the moment it begins to growl.

"He's hungry," Mikhail says. He has no fear. "I thought it was high time I fed him. Don't you agree?"

The wolf lunges at me, and I scream.

I manage to leap out of the wolf's way, but only by inches—I can sense its weight and speed as it skids past me. I catch a glimpse of its long, white teeth. Quickly I scramble to my feet and run through the opulent bath, looking for a door that isn't blocked by Mikhail. There isn't one, but one wall is lined with small wooden booths—for changing, perhaps? I don't care. They have doors, and maybe I can lock myself in.

When I run into the booth, I want to swear. This wood is so thin, so flimsy. But what did I expect? They're not meant to provide protection, only privacy. It's all I've got, though. I brace myself, back against the door, and wince as I hear the wolf running toward me—it's going to slam through, right through the door and through me—

But the wolf doesn't hit the door. It skids to a stop just short of the booth. I stare down at my feet, terrified it's going to crawl underneath the small gap there, or just bite at my ankles. It doesn't. Instead the wolf starts pacing, back and forth. Back and forth. I can hear it panting, its claws clicking against the tile floor.

Though I'm still so scared my whole body shakes, I finally have a moment to think. What is a wolf doing onboard? Surely no wild animals would be brought aboard a ship, or if they were, they would be caged in the cargo hold. This is Mikhail's doing, obviously, but I can't imagine why.

Is it the same beast I saw in Southampton? No—this one is sleeker, redder. But it is surely another wolf, and surely now even more dangerous. If only Alec would appear again to help me. Alec, or anyone. But there's no one here besides Mikhail.

He laughs again, though now it's quieter—slow chuckling.

As though he's seen all this a thousand times before, but it never fails to amuse him. "How long do you think that will protect you? Three minutes? Five?"

I don't answer. I have nothing to say to that worthless bastard.

"The wolf is very close," Mikhail says. "Close enough to smell your blood. But he doesn't remember how to be a wolf any longer. If he did, he would have devoured you already."

The wolf's pacing slows. I can hear it breathing.

There's a small bench in the little booth, and, keeping my hands braced against the door, I step atop it. That means the red wolf won't be able to drag me down by my ankles. It also means I can see Mikhail. He's still standing not far from the door—but he's taken off his jacket. His white shirt has begun to stick to his body from the moisture in the air; he's thick with muscles, so rippled and bulky that he looks nearly monstrous. No wonder I couldn't fend him off. Now he takes off his shoes. As he sees me watching him, Mikhail's grin widens, and he pulls open his shirt to reveal his hairy chest. I look away so as not to give him the satisfaction. It seems clear enough what he has in mind, but how does he expect to get at me with a wild wolf between us?

Mikhail says, "If he's forgotten how to be a wolf, then I'll have to remind him."

He growls—a low sound like an animal's. Just like an animal's. Then he screams.

I turn back toward Mikhail, half expecting to see the red wolf attacking him. But the wolf remains in front of my door, its red fur standing on end, a low growl scratching in its own throat. Mikhail is screaming, louder and louder, naked now, his body exposed—

And changing.

It's the steam playing tricks on me. The darkness. My own fear. But no. I *see* this. It's really happening.

Mikhail's body twists and contorts, shoulder blades spreading outward, back hunching so sharply it's as if he broke his spine. He falls to all fours, arching his neck back as his face stretches with a terrible sound like the butcher sawing through gristle. His jaws grow. His teeth seem to be stabbing their way out of his gums. And his skin is darkening—no. He's growing black hair all over his body. Fur.

*A wolf,* I think. Another wolf, as enormous as the first, but iron black. And this, I know, is the very wolf that chased me last night in Southampton. For the first time I realize that Mikhail is a monster, a thing out of stories told to frighten children, but it's real. He's real, and he's growling, and he began hunting me before this voyage ever started, and now—now he's coming to kill me.

The black wolf charges toward my stall, and I cry out in fear as I push back against the door, expecting him to burst through at any second. But then I hear another growl, and the impact of beast against beast.

I look back over the stall to see the red wolf lunge at the black wolf's throat.

They're like dogs fighting now—tearing at each other's flesh, snapping and snarling. The steam is so thick that I can't make out precisely what's happening, but the black wolf is larger, and so I feel sure it will win. Yet the red wolf stands its ground, sinking its fangs into the black wolf's shoulder and hanging on.

For one moment I think the red wolf must be defending me. But how stupid of me. It's just trying to claim prey for itself.

"Help!" I scream. "Somebody, help!" My voice echoes off the green and white tiles, and I know nobody is close enough to hear. The vapor catches in my throat again, and I pull off my white cotton cap—damp from the steam—and hold it across my face.

The fight lasts for what feels like eternity, though probably it's only a few minutes. I have no sense of time anymore; there's nothing in the world but my fast, hard pulse and the trembling in my limbs. Exhaustion has weighed me down since this day began, and now, weakened by fear, I feel as if it's all I can do to remain standing. But I keep myself braced against that door.

Eventually the black wolf retreats, walking backward from the red wolf, which is panting hard. I hear that sickening sound again, and the wolf twists violently, jerking up onto its hind legs; the iron-black fur begins to vanish, disappearing beneath restored skin. Although I know it's Mikhail—that this has been Mikhail the entire time—it's still a shock to see his cruel face once more. His shoulder is bleeding from bite marks, but it's as though I can see him healing where he stands.

Then his eyes flick up toward mine, and I see that he still has the flat, animal gaze of a wolf.

Mikhail laughs as he grabs his abandoned clothing and begins putting it back on. "Look at you," he says. "Too stupid to know what you've seen. To appreciate the miracle you've beheld. And all your pretty golden curls down in your face. Beautiful and foolish—very appetizing."

"You're nothing more than a freak from the circus," I say, with more bravado than I feel.

It outrages him. Mikhail snarls as savagely as he did while a wolf. "You don't know your betters. You don't know a god when you see one."

"You're no god!"

"My compatriot has worked up an appetite now," Mikhail says as he buttons his shirt. "And I think he wants you to himself." He opens the door, letting in a brief shaft of light. "Don't worry. I'll be back in the morning to gnaw your bones."

The door slams shut again, and I hear a key turn in the lock. I'm as trapped as I was before, but now I'm alone with only the red wolf.

The wolf doesn't come after me right away. Perhaps he's as hungry as Mikhail said, but as he paces I see him limping, clearly in pain. There are droplets of blood on the floor from the fight between the wolves, and not all of that blood could be Mikhail's. He's injured. Badly?

Badly enough for me to escape?

Tentatively, I step to the floor, then slowly open the door of the booth. Just as I open it enough to step through, the wolf turns to stare at me. Its green-gold eyes are bright amid the steam. The wolf's head droops low, like that of any hurt creature, and I remember everything the groundskeeper at Moorcliffe told me about wounded animals being the most dangerous.

I dare not risk it. Instead I dash back into the booth and shut the door again. The wolf steps closer, pacing in front of my door again, and then stopping there—close enough for me to hear its panting once more.

My whole body is shaking from weariness and fear, but I force myself to think rationally. The beast is wounded. Weak. Probably the wolf no longer has the strength to get through the door of the booth, and it's too enormous to get underneath. No doubt it will recover—and be very hungry when it does—but that will take time. And time is on my side.

Gentlemen from first class will want to use the Turkish bath tomorrow. Probably the bath opens not long after the breakfast service. That means the attendant will come to make this area ready around breakfast time, if not earlier. Help is coming. All I have to do is wait.

The heat is unbearable. Sweat and condensed water have slicked my skin, and it feels as though I can't catch my breath. I hesitate, because the thought of undressing makes me feel less safe—but the thought of wearing wet, heavy clothes in this suffocating heat is even worse. So I peel off my damp, sodden uniform so that I'm wearing only my thin vest and slip. That's a little better.

I pull my knees up so that I can lie down on the small bench inside this booth, and crumple my uniform into a ball beneath my head. The wooden slats are hard against my side, but I don't care.

Outside, the wolf lies down outside my door. I can see nothing except his red fur. He's waiting for me. He doesn't mean to let me get away, even when he sleeps.

The thought is horrifying, and it keeps me awake for hours as

I tremble and cough. But eventually sleep wins, and I drift into dreamless oblivion.

*April 11, 1912*

I awake knowing only that I am stiff and uncomfortable, and that I want more sleep. Then I open my eyes, and my strange surroundings—and the unbelievable memories that explain them—jolt me to alertness. I sit upright and push my hands against the door almost before I remember that I'm doing it to keep the wolf back.

There's light now—thin and gray. Dawn, then. There must be portholes to let the sunlight in. I look down, but the wolf isn't lying in front of the door any longer. I can't hear him panting, either, nor any claws against the tile. Might it have left? Died in the night? Or is it at least far enough away that I could run to the door and pound against it? Someone might be closer now.

With a shaking hand, I pull the door open, so slowly that it seems to take forever. No movement. No sound. So I dart out, thinking to run for the door that leads to the hallway and do whatever I can for myself—

—and I jerk to a halt within two steps.

Lying on the floor, entirely naked, perfectly formed, and dazed nearly to the point of unconsciousness, is Alec Marlowe.

The red wolf.

# ⊰ CHAPTER 7 ⊱

FOR A MOMENT I CAN'T MOVE; I CAN ONLY STARE.
Last night, as I drifted between waking and sleep, I had realized the
red wolf must be another version of Mikhail—another transformed
human being. But with all his talk about his "friend" and his "compatriot," I believed it had to be one of the men he'd been walking
with that night in Southampton. Never did I suspect Alec Marlowe.

Alec comes to enough to recognize me standing over him, and
he rolls onto his side, slightly away from me—maybe to show me
that he doesn't want to hurt me, maybe just because he's embar-
rassed to be naked in front of a girl he hardly knows.

Maybe I should run. But seeing how he moves—slowly, still
confused—it seems too cruel to leave him like this.

He says, "What are you doing here?"

"You—you don't remember?"

"It's all a blur." Alec tries to push himself up, but he can't. His
muscled arms shake too much to bear his weight yet. "What happened?"

"Your friend, Mikhail—he dragged me in here. He . . . " How

do I say this? "He changed. The two of you fought, and I couldn't get out until—until you changed back."

Now that it's light, and the steam has finally run out, I take a good look around the Turkish bath. There's a cabinet I'd bet anything is for linens, and sure enough, when I open the door, there are towels and plush robes folded inside. I take a robe to Alec and kneel by his side. The tiles are cool against my bare knees. "Here," I say gently. "Are you all right?"

He snatches it from me, though he's apparently still too weak to put it on. He just drapes it over his lap. "There's no need to worry, Tess. Nothing's happened here. Just leave me. And tell no one."

I almost want to laugh. "Are you really going to pretend I don't know?"

Alec turns his head toward the corner; his firm jaw clenches, as he struggles against some deeper emotion: shame, I realize. He's ashamed to be seen as what he is.

"Most people . . . prefer to forget, instead of admit what they've seen," he says roughly. His voice sounds terrible—as though he had been screaming for hours. I remember how he growled and snarled. "You should go."

"I can't."

"Because you want to stare at the monster?" Alec's green eyes blaze, but with a wholly human fire now. "Or because you pity me?" I couldn't guess which possibility he loathes more.

I fold my arms. "I can't leave because the door's locked. Believe me, I would've gone hours ago if I could have."

"Oh. Of course." Then he looks so abashed—so boyish, and so handsome—that I almost want to laugh.

But the strangeness of the situation keeps me quiet. I am still frightened of Alec, knowing what he truly is. And yet this morning he is weary, bruised, naked, and exposed on the floor of the Turkish bath. Vulnerable.

If I want answers, I had better get them now.

"You're a—" I hesitate on the word, one I've heard only in stories to frighten the gullible. "A werewolf."

Alec lifts his head to face me. His chestnut curls glint slightly red in the dawn light. "Yes."

"And Mikhail, too."

He grimaces with pure dislike. "Yes. Older. Stronger. More powerful."

"Did he . . . do this to you?" I wouldn't put it past Mikhail to do something so wicked. "Or were you born a werewolf?"

Taking a deep breath, Alec pushes himself up to a fully seated position, then struggles into the robe as I avert my eyes. Only now, as he puts something on, do I remember that I'm still in my underclothes, which are made of flimsy linen. Should've gotten myself a robe while I was at it, but now I simply draw my knees toward my chest, for a little modesty.

Once the robe is on, Alec slowly rises to his feet. Movement still seems to hurt him, and he sways as he straightens for the first time. Before I can rise to help, though, Alec steadies himself.

He looks down at me. "I've never told anyone this. Anyone besides my father, I mean."

Mr. Marlowe knows? I wouldn't have expected that. But how would I have expected any of this?

"I became a werewolf two years ago," Alec says. "My father and I were on a hunting trip in Wisconsin."

I've never heard of this "Wisconsin," which is apparently a dangerous place. So I imagine it like the great woods near Moorcliffe, where the Viscount sometimes goes to shoot—ancient trees that stretch up toward the sky, their leaves so thick that they almost blot out the sun. The ground covered with clouds of ferns and carpets of moss. A profound silence broken only by the flapping of birds' wings.

A bitter, rueful smile plays on Alec's face. "It was just after sunset. My father had told me earlier to come in for dinner, but I hadn't shot anything all day. I refused. I was going to prove what a great hunter I really was. But there was a better hunter in the forest, waiting."

"Mikhail?"

"Another. I'll never even know his name, or what he looks like as a human, unless he someday chooses to reveal himself." Alec's tone makes it clear that this would be extremely unwise for the werewolf to do; he wants revenge so badly that I can feel it in the room with us, as tangible as the walls. "I didn't understand what had happened to me at first. I thought I'd simply been bitten by a wolf. But immediately I became sick—so sick—God, the fevers. I remember tossing and turning in bed, thinking that I knew what meat must feel like when people cook it on a spit."

I've been sick like that—well, not *exactly* like that, but I know what he means.

"Then the full moon came," Alec says. "And for the first time,

I changed into the wolf. Luckily, I was in our stables at the time, and only my father was with me. He was able to shut me in alone. Of course, we lost all our horses."

Meaning, he killed them.

He sounds so disgusted with himself that I feel more sympathy than horror. But there's one thing that's confusing me: Something from the old wives' tales, and from what he's just said, that doesn't add up. "I'm sure last night wasn't a full moon."

"You're right. It wasn't. The full moon is important to our kind—that's when the curse finally awakens in us. When our powers are at the zenith. And it's the one night we can never escape from; no matter what, on the night of the full moon, we have to change into wolves."

"The rest of the time, you can choose? You chose to change and attack me last night?" The fear shivers inside me again, and I wonder how long it can be before the morning staff finally arrives. Alec is still weary, but I can see him growing stronger by the second. Restoring himself.

"No. God, Tess, no. I don't have any control over when I change. I have to transform into a wolf every night, dusk to dawn—no matter where I am. That's why I always try to be alone, someplace safe. But Mikhail must have found me. He had other plans." He rubs a hand across his temple, as though his head hurts. "For both of us."

I think back to the night before, to the casual way Mikhail tossed aside his clothes before he transformed into a wolf, and how he changed back long before the sun rose. "You mean—Mikhail can choose whether or not to change."

"He has that power. Because he's been initiated into the Brotherhood."

My Lord, the hate in his voice as he says it. It frightens me, even though I know the hatred is directed at the Brotherhood and not at me. That kind of hate is terrifying no matter where it's aimed. I shrink down, hugging my knees closer.

Alec doesn't seem to notice. He's staring out the porthole at the early morning light. "The Brotherhood is the dominant group of werewolves. The ruling pack. There are other groups—smaller, weaker, hunted by the Brotherhood. And there must be lone wolves hiding out, the way I did at first. But the Brotherhood will stop at nothing short of absolute power. They control henchmen in the streets. They control members of Parliament and Congress. There's no one too low for them to notice or too high for them to command. Sometimes I think they might have targeted me—sent the werewolf that attacked me, the better to bring Dad's money and influence under their control." He shakes his head tiredly. "My father thought he was helping me, taking me to Europe. We wondered if there might be . . . men of learning there. People who understood what was happening to me and could make it stop. We meant to search for them, no matter how long it took. Instead we found Mikhail and the Brotherhood waiting for us."

"Why do they want to kill you? Why do they hunt other werewolves?"

"They only hunt the ones they don't want to join the Brotherhood," he says. "But they want to initiate me. That's why Mikhail's on the *Titanic*. To force me to join them."

Alec says it as though there could be no worse fate. I don't understand. The Brotherhood sounds scary to me, but if Alec is a werewolf, like them, why wouldn't he want to be one of the "ruling pack"? It makes no sense. "If that would give you the power to . . . change, or not change, as you wanted—then why don't you join them?"

"Because they're monsters." Alec glances over his shoulder at me; one corner of his mouth lifts in an unwilling smile. "But you think I'm a monster too, don't you?"

"Tell me the difference." As long as I'm trapped on the same ship with both Alec and Mikhail, I need to know.

"The Brotherhood kill people, to eat, or just for fun. They terrify and torment them for their amusement—especially women. And if a woman becomes a werewolf, the Brotherhood never considers recruitment. Just murder. They claim female werewolves would 'weaken the pack.' It's not as though I could undergo the initiation and then do as I pleased, either. The older members can exert power over the others, once they're initiated—perhaps even control their minds. I'm not sure. I don't intend to find out."

Alec, at least, is not a random killer. I still don't trust him, but I now feel brave enough to rise to my feet.

No longer am I looking up at him as a little huddled wretch on the floor. I realize that I am one of the only people in the world who knows his secret, and that gives me power. Not much power, perhaps, and the knowledge is more trouble than it's worth—but if I have a hunter after me, I have to take what strength I can.

"When I first saw the two of you," I say, "near the grand staircase,

72

yesterday morning—that was when you first realized Mikhail had followed you onboard, wasn't it?"

"Yes." Alec leans against the wall, still tired, though I think this is now more emotional than physical. "My father and I booked passage at the last moment. Yet somehow they knew. The Brotherhood has spies everywhere."

So, they aren't working together. But maybe Alec at least knows this: "Why did Mikhail come after me? What's in the box I was carrying, the one he wanted so badly?"

Alec sighs. "I don't know, though I've been wondering. The man is hugely wealthy, so he wouldn't bother stealing if it were merely a matter of money. There's something special inside that box. Something unique. Something Mikhail can't get any other way." His green eyes search my face. "You didn't look inside?"

"No. It locks, and I don't have the key."

"I don't suppose you've ever heard of any connection between the Lisle family and werewolves."

I can't help but laugh. "Not hardly."

He lifts his chin. "But of course, you don't know all their secrets, do you? You're merely a servant girl."

Although Alec says it matter-of-factly, with none of the contempt Layton or Lady Regina puts in those words, hearing him dismiss me that way stings. "Who do you think knows more about what happens in a house than the servants? No one. I know things about every person at Moorcliffe that the other members of the family could never guess."

Now, that sounds like I'm bragging, or threatening to tell, and

I wish I hadn't said it. But Alec doesn't pry for more. He looks as though that threw him off his guard.

So I press my advantage. "Why are you going back to the United States, when you haven't found the cure you were looking for? To get away from the Brotherhood?"

"Partly." His expression darkens, not with anger but with sadness. As he turns toward me, I realize how desperately lonely Alec is; he's talking to me not only because he feels he must, but because—no matter how ashamed he is of his secrets—it feels good to talk to someone. "But . . . I'm too dangerous for polite society. For any society. Look what I nearly did to you last night. What I might have done if I hadn't been sure to eat just before sundown. I penned myself in here because it was one of the only places onboard with nothing to damage and no other people around after dark, but even then, you've told me, I nearly—" The words choke in his throat. Alec takes a deep breath before he continues. "I want to find an isolated place on the frontier. Someplace remote, where I can live without hurting anyone. My father will take me out West, help me get established, and then leave me behind. It's past time he had a normal life again. At least one of us can. Maybe there I'll finally be beyond the Brotherhood's reach."

Then he focuses on me. "But Mikhail's after more than the box. That first night, in Southampton—you must have realized by now that he was the wolf who tried to attack you."

I nod. "But why would he be after me? If it's the box he wants."

"For fun. The box—that's only why he first began following the Lisles and you as their servant. After that, he wanted to kill you for fun." The simple way Alec says it makes it all the more horrifying. "I thought if I helped you then, he'd probably never see you again. That he'd be looking for me and forget about you. When he saw you aboard the *Titanic*, though . . . now you're something he wants and couldn't get. Proof he's not all-powerful: Believe me, there's nothing Mikhail hates more. You have to be careful, Tess."

Alec steps closer to me; though I feel a shiver run through my body, it's not exactly fear. The morning sunshine grows brighter, bathing his sculpted face in almost dazzling light. "You probably wouldn't tell anyone about this, regardless of what I say or don't say. Who would believe you?" Then he sighs. "But all the same—help me keep this secret. I only need a few more days." He finishes with a word that almost seems to be torn from him: "Please."

Our faces are very close. I try to imagine his face, his eyes, his body as the red wolf I saw last night. The beast is there, just beneath the skin; I'll always be able to see it now. He's very kind now that I've got something on him, with his asking me nicely, but I wouldn't like to find out what he'd do if I didn't agree. "I won't tell."

He steps back, suddenly distant again. "Stay away from me as much as possible." This is the voice of a gentleman again, one used to giving orders and having them obeyed. "It's for your own good. Mikhail clearly likes the idea of using you to bait me. If he realizes we've spoken—that you know the full truth—it's even more dangerous for you."

"If you can steer clear of Lady Regina, I can avoid you well enough." I think that over. "But I warn you now, steering clear of Lady Regina is easier said than done."

A moment of humor flickers in those green eyes, but he grows serious again in an instant. "If you ever see me in Mikhail's company, and I don't appear to be . . . troubled, or arguing with him, anything like that—abandon your duty. Leave the Lisles to their own devices, and hide until the *Titanic* makes port."

"Why?"

"Because that will mean I've been initiated into the Brotherhood. They might have ways of forcing me to do it—Mikhail's hinted at it before. If the Brotherhood can control me as completely as they claim after the initiation, then he could order me to murder you, and I'd do it."

He looks me dead in the eye. He means it. Alec can't swear that he wouldn't kill me. There's nothing I can say in response; I simply nod.

After a moment of terrible silence, Alec says, "I wish we might have met in different circumstances." Then he pauses before he adds, "Thank you for keeping the secret." Then he walks across the room to another of the booths, where he pulls out a small bundle—his clothes, I realize, set aside for the morning. But he's obviously eager to be gone, and heads directly for the door, perhaps planning on sneaking up to his room to change.

I call to him, "The door's locked. Remember?"

"I know." Alec flashes me a grin that shows me just how handsome he could look, if he were ever happy and carefree. "I've got a key." He unlocks the door and goes through, leaving it cracked open behind him.

He could have let me out when he first woke up. I can't decide whether to be angry or laugh. My head spins from everything I've learned in the past few hours, from the fact that the world isn't at all the place I thought it was—it's a thousand times more dangerous and strange. As I walk over to fetch my own clothes, I'm practically sleepwalking.

But seeing my damp, crumpled uniform reminds me that I've got to put it back on. I have to return to first class, and in a hurry. Even after all this, I still have to go to the Lisles and get to work.

# ⊰ CHAPTER 8 ⊱

I STRUGGLE BACK INTO MY EVENING UNIFORM, which is a wrinkled, damp mess, and dash out into the corridor, where I promptly run into a steward, perhaps the Turkish bath attendant. "Hello, what are you doing in here?" he demands. *Now* the staff shows up.

"Marvelous timing," I pant. "I've got to get back into third class. Pardon me, would you?"

He doesn't look amused, but I'm only asking to go back where I ought to be in the first place, so he lets me go. I take off at a run. On one hand, it seems almost absurd to be worried about angering Lady Regina, after I've learned that werewolves are real and at least one of them is eager to kill me. But not even that can make me forget that I want this to be my last week as a maidservant. If I'm going to start a new life in America, I need to be able to collect my last wages. Every penny counts.

And now I have even more incentive to get away: The sooner I leave the Lisles' service, the sooner I will vanish from Mikhail's sight.

Now that it's daylight, I can see my way around better, and soon I've found my cabin. I dash through the door to find the rest of my bunkmates staring at me. The old Norwegian ladies are still tucked in, red-and-white blankets pulled up to their chins, but Myriam has already made her bed and dressed. She sits atop her bunk, vigorously brushing her hair, and when she sees me, she doesn't miss a stroke.

"I've always heard how very proper Englishwomen are," she says. "Who could have guessed I would get so much proof, so quickly?"

"I don't want to hear a word about it." Quickly I start stripping off my uniform—which is only for evenings. There's another uniform for morning wear, and that, thank goodness, is still folded neatly.

"Oh, look." Myriam's still brushing, a smug smile on her face. "You made it home with your underwear. Well done."

I glare at her, but I have no time to spare. If my cabinmates are waking up, the Lisles will be too, and I'll be expected to have Irene all decked out before breakfast.

One of the old ladies looks at me through narrowed eyes, then mutters something to her sister—no doubt about how fast young girls are these days. To my surprise, her sister chuckles and says something knowing in reply; the first lady actually blushes. Though I don't speak a word of Norwegian, I'd bet anything she just got a reminder that they were fast in their day, too.

"Really, it's disgraceful . . ." Myriam's voice trails off, and she stops brushing. She leans forward, studying my face more carefully, and her smirk vanishes. "My God. What happened to you last night?"

"Nothing." But what a ridiculous lie. Myriam knows better already. "I can't explain now." As if I could ever explain.

"Has anyone harmed you?"

"I'm fine, I promise!" I groan as I look at my crumpled evening uniform. "Or I will be until Lady Regina sees this later on." I'll need to change in the afternoon, if I'm to look proper, but I haven't any time to press it.

"Give that here," Myriam demands. When I just stare at her, she repeats, "Give it to me!"

So I throw it at her, still hardly understanding. It's not as though she can make it any worse.

Myriam inspects the fabric carefully. "It's not dirty. Just wrinkled. I can use the iron on it this morning, get it ready for you."

Using an iron is no fun—heating the heavy, cast-iron thing at a fire or stove, covering the handle with a damp cloth to try and keep from burning your palm, going over and over the wrinkles five or ten or twenty times each to finally get them out. It's no small favor, and I'd never have predicted Myriam would offer. "I—thank you. Really."

She tosses her thick hair. "It's a good excuse to send a note to George. Ask him about the ship's laundries." But I don't believe that's all there is to it, and for the first time, I give her a true smile. It feels as though I haven't smiled in years. Myriam doesn't return it, instead cautiously spreading my uniform on her bunk, showing that cloth the kindness that she apparently doesn't like to admit to.

Our cabin has no mirror, but what does it matter? I can see that my morning uniform looks right, and though my hair is undoubtedly a frizzy blond nightmare, it won't matter once I get it pinned up and put on my linen cap, which by now I can do in seconds. "I'll see you after lunch," I say.

The mere mention of food makes my stomach rumble, and all at once I realize I haven't eaten since lunch yesterday. Fear had banished my hunger, but now it comes back, so hard I nearly swoon.

"Are you sure you're all right?" Myriam's face suggests that I must have gone pale, too.

"I will be." I hope it's true.

Thank God for Miss Irene. When I arrive in her room, she offers me some sweet cakes from a tin. "I thought you might've missed dinner last night," she says as I gobble one down. "Mother kept you so dreadfully late."

"You've got to stop sympathizing with the servants, miss." I hate to say it, but it's true. "The two of us get on, but when you run your own house, if you worry this much about everyone who works there, they'll run roughshod over you."

Even at Moorcliffe, we already know that if a mistake must be admitted, it's best to admit it to Irene first. She'll plead with her parents on our behalf—which is useless with Lady Regina, but sometimes works on the Viscount. For every one of us who respects Irene for her kindness, like Ned and me, there's another who thinks her weak for it. If there were no higher authority in the house, no doubt half the staff would pay her orders no attention at all.

"I don't want to think about that now." She looks so pale, so drawn. I want to ask her if she's well, but at that moment, Lady Regina glides in—already turned out to perfection by the damnably efficient Horne. Hurriedly I turn away, as if examining Miss Irene's wardrobe, and lick the last of the crumbs from my lips.

"Still dawdling, Tess." Lady Regina sounds more annoyed than angry; it's Irene she's focused on this morning, not me. "Irene, I want you in the yellow dress today. It's so fresh and delicate."

That pale yellow washes Irene out until she looks sickly. I venture, "Maybe the pink, milady?"

"It's not your place to argue with me," Lady Regina snaps. "You think I don't know what's best for my own daughter? Or that I don't understand the latest fashions better than some servant?"

*I think you keep trying to dress your daughter in the colors that suited you when you were young, without ever asking yourself if Irene needs something different.* "Yes, milady."

Irene sighs, so softly her mother doesn't hear. But I do.

Lady Regina remains in Irene's room throughout the entire process, critiquing everything I do—from whether Irene's shoes have been polished brightly enough (even though they reflect back as well as a mirror) to how I comb her hair (too gently for her taste, as if ripping at the poor girl's scalp would somehow magically make her hair curl). But the worst of it is how Lady Regina keeps on at Irene—and what she keeps on about.

"We ought to have had Layton travel separately from us," Lady Regina says. "He might as easily have come over on the *Lusitania*."

"It would be less embarrassing," Irene agrees, as I slide the white silk hose up her leg. "He really did get dreadfully drunk at dinner last night, Mother. Can't you speak to him about not having so much wine?"

"Layton is a young man. Young men have their foibles. Only the most foolish sort of woman tries to break a man's spirit. When the time is right, Layton will take a wife and behave properly," Lady Regina says, as if marriage ever made a man change. But she sounds weary; Layton's dissolution the past two years has tasked even her patience with her favorite child. "Once again you've completely failed to understand my meaning, Irene. Are you so blind to the opportunities we would have, were we women traveling alone? Any number of gentlemen onboard would have offered us their protection."

The idea is that women can't possibly manage traveling on their own, so when they have to, men usually offer their "protection." This means that they'll arrange social introductions, dine with the ladies at meals, so on and so forth. A friendly enough custom, though I notice it applies only to gentlewomen; a poor girl or a servant like me can be sent on any number of difficult errands alone, and none of these men will think to "protect" me from lifting heavy boxes, or from the jeering of sailors.

"Howard Marlowe would certainly have offered." Lady Regina watches as I hold out the skirt of the pale yellow dress for Irene to step into. "Then you would have been sure of spending every meal dining beside his son."

My hands fumble with the buttons on the back of Irene's dress at the mention of Alec. I keep my face very still.

*You have to stay away from him, Irene. Because he's dangerous in every way that a man can be dangerous. Because he's a monster. Because he could destroy you and your family, all of us, by bringing us closer to the Brotherhood.*

An even smaller voice within my mind adds, *Because you don't really know him, and I do. I understand him.*

*I want*— No. Not even in my mind will I allow myself to finish that thought.

"Alexander Marlowe showed me no special attention, Mother." Irene suddenly seems very interested in her skirt, smoothing the fabric with her hands; it's as good a way as any of avoiding her mother's eyes. "He's certainly a very eligible young man, but I don't see why he more than any other—"

"Do you not see the need for haste, Irene? Truly, after all that has happened?" Lady Regina's expression is very strange. Were I to see it on anyone less formidable, I would say she looked . . . sad.

Irene hangs her head, and she actually sways a little on her feet. I balance her elbow with my hand, but otherwise I give no sign that I can hear this conversation, or notice anything in the room but her appearance.

Servants are sometimes thought to be deaf, blind, mute, and stupid—or so you'd guess, to judge by what lords and ladies will say in front of us. We can choose not to listen, but we listen often enough. I was telling the truth when I said to Alec that nobody knows more about the secrets of a household than its staff. Probably this is Lady Regina's way of referring to the reduced circumstances of the Lisle family, and the need for Layton and Irene to marry as well as they can.

And yet Lady Regina's voice was so strange, and Irene is so shaken—

"You must marry," Lady Regina says as I tie a broad lace sash around Irene's tiny waist, emphasizing what good features I can. "You must marry soon. If you won't pursue the most eligible young man fate has offered you, then whom will it be?" Her eyes flash, and there's something dangerous in the room, something I don't fully understand. "Who is good enough for you, Irene?"

"I'll try harder," Irene promises. She sounds close to tears. "I promise."

As I kneel on the floor to button Irene's shoes, Lady Regina continues on, as blithely as though she'd been in a lovely mood all morning. "Alec Marlowe would do quite well. Marlowe Steel is a fortune to rival that of the highest English nobility. True, they're Americans, but one can't have everything."

"What else do you know of him, Mother?"

*Not as much as I know of him*, I think. How would Lady Regina react if she knew who—no, *what*—she wanted her daughter to marry?

"Not very much. Naturally one hears more about the father. Tess, her hair isn't right at all; do it over. Let's see, Alexander Marlowe. He was attending one of the better American universities before the family moved to Paris. Presumably he took up studies at the Sorbonne. There was a hint of scandal not long ago—"

I realize I'm holding my breath.

"—something about that French actress Gabrielle Dumont.

That ended badly." Lady Regina shrugs. "But as I said before, young men have their ways. No doubt he's returning to his home country with thoughts of joining his father's steel business and finally starting a family of his own."

I remember Alec as he looked this morning, his expression bleak, his profile outlined by the dawn light. He wants to set his father free. He wants a cabin on the frontier where he can harm no one. He's nothing like the dream Lady Regina is chasing.

And yet, Lady Regina knew something about him that I didn't. As I fix Miss Irene's hair all over again, I wonder who Gabrielle Dumont is. A French actress. Sounds glamorous. I wouldn't have thought Alec would find it easy to run around with women, as he changes into a wolf every night. Yet any young man as handsome and rich as he is would attract female attention.

Just as he's attracted mine.

*Don't be stupid*, I tell myself. *Alec is a monster, and no matter how badly he wants to escape that, he never can. A killer is stalking him. You don't want to be a part of his world.*

But all the reasons I have for not wanting Alec Marlowe don't seem half as real as the stinging knowledge that he would never want a servant girl like me.

I step back from Irene to let Lady Regina inspect my work again. She sniffs, not impressed, but apparently she'll accept it. "I'm going to see if Layton is fit—I mean, whether Layton is ready to take breakfast with us. You may finish here."

When Lady Regina steps out, the silence in the room is awful. Irene looks utterly wretched, and her misery draws me out of my own concerns for a moment. Couldn't her mother have said one kind word to her, just once? I try to make a bit of a joke of it, for her sake and for mine; it's the sort of thing I do to cheer her up sometimes. "Her Ladyship's practically picked out your wedding bouquet, hasn't she?"

Irene's eyes well with tears.

"Oh, no, Miss Irene. Don't do that. You're all right." Quickly I fetch her a handkerchief and pet her arm. "No need to cry."

She fans her face, takes a deep breath. "I'm all right," she repeats. "Let's find some pretty jewelry. Something really nice, so Mother can't claim I'm not trying."

I move toward her jewelry box, but Irene shakes her head and picks something up from her bedside—a key on a chain.

"No, Tess. Something really special."

We go into the sitting room of the suite, with its gleaming oaken paneling and green marble fireplace. Irene kneels in front of the safe, and I repeat the combination in my head as she turns the dial, making sure I've still got it memorized. I take the heavy box out for her, and Irene uses the key to open it.

This is what I was nearly robbed for. This is what Mikhail's actually after.

This?

It's a mishmash of fine metalware, gold and silver and bronze: candlesticks, jewelry, an ancient dagger with a peculiar asymmetrical design scratched into it, a few old coins. The Lisles have brought along a fair amount of the family's heirloom loot. How much are they planning to sell while they're on this journey? Maybe their family fortune has dwindled even more than I'd realized.

Any single item in that box is worth more money than I'll see in a lifetime, but the most valuable thing there must be what the Brotherhood needs. I can't guess why, though. What would the Brotherhood want with a couple of candlesticks?

"There," Irene says, picking up an ornate gold pin. "We can clip these on either side of my neckline. That will look nice, won't it?"

She puts the pin in my hand. I trace the whorls of the old-fashioned design with my thumb. It's extraordinarily beautiful. It's very familiar.

"But—there ought to be two of them." Irene begins raking through the box with her hands. "I'm sure there are two. I remember Mother wearing them both at that ball two years ago. Why isn't the mate in here? Has it been lost?"

"Don't worry about it, Miss Irene." My mouth is dry, and it's all I can do to keep from shaking. "I think these earrings are much more flattering. Sapphires, aren't they?"

"You don't think they're too flashy for morning?"

"Not a bit, miss." At this point, I'd put a tiara on Irene's head if it would get her out of here and off to breakfast sooner. I can't pretend to make small talk much longer. I feel like I want to scream. A long-held fear of mine has awakened into certainty, and I've never known anger like this in my life.

Because I know where I've seen that pin before. I know where I've seen its mate.

I saw it on my sister.

## CHAPTER 9

THE WHOLE MORNING, I GO THROUGH MY TASKS as if I'm sleepwalking. I pay no attention to Horne's bad temper, or Layton's bloodshot eyes as he finally saunters out of the suite. Sometimes, the more ghastly moments of the night before flash in my mind—Mikhail's brutality, Alec as a wolf—but now I have my own horror to add to that.

From the moment I recognized that gold pin, I've been trapped all over again, just like I was last night—but this time, I'm trapped in the past.

Four years ago, I came to Moorcliffe with my sister, Daisy. She was three years older than me and had stayed in school; she badly wanted to finish, as did I. But our father had less and less work at the stables as horseless carriages become more popular, and our gran was going to have to come live with us, and money was short. So we trudged all three miles down the muddy country road that led to the great estate of the Viscount Lisle.

"Is that really just a house?" I whispered to Daisy as we walked toward the back, where servants and tradesmen entered. Moorcliffe was so enormous, so splendid with its marble columns, that I thought surely it must be some kind of church. Maybe the great Salisbury Cathedral I'd always heard about, but never seen. "Are you sure?"

"Yes, that's where the Lisles live. Where we'll work, if we're lucky." She gave me an encouraging smile. Daisy's fair hair, even more golden and curly than mine, caught in the spring breeze, and I thought she looked like an angel. She was a few years older than most girls were when they entered service; at thirteen, I was just the right age. But I never doubted that the Lisles would want someone as pretty and clever as Daisy to work in their house. Both of us "spoke proper"—thanks to our mother's education, and her tireless correction of any errors, our accents betrayed less of our country origins than our neighbors' did. I figured that was my main advantage. Though I was scared to walk into such a grand place, much less start in service, I felt safe knowing she was by my side.

I didn't realize she was the one who needed protection.


"No!" Little Beatrice throws her silver spoon across the nursery, spattering Horne's apron with applesauce. I manage to dodge it. Beatrice giggles in delight. She's getting too old for such naughtiness, but nobody seems willing to bring her in line. Which is a shame—her high spirits will turn nasty if she's spoiled.

"Honestly!" Horne's face shrivels up in a grimace that makes her look like a dried apple. "Why they couldn't have brought Nanny along on this trip is beyond me."

"Because they couldn't afford it," Ned calls from Layton's bedroom, where he's busy shining shoes. "We're lucky we've got cabins to sleep in at all. Probably Lady Regina would just as soon have tied a rope around us and towed us to America."

"I don't want to hear that disgraceful rumor again, Ned." Horne draws herself upright and looks as imperious as it's possible to look with applesauce on her apron. "The way some of you talk. The Lisles are among the noblest and most ancient families in England."

Ned replies, "And soon to be among the poorest!"

On any other morning, I'd be hard-pressed not to laugh at his joke, or at Horne's indignant face. This morning, I just keep darning Layton's socks, seeing not the tasks before me but the labors of long ago.

When I came to Moorcliffe, I started as a housemaid—sweeping grates, beating the rugs, washing the floors, that sort of thing. Daisy was brought on as a nursery maid, the assistant to the nanny, to help with then newborn Beatrice.

We both worked from before dawn until almost midnight, seven days a week, with one afternoon off a month for walking back into the village and visiting our parents. At least they let us share a room, which was the only thing that made that attic bedroom bearable. It was at the highest point of the house, but with no window to provide a pretty view of the grounds. Hot in summer, so cold in winter that the water in our bedside jug often froze overnight—the first thing we did, on waking up in December and January, was take a stone and crack the ice, so we could wash our faces in the frigid water beneath the surface. The bed was rather small for both of us, but we'd shared one as small at home; the crowding was worse only because we were growing older, and in my case, growing taller. At least at home we'd had the luxury of packing our mattress with clean, fresh straw once a year. From the musty smell of the one we had at Moorcliffe, it had last been restuffed decades ago.

"Look on the bright side," Daisy said to me one night, when I was crying. I'd had to scrub the front steps with lye, which had blistered my hands. The pain of it bothered me less than the fact that I'd have to scrub the back steps the next day, and blister them again and even worse. "We don't have to listen to Dad preaching at us day and night, not here."

"It wasn't so bad." But I didn't really mean that. Ever since our little brother had died of influenza a few years before, our father had become almost frighteningly religious. We were never naughty anymore; instead we were wicked, or sinful. It was hard to be told you were sinful all the time. But it was also hard to feel the skin on my hands cracking from the lye.

"We're making money to send home to Mum," she said, stroking my hair. The light of our one candle flickered, blurring the silhouette of her hand against the wall. "And we have chances to get ahead here, you know. Ways to improve our station."

"If I work very hard, maybe someday they'll make me a head parlor maid." So I could wear a slightly less ridiculous uniform, and instead of burning my own hands, I could make the poor little housemaids under me burn theirs. It didn't sound so marvelous to me.

"That's not what I mean." She pulled the thin blanket more snugly over me, as if the chill was my biggest problem. "I just mean—chances, is all."

I ought to have asked her what she was really speaking of, but I didn't.

"Be careful with that!" Horne demands as I restitch the lace on the sleeve of the gown Lady Regina wore last night. Really, this is Horne's job, but she's busy doing the absent nanny's job and wrestling Beatrice into her pinafore. "She'll inspect it today, probably as soon as she comes back to the suite."

I'm a better seamstress than Horne, and she knows it. But the truth is, my fingers are shaky, and it's all I can do to keep my stitches straight. I try to focus only on the lace in my palm, only on the needle between my fingers.

I need sleep. I need a proper meal. I need to feel safe from Mikhail. I need to know what the Brotherhood wants. I need Alec to—to be someone he can never be. I need to go back to before, to warn Daisy. The things I need, I can't have.

When it began, just over two years ago, I thought Daisy was merely sick. No great surprise, given the coldness of that winter and the chill in our attic.

She was losing her breakfast nearly every morning; I'd awaken to the sound of her vomiting into a basin. "Tell Cook," I would say, as I held back her hair. "She's not as mean as old Horne. She'll save you something easier for tea. Chicken broth, maybe."

"Don't tell Cook," she choked. "Don't tell anyone. Not anyone, Tess."

We had so little privacy with our small room and our one chamber pot that I should have guessed before. But it wasn't until spring, until the morning I realized Daisy's uniform was becoming tight in the waist, that I realized the truth.

"Oh, my God," I said, staring at her. At first she didn't understand, but then she saw my face, and hurriedly tied on her apron. But it was too late. "Daisy, you aren't—are you—are you going to have a baby?"

"Don't say anything!" she hissed.

"I wouldn't! But Daisy, if I can see it, others can too. Horne will see. Everyone will eventually." And what did she expect to do when she actually had it?

Daisy slumped onto the corner of the bed. I'll never forget the utter desolation in her eyes. "We have to hide it as long as we can. I know it can't be much longer. But help me, Tess. Please."

I knew how women got with child; you can't grow up surrounded by farms without noticing what the rams and ewes get up to. But I couldn't imagine who the father might have been. We were discouraged from having male "followers," and with only one afternoon free a month—spent at our parents' home—how would she even have found the time to meet anyone?

That answer, at least, came to me quickly enough. "It's someone here at Moorcliffe. The father, I mean."

"Don't ask me about that."

"Is it Ned?" He was nearly the only young man we knew, and always friendly to us. Was he maybe more than friendly to Daisy? I'd never thought there was anything between them, but then again, I'd never suspected Daisy wasn't a virgin.

"It's not Ned," Daisy spat back at me. "Don't be absurd."

"Holloway?" He was the under butler, and a handsome figure of a man, though a few years older than her.

"No."

I racked my brains. There were nearly forty servants at Moorcliffe, most of them male, so the list of suspects was rather long. The chauffeur was always winking at us. "Is it Fletcher?"

"No! Good God, Tess, do you think I've slept with half the household?"

"I didn't mean that, Daisy! I just meant—whoever he is, he has to help you."

"He won't." She spread one hand across the faint swell of her belly. "I asked. Repeatedly. If I name him, he'll just deny it and hate me so much there's no chance this child will ever—he'll deny it. So I'll never tell, not you nor anyone else." The way she said it, I knew she truly never would.

I started to cry. "What are you going to do?"

"I don't know." Daisy leaned her head into her palm. "I don't know."

Horne figured it out two weeks later. She called Daisy a slut and a whore, and of course she went right to Lady Regina with the information. Lady Regina did what any other fine Christian noblewoman would have done upon learning that one of her unmarried servant girls was pregnant: She fired Daisy and threw her out of

95

the house that very day, with only a fraction of the wages she was entitled to. I cried as I watched her walk down the long path away from the back of the house, until Horne boxed my ears and told me to get back to work.

I knew there would be no question of her returning to our parents' house. As soon as my father learned she'd become pregnant out of wedlock, he'd call her worse names than Horne did, and throw her out even faster than Lady Regina had. On my next afternoon off, instead of going home, I sought her out in the village. What few coins she'd had, she'd used to rent a room in a disreputable boardinghouse. When we saw each other, she was so much bigger, and so much paler and wearier, that I sobbed just to look at her.

Once I'd calmed myself, Daisy handed me a knotted handkerchief that held something heavy inside. "When you get your next afternoon off, don't come back here. I need you to go to Salisbury."

I'd never been anywhere as enormous as Salisbury in my life. And so far away—perhaps even five miles! "What do you want me to do there?"

"Pawn this." With that, Daisy opened the handkerchief to reveal an ornate gold pin.

I gasped. "You didn't—Daisy, you didn't steal it, did you?"

"I'm not a thief!"

"I wouldn't blame you if you were," I said, and that seemed to pacify her.

But still she insisted, "I didn't steal it. It was given to me. I need the money now, and I think it's worth a lot."

"I'll do it," I said. "I promise."

Probably the pawnbroker gave me a poor deal, but he gave me fifteen pounds, as much money as I'd ever seen in one place at one time. That money kept Daisy going, and little Matthew once he was born, until earlier this year when she married Arthur the butcher. Arthur's a good man; in fact, he treats Matthew as though he were his own son.

So Daisy's all right now, I tell myself as I finish mending Lady Regina's sleeve. And maybe she did steal the pin. I'd always thought so.

But if it was kept in that box, Daisy would have needed the key to get inside it. Nobody gives a nursery maid a key like that. So she couldn't have stolen it after all. Somebody had to give the pin to her, just as she said.

Only two men would have been in a position to give it to her. One of them is the Viscount Lisle, but he was in London that entire winter, not to mention that he's so fat he hardly has the energy to climb up the staircase, much less chase girls.

The other—

I lay the dress out neatly for Horne's inspection, then slip into Layton's room. If anyone asks why I'm in there, I'll say I need to borrow some blacking. But Horne's busy chasing after Beatrice, and Ned's taken himself off on some errand, so I have a few moments alone.

On Layton's desk is a packet of his calling cards. I glance down to see that they read LAYTON MATTHEW LISLE.

I'd thought that was his full name, but I was never sure—my job keeps me busy with Irene's doings, not his. Back in the days when I was a housemaid, I was always away from the family as much as possible. Horne even made us take the rickety old back stairs all the time so the Lisles wouldn't have to see any evidence we existed, as though their house stayed clean by magic.

But Daisy would have been near the family all the time, as a nursery maid. Layton must have stopped in often to see his little sister, when she was merely a cute infant to be cuddled a bit and then handed aside for someone else to care for. He was more dashing then; he drank less. Perhaps he was charming to her. Perhaps he made her promises.

However it came to pass, now I know: Layton is the father. They didn't throw her out just for having a baby; they threw her out for having *his* baby. For being the mother of their grandchild.

I always knew how cruel the Lisle family had been to Daisy; now I see what hypocrites they are too. Anger boils inside me, clenching my fists and throbbing at my temples. To think I grew up admiring them as the noblest family for miles around. They're wretched. They're vile. I've spent the last four years of my life mopping floors and scrubbing laundry for people who are lower than dogs.

The door to the bedroom opens, and I try to compose myself before Ned or Horne sees me. But when I turn, I see Layton himself.

Mikhail is with him.

# ⫷ CHAPTER 10 ⫸

"WELL, WELL," MIKHAIL SAYS. HE'S LOOKING AT ME, but he speaks to Layton. "May I congratulate you on how charmingly you've decorated your cabin?"

Layton replies, "Nothing brightens up the boudoir like a pretty girl."

They roar with laughter like they think that's the most hilarious joke in the world, and maybe Layton really does, since he's the one who made it. But Mikhail keeps his gaze on me the whole time. I can see the wolf beneath the surface; there's more beast to him than man.

For one moment, I'm afraid he's going to attack me where I stand—but no, he wouldn't, not in front of Layton. Still, I have to grab the back of the nearest chair to support myself, and I see that my panic pleases Mikhail immensely.

"This will only take a moment," Layton says, as he changes jackets, tossing his first one in a heap on the floor for Ned to deal with later. "You must meet my mother at luncheon, Count

Kalashnikov. Though, I warn you now, she'll start by trying to marry you off to my sister."

"No doubt your sister is utterly charming," says the man who is apparently Count Mikhail Kalashnikov. The thought of him touching Irene, coming anywhere near her, makes me sick. To me, he says, "How very . . . healthy you look, my dear."

Mikhail must have assumed that Alec would kill and eat me.

I realize that Mikhail and Layton have only just met, and almost as quickly realize that this is how Mikhail has planned it. Having failed to rob me, he's going to befriend the Lisle family— all to get closer to that box and the treasures inside.

As much as I hate Layton at this moment, I know I ought to warn him, for Irene's sake if nobody else's. But how can I? I can't tell the Lisles the truth about Mikhail without revealing facts that will make me look like a lunatic. Even if I said only that he tried to rob me, they'd think it was absurd. He's in first class, just like they are; why would he try to rob anyone?

"It's a pleasure to make such a congenial acquaintance as your-self aboard ship," Mikhail says as he strolls around the small room. "So many pompous toads upstairs. I like men about me who are young and vigorous. Who want to drink deeply of the pleasure of life."

"Hear, hear," Layton says with relish. Is he thinking of my sis-ter? Some other girl he ruined just for his pleasure?

"And to think I knew your dear uncle. Humphrey was a most ingenious man."

"We all thought he was a bloody fool, to tell you the truth."

Layton's honesty is as disarming as his smile; he looks almost handsome again for a moment. He can appear to be a good man when he chooses, but I know now that is nothing but a sham.

"I shall redeem his memory, then, as we improve our acquaintance. I look forward to spending more time with you and your family while we're aboard." Mikhail is standing slightly behind me now, and I can feel his gaze on my back. "And as I said before, your room has lovely . . . accommodations. Tell me, Layton, how accommodating is she?"

Layton laughs as hard at Mikhail's joke as he did at his own. I am torn between anger so great that I want to slap him and the horrible, crawling sensation of Mikhail stepping closer to me.

But I reveal nothing. I stand straight and tall, and my face remains still. I'm stronger than these worthless men will ever know.

"Excuse me, sir." Quickly I walk out of Layton's room, and neither of them bothers to stop me. Maybe I should have grabbed the tin of blacking to cover my tracks, but now that I've left Layton's bedroom, nobody's likely to ask me why I was in there in the first place.

"There you are," Horne says. "Lady Regina sent word that she wants her Italian shawl. She's up on the boat deck. Take it to her, and look lively about it."

I'm eager to get out of here, and as far away from Mikhail as possible. But it strikes me as odd that Horne's sending me instead of going herself and leaving me to deal with Beatrice for a while. The child's a terror this morning. I can see that she's already managed to smear jam over the entire front of her pinafore. One thing you learn in service: Anytime you're asked to deviate from your expected duties, try to find out why. "Don't you want to go?"

That's Horne's cue to snap at me as she usually does. Instead she pauses, and her rheumy eyes become distant. "I don't like being up on deck. Seeing the waves."

"Why ever not?" You'd think it would at least make a change from the same old suite of rooms, however elegant they are.

"It gives me a bad turn, is all. I don't like the look of it." She tries to brush it off, but I know what I just saw. Mean old Horne, whom all of us fear, is scared of the ocean.

Maybe I ought to pity her. Remembering what she said to Daisy, maybe I ought to laugh at her. But mostly I want to get out of this place. I snatch Lady Regina's shawl from the table and practically run through the door.

For the next few minutes, I argue it out with myself—partly because I have to know, and partly because, upsetting as it is to think of my sister's plight, it is a great deal less scary than Count Mikhail Kalashnikov.

*Did Layton force Daisy?* He's no prize, but surely he's not as nasty as that. And she'd hardly have named their boy after him if he had. All those things she said about having chances to advance ourselves—she was talking about Layton then, I'm sure of it. Daisy can't have been stupid enough to think he would actually marry her. But maybe he talked about setting her up in an apartment in London. He gave her the pin; probably he gave her some other money as well, because she must have lived on something before

I pawned it for her. When she became pregnant, she would have known that was the end of that. Did she ever tell him, face-to-face? Hardly matters—he has to have known, when the family fired her if not before, and he never lifted a finger to help her or my nephew. Probably she named the boy Matthew to shame him into giving her a few more pounds.

These thoughts weigh me down as I hurry along the boat deck, salty ocean breeze whipping my black uniform dress around me, with the shawl under one arm. I'm so distracted and nervous that I think I could walk by Lady Regina and Irene without even noticing them.

But perhaps that's wrong, because I recognize the next familiar face I see instantly.

Alec.

He looks as impeccably put together as he did yesterday, in a charcoal gray suit cut perfectly to his body; the transformation from animal to gentleman is complete. The only elements of his appearance that are out of place are his wild chestnut curls and the sadness in his green eyes. It's almost startling, how alone he seems. How did I miss it yesterday? How did the glamour of his handsomeness and charm disguise the pain he's in? Now that I know it's there, it seems to surround him, a kind of halo in reverse.

But a man in pain is more dangerous, not less. I must never forget that.

Alec's gaze meets mine. In that first instant, warmth spreads through my chest, like a flower blossoming into fire.

But he looks away almost instantly and begins walking in the opposite direction. Of course—he said we had to remain apart, for my own good.

When he said that, though, Alec didn't know what I know now.

I decide to call to him, and I nearly shout *Alec* before I think better of it. "Mr. Marlowe!"

He stops at once. As I hasten to his side, he whispers, "Tess, I told you—"

"Forget what you told me. Mikhail's made friends with Layton. He's in the Lisle family cabins now."

"Has he threatened you?" Alec's eyes narrow, and there's the wolf again. My breath catches in my throat.

"Not yet."

"He will."

"He's going to get whatever is in that box," I say. "He's determined to get it no matter what, and he's willing to go through me to do it. Eager, I think. Are you so sure he's on this ship to initiate you? Perhaps he's been after the Lisles the whole time."

A few people are glancing in our general direction, and Alec notices at almost the same time I do. "Follow me," he says.

We walk a few steps along the deck—me slightly behind so it won't look as though we're together—and I follow him through the next door. This turns out to lead to a very peculiar sort of room with odd machines all about. And strange metal weights are on the floor; I remember that the strong man at the county fair lifted them. Barbells, I think they're called.

My confusion must show on my face, because Alec says, "The ship's gymnasium. The men come here to practice rowing, or box.

You know, to build their muscles."

Only gentlemen leading a life of leisure would need to go someplace special to build muscles. After spending four years toting buckets of water up multiple flights of stairs, I bet I could successfully arm-wrestle most of the first-class male passengers on this ship.

Thinking of the gap between gentility and servants reminds me of Daisy, and what's become of her due to Layton's irresponsibility. It must show on my face, because Alec's expression softens. "Are you all right? You look as though something's troubling you. Something besides Mikhail, I mean."

His concern touches me more than it should. "You're very perceptive."

"You're pale." I can tell that Alec doesn't want to be worried for me, and yet he can't stop himself from asking, "Can I get you— water, or a glass of sherry, maybe? We should find someplace more comfortable for you to sit."

He thinks I'm weaker than I am, and it ought to irritate me. Instead, I stare at him almost in shock, because—he's treating me like a lady. Not like a servant. Alec wants to take care of me, I who have always had to see to the needs of others. As small a gesture as it is, I never expected even that much from a wealthy man. From anyone, perhaps. And in this moment, I realize how good it would feel to have someone take care of me once in a while.

But Daisy's secrets are hers, not mine, and there are more pressing matters at hand. "I'm all right, truly. Mikhail—he says he's a Count Kalashnikov. Is that true?"

"Entirely true. He's one of the wealthiest men in Russia, a friend to the tsar."

"So he says."

"I believe it. The Brotherhood's influence stretches to the highest rungs of society, Tess. There's no one too high or too low for him to reach."

"We've got to figure out what Mikhail's after, then. If they're as mighty as you claim, and they're sending someone that influential after a dusty old box of the Lisles—then there's something enormously important in there. And who knows? Maybe it's something you could use."

Alec looks at me with new respect. "I like the way you think, Tess. But I told you before; I have no idea what he's after. Who knows what's in that mysterious box?"

"I do. I got a look inside this morning. Miss Irene turns out to have the key."

"Good," he says, almost fiercely. He wants to know Mikhail's secrets even more avidly than I do. Perhaps we are both only speaking together to save our own necks, but that's reason enough to cooperate. "All right then, what did you see?"

"Nothing that looked extraordinary, honestly." I need to think about this very carefully, and truth be told, I am feeling a bit shaky. I sit down on the nearest machine, which is the closest thing the gymnasium has to a chair. The seat slides, jerking me to one side.

"That's a rowing machine," Alec says. Now that he says it, I can see how a man could sit in this contraption and work the handles, going back and forth to row as if he were in a boat. For now I simply steady my feet on the floor.

"Let me think," I say. I close my eyes and imagine the box as it looked when Irene went through it. "Some candlesticks, valuable but awfully plain. Probably a hundred years old at least."

"I doubt Mikhail's after candlesticks."

I peek at him long enough to glare. "Shhh, let me go through it, would you?" I've never fussed at a gentleman in my life—and while Alec might be an American millionaire instead of a member of the nobility, he certainly counts as a gentleman. He doesn't rebuke me, though, just accepts it as his due with a small smile. I close my eyes once more. "Some old coins, Spanish maybe. A few pieces of jewelry: sapphire earrings, a pearl choker, the tiara with the opals, and . . . and a golden pin." I swallow hard. "One in a pair, but missing its mate. And then there was a very old sort of knife, maybe a dagger—I wouldn't know."

"A dagger?" The tone of Alec's voice opens my eyes. His entire body is tense, and as he stands above me, I again sense the presence of the wolf. "Describe it. In every detail."

"About so long." I hold my fingers perhaps nine inches apart. "A long, thin, triangular point. The hilt might've been made of gold, but it was so old it was half gray. The scabbard had some etchings on it, illuminated with gilt. The etchings looked sort of like letters, but not proper English letters. And there was something else on the hilt, this weird scratched shape. Nothing I could read."

I hold up my hand to trace the shape, but as I do, I realize I've seen it before: It's that peculiar asymmetrical Y—the one I first saw on Mikhail's watch.

"That's the symbol of the Brotherhood." Alec slams one hand against the wall so hard I jump. He doesn't seem to notice as he paces the length of the gymnasium. "It's an Initiation Blade."

"A what?" The word "initiation" resonates, reminding me of what Alec and I spoke about this morning. "You mean—for the Brotherhood initiation?"

"Exactly." Alec leans against the wall next to me, letting his head fall back. I can see his Adam's apple work as he swallows hard. "You don't know all the family secrets, Tess. Somebody among the Lisles, maybe generations back, was connected to the Brotherhood."

Who could it have been? Of course—Uncle Humphrey, supposedly Mikhail's old friend. The Viscount has never liked to discuss Uncle Humphrey; he lived far out in the country, on a much humbler estate than his station in life would have demanded. The Viscount called him a crackpot, and perhaps that's as much as he knew about it. Now I wonder if he was a werewolf too. Or did he fight against them?

I abandon those questions; they'll get us nowhere. "What's an Initiation Blade? Why does Mikhail need it?"

"They were forged long ago, so long that the date is lost to memory." Alec looks down at me, sadder even than he was before. "And nobody remembers how precisely they were made, which is why they are so rare and valuable now. The core of the dagger is silver." He pauses. "Silver has the power to kill a werewolf. Remember that."

Is he telling me this so I can defend myself against Mikhail, or so I can defend myself against him?

He continues, "Within an Initiation Blade, the silver dagger is then plated with gold, which allows werewolves to touch it. When one of our kind is cut with the Blade, and the old magic is called on, the supernatural energy that rises from a werewolf's nearness to silver creates a change—something no one fully understands. But it's the change that allows us to transform into a wolf if and when we will, except on the night of the full moon. The Brotherhood controls all the Initiation Blades and has done for centuries. This one must have been lost until now."

"And that's what Mikhail is after."

"I can't believe I was fool enough to think he booked passage on this ship only to come after me. They'll want that Blade more than anything, Tess. They must have learned of it recently; if they'd known about it before, they'd have stolen it from the Lisles. Burned their house down, if they had to. There's nothing Mikhail won't do to get his hands on it." He slides down the wall, forearms on his knees, so that we're eye to eye again. "You realize that Mikhail now knows he can do this without killing you. And he won't care."

It's not like I wasn't scared before, but it's a hundred times worse now. Before I thought that maybe I was just a toy for Mikhail to bat around, in danger from him but perhaps able to buy safety with my silence. Now I know that killing me isn't something he would have to do to accomplish his task; it's something he *wants*. Something he'll seize any excuse to do.

I don't have to say anything; Alec can see what I'm feeling, or sense it somehow. "Mikhail's anything but stupid," he says. "He won't attack you in front of witnesses. He only went after you in front of me that first day onboard because he thought he could coerce me into joining him, and now he knows that won't work. You've simply got to avoid being alone as much as possible."

"Won't be hard to stay near the family, with Lady Regina wanting something every five minutes," I try to joke. The Italian shawl is still draped over one of my arms; when I reach her, she'll be furious. Let her shout at me forever, so long as I don't have to be alone. But then I gasp. "Oh, no! Tomorrow!"

"What's tomorrow?"

"My afternoon off."

I'd been so looking forward to it. Horne, Ned, and I would each get one afternoon off during the trip to America—Ned's is today. Lady Regina told us as though she were doing us a special favor. What she really wanted to do was make us use our free afternoon for the month while the family is still onboard and has ship's stewards to do their bidding. That way she could work us harder once we reached the United States. Her motives didn't matter to me when I thought I'd have an afternoon to lounge about on deck and feel the sunshine on my face—especially given my plans to quit shortly thereafter. Now all those hours away from the Lisles feel like a death sentence. "He's close to Layton now. He'll realize I'm not with them, and come after me."

Alec weighs the problem, then nods. "You'll simply have to spend the day with me. Given the people I've . . . endangered, by being what I am, I ought to protect someone at least once. So we'll stay together."

There's a fluttering in my belly when he says that, but I don't trust it. I might have more faith in Alec than I do in Mikhail, but he, too, is a monster. "You said I was to stay away from you. For my own good."

"The situation has changed now." He tries to sound practical about it, but I realize he feels it too—that illogical, powerful need for us to be together. "You don't have to be afraid. We'll stay in the public areas of first class. People will be around us the whole time." His voice grows softer. "Safe as houses."

"Safe as houses," I repeat. "But—sir, you can't be seen socializing with a servant. It isn't done."

"I don't really care what people think of it. Nobody will have the courage to confront us directly. So we'll snub them right back, pretend they're not even there." Can he really not see the divide between us? I must be gaping at Alec, because he shrugs and adds, "After you become a werewolf, you give up on the idea of fitting in."

I notice that he didn't suggest going down to third class, but if I were him, I wouldn't want to trade down either. The Lisles might see me up there, which would be awful—but then again, this is a large ship. It's not as if I was able to find Lady Regina with her shawl even when I was looking for her. "I could wear something nice. So it wouldn't be too obvious I'm a servant."

"When will the Lisles let you go?"

"Just before luncheon."

"Then I'll meet you at the grand staircase just before luncheon."

"I haven't said yes yet. We've got to think this through. Isn't the first-class dining room opposite the staircase? What if Mikhail sees me?"

"What if he does? It might be better, actually, if he knows I'm

111

guarding you. Then perhaps he'll back off for a while." Alec rises once more to his feet, and this time I stand with him. It's nice that he's taller than I am; so few men are. He becomes more formal now. "Will you accept my invitation?"

*Don't be stupid. This man is cursed to be a monster. He's tied to dark powers you can never understand. Even if he weren't, after what you've learned about Daisy and Layton, don't you know that no servant girl can ever trust a wealthy man?*

The stupidest part, I realize, is that I'm considering denying myself the only protection I have—because I'm afraid of my own heart.

"Yes," I say. "Tomorrow, before lunch, at the grand staircase."

He doesn't reply, but I can see the reflection of my own gladness and confusion in my eyes. In some strange way, we are alike. A boundary has been crossed.

# ⊰ CHAPTER 11 ⊱

AFTER FINALLY LOCATING LADY REGINA, AND BEING scolded for taking so long with her shawl, I'm released to change from my now-dusty morning uniform into my evening uniform, and to eat something for dinner if I'm lucky enough to have the time. Hopefully I will; that one sticky bun Irene gave me wasn't much to go on after missing tea last night. I must be the only person going hungry on the *Titanic*—the richest ship in the world.

Making sure to remain in sight and hearing of others the entire time, I dash down to F deck, through the doors that separate the classes, and enter my cabin, which is empty. None of my bunkmates are inside, and neither is my evening uniform. Just as I'm getting ready to curse worse than the groundskeeper when he's had a pint of gin, the door opens behind me and Myriam walks in. Her thick dark hair is a frizzy mess, the way it gets when you've had to spend too much time in heat and moisture. But in her arms, neatly rolled, is my uniform.

"I hate ironing," she says.

"Oh, thank you!" I take the uniform up and see that Myriam's done a wonderful job; this is as neatly pressed as I could manage, or perhaps even a professional tailor could do. "Really. It's marvelous."

"Do you intend to spend all of luncheon changing clothes, or would you like to hurry so that we can actually eat?"

I ought to correct Myriam: The midday meal is luncheon only for the rich. For us, it's dinner—the main meal of the day. At night, when they get dinner, we only have tea. Sometimes it's no more than bread and butter washed down with a cup of tea. But who knows, perhaps it's different in America.

Her unspoken assumption is that we'll have dinner together, and I suppose we will. As I hurriedly change, brushing and hanging my morning uniform so that it will be presentable tomorrow, I realize that—with hardly a kind word spoken between us—Myriam and I have somehow become friends. I've never had a friend outside my family or the other servants at Moorcliffe before; it feels almost strange, but kind of interesting, too.

The third-class dining hall isn't anything so grand as the one for first class, of course, but it's still a bright, cheerful space, with gleaming white walls and well-polished floors. Myriam informs me that last night there was an impromptu dance after the meal, because a piano has been provided even for the third-class passengers. An Italian who had brought a violin and a German who had brought an accordion joined in with the volunteer piano player, nationality unknown, to play tunes for hours. "Some of the ship's officers joined us," she says, as if it were an afterthought. "Not the captain, of course. I'm sure he'd never show his face down here."

"Just some of the lower officers." I take a big bite of my roll, gulp down some tea. "Like, for instance, the seventh officer, a Mr. George Greene?"

Myriam doesn't deny it. She rests her chin in her hand, half lost in thought. "He is not at all the sort of man I would once have imagined for myself. I thought another man from Lebanon, some friend of my brother's in New York, perhaps. George is—oh, Tess, he's been everywhere in the world. Even India."

It's funny to see her so starry-eyed, though I don't mock her. After the past couple of days with Alec, I understand that feeling better than I used to. "He seems awfully nice, too. He's gone out of his way to be kind to me."

"Is it true that sailors have girls in every port?"

"George doesn't seem the type." Though who am I to know what type George is or isn't? After everything I've learned in the past twenty-four hours, it feels as if I hardly know anyone, even some of the people closest to me. I think of Alec—man and monster—and the hours I've promised to spend with him tomorrow. "But it's hard to know when to trust a man."

"You say that like someone who has reason to doubt a man's intentions." Myriam raises one eyebrow, as perfectly shaped as a bird's wing. "And here I thought your overnight adventure probably had an innocent explanation."

Our eyes meet across the dining room table. For a long moment, neither of us speaks. We're surrounded by the clinking of plates and forks and chattering in half a dozen different languages, but the silence between us seems louder than all the rest. She's teasing me, but not; what Myriam's really doing is giving me a chance to confide in her about last night, if I want to. In some ways I do want to. But who would ever believe me?

"Nothing improper happened last night," I say.

"You are keeping a secret."

"What a brilliant deduction. You're a regular Sherlock Holmes."

Myriam frowns. "Who is Sherlock Holmes?"

They must not get Arthur Conan Doyle's books in Lebanon. "He's the most marvelous detective. I'll give you the titles of some of the best novels. When you get to New York City, you can look for him at the bookseller's." Though after last night, I'm never rereading *The Hound of the Baskervilles* again.

This was my best effort at changing the subject, but Myriam's forehead is still furrowed with concern. So I add, "It's not my secret I'm keeping. It's someone else's. That's why I can't tell you."

Accepting this, Myriam says, "Well, if you weren't having amorous adventures throughout the night, which man do you distrust, and why?"

The least complicated layer of the truth will have to do. "Tomorrow I've got an afternoon off. Someone has asked me to spend it with him. Alec."

"Shipboard romance has its charms." Her silky smile reveals that she's familiar with these charms already. "I'm surprised you had time to meet anyone here in third class, though. They've kept you working every moment."

"He's not in third class." I look down at the potatoes on my plate instead of at her. "He's a first-class passenger. Alec Marlowe."

"First class!" She doesn't sound impressed; she sounds wary. "I doubt the motives of rich men who pay attention to poor girls."

"That's not how it is," I say as firmly as I can.

Doubtfully, Myriam replies, "Maybe Americans are different."

"Maybe."

"I will be an American soon." She takes a deep breath, and there's something different about her smile now. Her anticipation is so fierce and unguarded—so like my own. "My brother says it's a wonderful place. Nothing like the old stories. Instead it's loud and crowded and dirtier than you can imagine."

"I think that's just New York City."

"That is where I'm going to live, so what's the difference? Loud, crowded, dirty, and wonderful. And new, always new. That's what I want. Not the same life my mother led, like her mother before her, and her mother before her."

Come to think of it, I have one secret I can reveal. "I'm going there too. America."

"Yes, I believe that's where the boat is headed."

"I mean, forever." I've never said these words out loud before. Speaking them makes them more real. "I'm giving my notice to the Lisles at the end of this trip. So I'll be starting over in New York too."

Myriam's entire demeanor changes. Before, she's been willing to listen to me, even to help me, but now she sees me as truly someone like her for the first time. Her excitement doubles to cover the both of us. "Good for you! You must be sick and tired of being a maidservant. What will you do for work, when you get there?"

"Well, I might end up a maidservant again," I admit. "It's the main thing I know how to do. But at least I could work for a less odious family, if I did. And I'm quite good at sewing, embroidery, making hats, things like that. So—you know, I expect something will come along."

"That does not sound well planned to me." The criticism stings mostly because I know Myriam has a point. But how could I have sought work in America without tipping off the Lisles? Her eyes narrow. "You aren't expecting your wealthy man from first class to take you away from all this, are you? I would not have thought you that foolish."

"Believe me, I never dreamed of it. I know it's—beyond impossible."

I recall Alec as he was when I first saw him this morning, lying half-conscious on the tiles of the Turkish bath. How beautiful he was. How bruised. How he had been a murderous animal only hours before.

Yes, it's impossible. For reasons I can speak aloud, and for reasons I can't.

My duties that afternoon are the same as I'd have expected, as boring as ever, but after the time I've had on the ship so far, boring is almost a relief. I tidy up after Beatrice, hand wash Irene's fine silk-and-lace underclothes from France, and get her into a fancy dinner dress—this one in a sea green that's even more unkind to her complexion than the yellow was.

Horne insists that she intends to take tea in the third-class hall tonight, and assigns me to stay with little Bea. It's not so bad, though, because the child's temper has improved, and there's enough soup and cakes for both of us. She goes to sleep right on time, and I feel almost at peace for the few blessed minutes I get to myself.

Though I'm alone—and I know I shouldn't be—this is the one place I think Mikhail wouldn't strike. He's trying to cozy up to the Lisles, but they're hardly going to be in the mood to chitchat with new acquaintances if they find a dead body in their rooms. Not even Lady Regina's as cold as that, and surely not even Mikhail would risk losing his chance of getting the Blade just to kill me for sport.

He could just throw my body overboard, though. A chill sweeps through me as I realize how easy that would be for him to do. Who would ever find my body, floating out in the middle of the dark ocean?

But no. He wouldn't. I've seen his fangs, heard his taunts. Mikhail wouldn't just kill me. He'd—he'd eat me.

*Well, he wouldn't do that here*, I tell myself. *Not without leaving an awful mess, and good luck getting bloodstains out of this carpet.* But the briskness doesn't work as well as usual; the fear remains curled within my belly, making my last meal feel crowded and my lungs feel tight.

Since I was thinking about Mikhail being so friendly with Layton, I ought to expect what comes next, but I don't. When the door opens, I quickly rise from the chair I'd been resting in to greet the family—and Mikhail, who is escorting Lady Regina through the door.

"How curious that you should have heard of Uncle Humphrey

119

so far away as Moscow, Count Kalashnikov," she says as she tosses her fur stole aside for me to retrieve. "He was a noted collector, but I admit, I always thought him a bit of an eccentric."

"Sometimes the eccentrics are the true geniuses," Mikhail says.

He says it the way any fawning gentleman would, but his eyes don't match his carefree tone. From the moment he walks into the suite, Mikhail stares at me. Only at me.

I hurry to put away Lady Regina's stole, hoping he won't see how frightened I am. Instead of acknowledging his attention, I look at the others in the room: Lady Regina, thrilled to have a new admirer; Layton, drunk again; and Irene, who looks so exhausted that she might have been the one working all day instead of me. Clearly none of them have any idea why Mikhail would be asking about Uncle Humphrey, or suspect anything; whatever ties the man had to the world of the supernatural, they're ignorant of it.

"Such a pity you could not meet Viscount Lisle," Lady Regina says. "He would have so appreciated knowing a friend of his late uncle's."

"A pity indeed, Lady Regina." Mikhail smoothly takes another step closer to me. "What kept the Viscount from the journey? Not ill health, I hope."

"He had business matters to attend to in London." Layton says it too quickly. He might as well hold up a sign saying, *He's trying to negotiate with the family creditors so we can keep living like rich people though our money's run out.*

But Mikhail handles the momentary awkwardness as easily as any gentleman would. "Business matters are such a burden.

Hopefully he will soon join you in the States, and I shall have the pleasure of his acquaintance there."

Irene sees me, no doubt white as a sheet, and gives me a wan smile. "You may go, Tess. I mean, Davies. That will be all."

"I should be leaving as well," Mikhail says. "Though it has been a charming evening, I must bid you *bonsoir.* Promise me, however, that we shall discuss the matter of Uncle Humphrey's collection another time, very soon."

*Oh, no, don't let him walk out the same time I do!* We probably wouldn't be alone in the corridor, but we might be, and then—I don't want to think about what would happen then.

For once, Lady Regina's snobbery works in my favor. There's no way she's going to let a Russian nobleman out of her sight that easily. "You must stay for a brandy with Layton."

"Damned right," Layton says, steadying himself as best he can.

"We already had a brandy in the lounge, and that is quite enough for me—" Mikhail's mask of perfect cordiality is slipping; I can sense his impatience as I hurry toward the door.

"Irene, do help me persuade the count. It is so rare to find properly sociable young men these days. I swear, that Alexander Marlowe appears to be in hiding. Does he intend to skip every dinner while we're onboard?"

Mikhail watches me as I leave, but knows as well as I do that, for the moment, he's caught in his own trap. While I walk out, I hear him say, "Perhaps Mr. Marlowe doesn't know how to enjoy himself. Unlike me."

The moment I'm alone in the corridor, I take off running.

Every step pounds despite the soft carpet, and a few well-dressed ladies and gentlemen have to flatten themselves against the walls to avoid being run over. I'm making a spectacle of myself, but I don't care. I've got to return to third class before Mikhail can get himself free of the Lisles.

I make it to the lift, where the operator is my companion and my safety—though he is hardly more than a boy. When he gives me a smile, I feel guilty. Am I endangering him, just being close? Would Mikhail kill someone else to get to me?

As soon as he drops me in third class, I start running again. Stupid of me now; I know he couldn't have followed me. And yet the light in the corridors doesn't seem as bright at nighttime, and I'm imagining footsteps behind me.

No. There are footsteps behind me.

I run faster and faster, and the footsteps go faster too. The door to the third-class area lies directly ahead; I'll have to stop to unlock it, and in that time, he'll catch up. My pulse hammering, I decide to turn and fight—

—and whirl around to see nothing. To hear nothing.

*It was the echo*, I realize. *The echo of my own footsteps.*

I laugh at my own foolishness, though the laughter is weak, and my heart still pounds. My legs wobble the whole way back to my cabin.

When I get there, the room is dark and the elderly Norwegian ladies are already fast asleep, but Myriam's not in yet. Maybe I'll get to tease her about her own "overnight adventures"? But no, it's not actually that late. Probably she and George are simply enjoying a stroll along the deck. I could go to the dining hall and see if another dance has started, but I'm far too exhausted to enjoy it. Tonight, all I want is sleep.

I change into my nightgown. As the thin cotton slips over my head, I remember what I slept in last night—my underclothes, damp with steam. And I remember Alec, who is back in that Turkish bath, a wolf again. Howling. Monstrous. Terrifying.

Yet when I think of the evident pain of the transformation— when I imagine him going through the agonies Mikhail did, with no choice in the matter, no hope—I can't be afraid of Alec. I feel only compassion.

Just as I prepare to clamber to my top bunk, there's a shivery sound beneath the door. I look down to see a folded note that's been pushed beneath.

Is this some sort of ship's bulletin? I frown as I kneel to collect it. There's just enough light coming through the crack under the door for me to read it.

In heavy cursive, it reads:

*You're to help me, Tess. Not stand in my way. To prove it to you, within two days, I'll hurt someone you love. Not you. I'll hurt you when you disappoint me—or when it pleases me.*

He didn't sign it. He didn't have to.

And as I realize who wrote it, I realize there are breaks in the light beneath the door. Just where two feet would stand, if someone

123

were on the other side, about to come in.

I can't move. Can't scream. I can only remain there, clutching the crumpled note in my fists, as I realize that Mikhail is standing on the other side of my door. My companions are two old ladies, sound asleep, whom Mikhail could and would tear through to get to me.

And then he walks away.

I'm not sure how long I remain crouched there, but by the time I'm able to rise, every muscle aches. Trembling, I climb into my bunk and wrap the covers around me tightly. Who will he hurt? There's no one onboard to hurt me with—Myriam's my friend, but I bet he wouldn't assume that.

He couldn't mean Alec. He couldn't.

I fight against sleep, because I no longer feel sure how, or if, I'm going to wake.

# ⊰ CHAPTER 12 ⊱

*APRIL 12, 1912*

"Are you sure you're well?" Irene asks, for about the fifth time this morning.

"Certainly, Miss Irene." Though I'm not well, and I'm positive I look it. I finally fell asleep last night, but not deeply and not for long, and I nearly had a heart attack when Myriam finally came in. If I go much longer without sleeping or eating regularly, Mikhail won't have to murder me; I'll die before we reach port.

All right, I'm exaggerating a bit there; it's not as if I've never worked without adequate rest or food before. But I look pale, and obviously Irene sees it.

She lounges in a deck chair, one hand steadying the wide brim of her straw hat. Lady Regina is off sucking up to the Countess of Rothes or Lady Duff Gordon or someone like that. Layton is probably playing cards with Mikhail. Both of them would prefer for Irene to be out and about, either making good connections with the nobility or inviting the protection of interested men. Instead she has a book she's borrowed from the ship's library.

"Listen, Tess," she says. "It's your afternoon off today, isn't it? Then why don't you go on?"

It's at least an hour before I thought I would get to leave. "Are you sure, Miss Irene?"

"Quite sure. Just tell Ned to come and fetch me so I won't be late for luncheon." She smiles up at me, cheerful at the thought of simply being left alone. This is a treat for both of us, I realize.

"Thank you, miss." I drop her a quick curtsy and head back to my cabin. The idea of going there alone gives me a bit of a turn—but Mikhail wouldn't expect me to be free now, and besides, the ship is bright, awake, and alive. First class is elegant and refined, the promenade a regular boulevard of fashions; third class, when I reach it, is bustling with energy. Every single mother and father on board seems to be taking their brood out for a bit of sunshine. As I reach my room, a few little girls—Irish, to judge by their flame-red hair—run past me, one of them carrying a dolly half as big as she is.

Myriam's not in our cabin, but the Norwegian ladies are. They're sitting together on a lower bunk, looking through a tattered old scrapbook. We give each other the friendly, uncomprehending smiles we've settled on as our main form of communication. Then I get to work.

No uniforms at all for a few blessed hours. I first reach into my bag for what I'd planned to wear today, which is what I usually wear on my afternoons off: a simple dark blue dress that I sewed for myself, with a high neck and a fit loose enough to keep my father from suggesting that I'm a sinful woman likely to follow my sister's damnable path. It would have been fine for whiling away a few hours on the third-class deck.

But now I will be in first class. With Alec. Nobody would remark if I wore this, but I don't want to.

Instead I dig deeper into the bag, to the very bottom, until my fingers touch lace.

One of the few perks of being a ladies' maid is that you sometimes get to keep discarded items of their clothing. I have a pair of Irene's old leather gloves, a cheery red, even if the fingertips and palms are worn. She provided my good warm coat, too, when it went out of style; I don't care about that in mid-January. And then, a few months ago, Lady Regina decided this dress, the lacy one now in my hands, wasn't the sort of thing she wanted her daughter to be seen in.

But Lady Regina and I have very different ideas of style.

The satin is rose-colored, a deep, vivid shade. The beaded lace overlay is almost the same color, but slightly darker, so that the contrast better outlines the figure. The overlay drapes over the slim sleeves that end just above the elbow, providing a soft silhouette. A high waist, just beneath the bust, and neckline deep enough to attract attention but not so deep as to attract gossip. It's as beautiful a dress as I've ever seen, and I've only worn it the once, when I tried it on in my attic to make sure I could really keep it. The only alteration I had to make was to the hemline—Irene's shorter than I am—but there was enough extra satin at the hem to let it out. I took it mostly because I thought it was too beautiful to throw away; I never imagined having an occasion worthy of wearing it.

Dare I wear it on deck? To stand up for the first time and declare myself as something more than a servant? Yes, I decide. I dare.

First things first. I take a comb to my hair and give it some meaningful attention. Most days, I just pull it up under my linen cap, because with that thing on my head, there's no point in doing much else. But I've been styling Irene's hair for a while now, and I know my job. It's a little different, doing this to my own hair by feel, instead of to someone else by sight. But before long I've gathered my ample curls into a loose bun at the back of my head, fluffing up the front so that I have a perfect Gibson Girl do.

Now, my face. No decent woman paints her face, only prostitutes and actresses. But that doesn't mean there aren't a few tricks to try. This morning, I surreptitiously "borrowed" a couple of Irene's pink papers—little sheets of blotting powder that keep the skin from becoming too shiny. The powder is gently tinted pink to add some bloom. I pat one of the papers across my nose, chin, and forehead until I no longer look pale and drawn in my reflection in the porthole. Of course, the smile on my face might have something to do with that too.

Really, I don't have proper shoes, but the dress is long enough to hide that. I slip into the gown. Now, if I can only get the buttons done up. It's hard because they're in the back, but usually I manage.

Then one of the Norwegian ladies steps up and fastens the buttons. Her hands shake a bit with age. I smile at her over my shoulder and say, "Thank you." No doubt she understands my meaning, if not the words. She just nods.

The other lady goes through her bag until she comes up with

a knotted lace handkerchief. She unties it to reveal what must be her most precious possession—a pair of real pearl earrings, and not small pearls, either. Lady Regina herself would envy them. Then she holds one up to my ear and nods.

"Oh, I couldn't!" But they insist, screwing them onto my ears themselves. I've never worn any jewelry before, much less anything fine. Their style is extremely dated; they must have been handed down for generations. But I think I like their simple lines more than the ornate clips that are all the rage these days. The weight of the pearls feels strange on my earlobes. And yet it's a thrill too. When I go to first class, I'll look as if I belong there.

I feel a surge of defiance. All these years of tending to other people's hair and clothes, always feeling that I could outshine any debutante or socialite in the world if only I got the chance—well, now I've got it.

There's no mirror in the room, but I don't need one. I know how I look from the smiles on the old ladies' faces.

"Thank you," I whisper again. From the pocket of my uniform I withdraw my felt purse with my savings, and I press it into the hands of the one who has loaned me the earrings. It's my way of saying, *You trusted me with your most valuable possession, so I'll trust you with mine.* And I know she understands.

When I travel back to first class in the lift, the operator boy stares at me, his jaw slightly open. Obviously he'd like to ask about the transformation, but he doesn't—even the appearance of wealth makes people treat you differently, I realize.

That becomes even more clear to me when I walk to the grand

staircase. I've done it before, trailing after Irene or Lady Regina a couple of times. But then I was in servant's clothing and therefore invisible. Now I am myself. And I am seen.

Women's eyes examine the fashionable gown and the pearl earrings, and I can see them asking themselves who I am, whether they should have noticed me before, and trying to connect me to various fine families from *Burke's Peerage*. Men's eyes—that's different. Before, they either ignored me or sized me up the way they might a piece of meat. Their appreciation is less crude now, and yet more avid, because they think I have a title or a fortune to match my beauty. It might impress me more if I hadn't seen the other side of it. Whispers follow me along the staircase, tracing my path.

As I reach the bottom of the steps, one of the doors to the deck opens and Alec walks through. He wears a pale gray suit, as beautifully tailored to his body as the others he owns. The sea breeze tousles his unruly chestnut curls. He glances around the hallway, looking for me. It takes him a moment to recognize the well-dressed woman walking toward him, but I know the second he does.

It's less as if he sees me and more as if . . . something happens to him. Some of the loneliness falls away. Whatever it is, it happens to me too. The change in me goes deeper than my clothes; when I'm with Alec, I'm someone new, someone more like the person I always wanted to be. The space between us closes, and not only because we're walking toward each other.

"Obviously there's more to you than meets the eye," he says, instead of hello.

"That makes two of us, doesn't it?"

Alec laughs, half in surprise. "May I escort you to luncheon?"

It's as if he doesn't remember that this is about keeping me safe. But I can't blame him for it—I've all but forgotten myself. I put on an imitation of Lady Regina's prim face, which makes him grin even wider. "I would be delighted."

Alec offers me his arm, and I take it as if I had done so a hundred times before. I don't remember that I'm playing a role; I don't remember the danger Alec represents. Mikhail is banished to the realm of bad memory. I'm lost in the moment, and in my companion.


Instead of dining among the first-class passengers at the formal luncheon, we go to the à la carte restaurant. This allows us to order whatever we want from the menu, and have it delivered shortly thereafter—quite fancy. We sit at a table spread with linen and china as a waiter lays out a proper luncheon for us. I give the server a smile, though it's awkward; normally servers are ignored by the served, and both parties like it better that way. But I know only how not to be noticed—it's impossible for me to pretend a servant's not visible.

Soon, though, I can pay attention only to Alec. We have no need of small talk; we're so far past that already.

"I suppose you would have run your father's steel business someday, if you weren't—if you weren't going to live on the frontier."

"That was never what I wanted," Alec says as we sit together, watching the brilliant blue sea out the window before us. It's almost uncommonly still. We seem almost to be suspended in the sky rather than floating on the water. "Dad supported me, too, God bless him. So many fathers want their sons to fit into the mold they define for them."

"Not only fathers." I think of how Lady Regina puts Irene down for what she isn't, instead of appreciating her daughter for what she is. "Well, if you weren't going to take over Marlowe Steel, what would you have done?"

Alec seems almost shy. "My whole life, I grew up around my father's work, but it was never running the mills or selling the product that inspired me. It was seeing the blueprints and plans they would bring him. The idea that you could measure the weight and dimensions of a building that didn't yet exist, and then will it into being—that was like magic to me. So I've been studying architecture. First back home in Chicago, with a man named Frank Lloyd Wright, and then at Columbia University. In Paris, I tried to keep it up—even got to meet with Gustave Eiffel, but it wasn't the same." He smiles, though there's sadness behind it. "I had wanted to work with steel, just in a different way. I wanted to—bend it into arches. Sink it deep in the earth to hold up a building taller than anyone's ever seen before. Architecture is the best of art and the best of business. The marriage of beauty and purpose."

I feel his love for it as though it were my own. "You mustn't give it up."

"What choice do I have?"

"You were able to study in Paris, weren't you?"

Alec looks away from me, staring resolutely at the Atlantic. "I can't repeat my mistakes in Paris."

I remember the rumors about his romance with the actress Gabrielle Dumont. Did he break her heart, or did she break his? "You did your best—"

"My best wasn't nearly good enough." Guilt shadows his features now, so deep he looks almost sick. Does he regret breaking Gabrielle's heart? "I can never fall into the trap of living among people again. Of—hurting them. Others had to suffer for me to learn that lesson."

How he must have loved her. Stupid of me to be jealous, so I try hard to put it aside and stick to the subject. "You could design buildings no matter where you lived. Couldn't you simply mail them the blueprints?"

"It's not the designing I can't do. It's—making business contacts. Going out and winning new clients. Working in a noted studio. None of those will be possible when I'm in Montana or Idaho or wherever else I wind up."

"If only you knew someone connected to the construction industry," I say innocently. "Say, maybe, one of the world's leading suppliers of steel."

He half laughs at the joke but doesn't yet turn back to me. "I didn't want to use my father's name to get ahead. I wanted to make it myself, without any unfair advantages."

"Spoken as only someone with advantages can." I gesture at him with my fork for emphasis. "Listen to me. If I had a rich father or connections that would help me do whatever I wanted in life, do you think I'd be polishing Miss Irene's shoes? As far as I can see, in this world, you're a fool for not using whatever gifts you're given. It's not as though you lied or cheated or stole to get Howard Marlowe as your father. That's who he is; that's who you are. You got dealt a bad card when you were bitten—so use one of the better cards you have in your hand to make up for it."

He finally looks at me once more, and his eyes search mine. "You don't talk like a girl who plans to be a ladies' maid her whole life."

"I don't." I'm glad I admitted this to Myriam before; it makes it easier to say now. "I've saved enough money to give notice once we arrive in New York City. It took me almost two years, but I did it."

"That shows real courage, Tess. Real determination." Alec nods slowly as he picks up his tea, and the admiration I see in his face makes me feel warm and giddy. "I think you're a remarkable woman."

"And I think you're a remarkable man." I sound positively brazen. So I hasten to add, "In ways besides the obvious, I mean."

He laughs again. Did I say before that it felt as if we were suspended in the sky? That's not right at all. It's more like soaring.

We leave the restaurant to stroll along the deck, which turns out to be much more pleasant when I'm not following Lady Regina with shawls in hand. Alec doesn't point out anyone "worth knowing"—instead we talk about songs we both like ("On Moonlight Bay"), and buildings in New York I must try to view (the Candler Building, under construction, and he is wild to see it himself). I share some funny stories from my time in service. Though Alec doesn't find all of them as funny as I do.

"Wait, it's so cold in your attic that the water freezes at night?" He can't wrap his head around it. "They don't have heating there? Even a fire?"

"Who'd waste firewood on the servants?" Honestly, it never occurred to me to wish for a fire. Getting one was so obviously out of the question.

"But that's cruel. Who would do that to people, particularly those who live in your home with you?"

"Your family must have servants. Do they all have fires?"

I expect this to cow him, but it doesn't. "The three servants who live with us have decent quarters, heated by the same furnace that serves our rooms."

Surely I didn't hear that correctly. "Three?"

"The cook, the driver, and the housekeeper. My father and I don't need anything more, and honestly, I'm not sure what the driver's been doing with himself the past couple of years."

"But—how do you get dressed in the morning?" I think of Ned's grumbling about how picky Layton has become during his interminable preparations each day.

Alec laughs out loud. "I put my trousers on one leg at a time, and it works perfectly well, I promise."

Although the Lisles have cut down on their household in the past few years, there are still about thirty-five of us at Moorcliffe, and Lady Regina often complains that this is inadequate. She doesn't so much as lift a foot if she can help it; that's how society defines gentility, or so I've always been told. But the Marlowes have a fortune that eclipses the Lisles', and yet they manage most of their affairs themselves. I don't know if that's the way their family is, or the way Americans are. Whatever it is, I like it. Half the reason the Lisles have servants is so they can show they're better than someone. Alec and his father don't need to prove that.

Then I realize there's someone he hasn't mentioned. "What about your mother?"

Alec pauses before he answers. "She passed away six years ago. Influenza."

"I'm sorry."

He motions for us to sit in two deck chairs. So I settle myself in one, wishing I'd brought a shawl just for myself; the sunlight was bright and warming today, but it's only a few hours from setting now, low enough in the horizon to look as though it's drawing the ship westward after it. Alec takes his place next to me, then fishes in his pocket and pulls out a knotted lace handkerchief. "Open it."

I can't see any reason not to. When the knot finally comes untied, I see a small, ornately carved locket on a delicate chain. I glance up at Alec, and when he nods, I press the latch to reveal two photographs. One is of a lovely woman in her middle years, perhaps the final portrait of her, and the other is of a baby with wildly curly hair—the infant Alec, of course.

"This was hers," I say.

"She pressed it into my hand only a few hours before she died. Mom said—she said every time she looked at it, she remembered how much I loved her. So I should look at it after she was gone to remember how much she loved me."

"That's beautiful. What she said, I mean—but her too." And

his baby self, though I know it would embarrass him were I to say so. "And the locket."

"It would be if I could still touch it." I frown, and Alec explains, "It's silver. Pure silver." Of course. It would burn him. "This is the first time I've seen Mom's picture in two years. It was the only one we brought with us to Europe and—I could have asked my father to open it for me, but every time he sees her photograph, he gets so upset. So I've just carried it with me. That's all I can do."

I had thought only of the greater tragedies of Alec's change, never the little ones. But looking at his face now, I know that the small ones carry their own weight.

I want to comfort him, but I don't know how. He lifts his eyes from the locket, and almost unconsciously, we begin to lean closer—

"Ah, young Mr. Marlowe! There you are!" crows Lady Regina. Of all the bloody luck. I look up in horror to see her sweeping forward, Mr. Marlowe and Miss Irene by her side. At first she seems oblivious to my presence—of course, she doesn't recognize me.

But Irene does, and she gasps, in true surprise, "My heavens, Tess! How pretty you look!"

"Tess?" Lady Regina draws herself up, surprise changing to fury, and all at once I feel like an imposter. This is not my dress, only a costume. I've been nothing but a servant girl in a masquerade, and now the play is over.

# ⊰ CHAPTER 13 ⊱

WE'RE CAUGHT.

Lady Regina draws herself up rather regally. "Mr. Marlowe, I take it you failed to recognize my daughter's maidservant after she so cunningly disguised herself. What lies has she told you? Did she invent a new name?"

"I know who Miss Davies is," Alec says, completely calm.

I'm not calm. I feel like a fool, and though part of me protests that I've done nothing wrong, another part of me is sure that I have. My cheeks flush warm with shame as I hastily retie the handkerchief around Alec's locket and hand it back to him.

"Alec," says his father, "come and talk with me a moment." He doesn't sound angry, but he doesn't sound pleased, either. Probably it looks to him like Alec's womanizing with servant girls—during the daytime, which would be his only opportunity. Alec doesn't say anything to me, but he gives me a glance as he rises. Am I supposed to know what he means by it? I don't. I can't think, can't sense anything outside the hammering of my own pulse.

As soon as Mr. Marlowe has drawn Alec aside, Lady Regina leans over me. "Get out of that chair. Take yourself down to third class where you belong. And where did you get that dress?"

"You gave it to me, milady." I shouldn't say a word to her now, but I'll be damned if I let her accuse me of stealing. "As one of Miss Irene's castoffs."

"And now you're after Irene's castoff lovers, I see." Lady Regina glares at her daughter with as much venom as she had for me. "As my daughter can't be bothered to associate with proper young men, you have to dress up and play the role for her."

Irene's pale oval face crumples in humiliation. She honestly hadn't thought a thing of it when she saw me, except that I looked nice. Leave it to Lady Regina to turn even that into a way to insult her.

"Leave," Lady Regina repeats. "You will return that dress when you return to your duties tomorrow. Not that my daughter will wear anything so garish, but I won't have you using her hand-me-downs to help you impersonate a member of the nobility."

*It's mine*, I want to say. *You can't take it back.* But where will I ever wear it again? If I get a job in a factory in New York City, my wardrobe won't require any pink satin.

I realize I only kept it in the first place for the same reason I'm reluctant to give it back now: I wanted to pretend my life could be something that it can't. All day, I've been sipping tea and sunning myself and—and looking at Alec as though he could ever belong to me. Don't I know better?

What an idiot I've been, letting myself care about him. Even if he weren't a monster, he would still be beyond my reach.

"If we were not at sea, I would dismiss you on the spot, Tess." Lady Regina is enjoying herself now. Does she recognize how much pleasure she takes in lecturing people who can't speak back? "As it is, I suppose we must make do. But you can expect your wages to be docked. Severely."

One afternoon's dreaming has cost me some of the precious money I need to start over in America. I would be furious at Lady Regina if I weren't angrier with myself.

All this time I've been sitting in my deck chair as though I were frozen in place by Lady Regina's stare. Now I rise, curtsy, and start backing away, so upset that I'm clumsy and stupid. "I beg your pardon, milady. Excuse me, milady."

Blindly I hurry from the deck toward the lift that will take me down to third class, where I belong. My hands reach to the beautiful pearl earrings, to yank them off, but then I remember how hopeful I felt when they were first put on—the sweet smiles of the old ladies who lent them to me—and I just can't do it. In my cabin, I'll pretend I had the time of my life, change back into clothes that say who I really am, and find some private space to have a good cry.

Just as the lift door opens and I step in, though, someone pushes in beside me—Alec.

"What are you doing here?" I ask. "I'm headed straight to third class."

"I'm going wherever you're going," Alec says. He nods at the lift operator, who clearly isn't quite sure how to handle this.

But we start moving down.

"Won't your father object? I saw how quickly he snatched you back."

"He wanted to make sure I wasn't toying with you. I told him I wasn't."

"I'm not interested in serving as a way for you to slap your father in the face."

Alec breathes out, frustrated. "Tess, have you forgotten why we agreed to spend the day together? You need someone with you today. I'm not leaving you alone, not if I can help it."

I had forgotten. Mikhail seems a thousand miles away. Has Alec's rapt attention today been nothing more than a way to pass the time while he serves as my bodyguard?

"You've risked a lot for me," he says quietly, and he can't meet my gaze. "I knew you were in danger from Mikhail—but until this, I didn't realize what a chance you took even with your job. With your pride."

I'd like to say that Lady Regina can't wound my pride, but it's not true. It's impossible to spend  years of your life in a house with a woman who thinks you're lower than dirt and not let her get to you from time to time. And she got to me today.

Alec slowly looks at me again, more intently than ever before. "I've spent the last few years worried mostly about myself. Then here you are—so much more vulnerable, and so much braver—" He swallows hard. "You've reminded me what it means to care for someone else, Tess. Let me do this for you."

He's too hard on himself: I've seen his concern for his father.

But perhaps it's true that something deeper has awakened in him. Isn't it true for me?

"Yes," I say. No other words come to me. This moment is too intense—too intimate—for me to speak easily.

But then his green eyes sparkle with humor. "Besides, I hear the third-class accommodations are top-notch."

"As such things go." I'm too overwhelmed to joke with him just yet, though I appreciate the effort. "You're hardly interested in seeing the third-class dining hall."

"I'm interested in anything you have to show me," he says as the door opens on lowly F deck, just down the hallway from the door to third class. Once again, he offers me his arm, just as he had before when I was playing the part of a fine lady.

Alec's attention isn't for the role I played. It's for me.

I push aside my fears about what lies ahead. This is the time I have with him, and I intend to make it count.

"First things first," I say. "You're overdressed for third class."

He looks down at his immaculate deep-gray suit, as though it might have changed on him while he wasn't looking. "What should I wear, then?"

The lift operator keeps watching us, turning his head from one to the other until it looks like he's watching a tennis match.

"Doff the jacket."

Alec's smile goes wolfish as he removes his jacket. I wonder how much of the rest of his clothes I could convince him to take off, then wonder where *that* thought came from.

Well. I guess I know.

He rolls his shirtsleeves up halfway, unknots his tie, and tucks it into a pocket. Nobody would ever mistake him for some Irish tough, but he looks friendlier somehow. More comfortable, too—I realize he likes this better than the pomp of first class. There is something wild about him even in his human form, something that wants always to be free.

Once he throws his jacket over one shoulder, he says, "Better?"

"Much." I can't help smiling. The lift operator is openly staring now.

Alec offers me his arm again, and this time I take it. Lady Regina's nastiness is a world away. We're somewhere else now, in a world we can share.

Alec waits in the corridor while I change into my simple day dress, then we go looking for what fun third class has to offer. If you ask me, it's better than first class—and Alec seems to agree.

For a little while, we simply spend time on the third-class deck. The views may not be as spectacular as first class—we can see them above us, impossibly distant and fine—but the sea air is as fresh and the sunshine as bright. The little Irish girls I saw before have decided that one bench is their home: not the cute Wendy house I would have expected, but a fort, which is to keep out the Indians they expect to find the moment they step onto American soil. We are allowed to sit on it and chat if we agree to stand guard the soldiers say, introducing themselves between bouts of pulling each other's pigtails.

"Whom are we guarding?" Alec asks, very seriously.

"The prisoner!" says Colleen. She points at the dolly lying beneath it.

"She looks dangerous." Alec frowns. "What do we do if she makes a break for it?"

Colleen's elder sister, Mary, draws herself up more majestically than Lady Regina ever has. With gravity, she says, "Then you must shoot to kill."

"Yes, ma'am." I salute, and Alec joins me in the gesture.

These aren't the only children playing on deck. There are boys spinning tops, tiny babies being bounced in their mothers' arms, and slightly older girls who look at Alec with undisguised longing, and at me with envy meant to strike fear in my heart. But I can't stop laughing. The air grows cooler, and Alec drapes his jacket around my shoulders. The wool is so soft, so warm. I imagine this is what his embrace would feel like.

"Were you like this as a boy?" I point to one of the rowdier boys, who is on a bear hunt. His younger brother must be the bear.

"Not at all." Alec leans back, as do I. Our shoulders brush, barely touching. "I was the quiet one who hid in the attic and read pulp magazines. That fateful hunting trip was only the third I'd ever been on in my life. Maybe I should've stuck to *All-Story Magazine*."

"Now you're living a pulp story of your own."

Alec laughs so loudly that even more people stare at us. "Do you know, you're the only person who's ever joked about—ever joked about it?"

"It's not that I don't take it seriously. What you're going through."

"I know. But it helps to laugh, just the same."

Before I can answer him, I hear Myriam's voice. "I thought you were in first class today."

"Change of scenery," I say, looking over my shoulder. Myriam strolls toward us with her long black hair rippling in the breeze. She's so beautiful in the late-afternoon light that I feel a momentary fear—it would be no great surprise if Alec couldn't take his eyes from her after this.

But when Alec says, "Tess, will you introduce me to your friend?" he does so with only ordinary politeness.

"Myriam Nahas, this is Alexander Marlowe. Alec, this is Myriam. She's one of the women sharing my cabin."

Myriam recognizes the name and raises an eyebrow. She didn't expect to see him here, that's for sure. "What inspired you to abandon the pleasures of first class, Mr. Marlowe?"

"Please, call me Alec. And we like the company more down here."

"More than John Jacob Astor?" She folds her arms, determined to test him, as I realize she must test everyone.

"Astor's all right, so long as you don't cross him. But generally the group is . . . a bunch of stuffed shirts."

Her face clouds, and for the first time, Myriam's knowledge of English has hit its limits. "Stuffed shirts?"

"You know," I say. "Stuffed up so tightly they can't move." Alec impersonates this, puffing out his chest like some brandy-soaked cigar smoker in the lounge, and both Myriam and I laugh. She gives me a look like, *Well, he's not so bad.*

Just then, a figure appears on the deck, looking about madly. I'm shocked to recognize him. "Ned?"

"There you are. Whatever did you do to Lady Regina? She's mad as a wet hen." Then Ned notices Alec standing there; though he's not met Alec before, he can see at once that he's a gentleman. "Beg your pardon, sir. Not meaning to interrupt."

"I'm the one who's angered Lady Regina," Alec says, which is a rather generous interpretation of events. "You'll be all right, though, won't you, Tess?"

He says it with a surety that reminds me how soon I will leave the Lisles' service. Why do I let her scare me so much now, when her power over me is ending? I take a deep breath. "Yes. I'm all right. Did she send you down here after me, Ned? Oh, excuse me— Myriam, Alec, this is Ned Thompson, valet to Layton Lisle and my good friend. Ned, this is Myriam, my bunkmate, and Alec, who is . . . not a valet and yet also my good friend."

"Nice to meet you both." Ned's gone all stiff. "No, she's just in a temper—I mean, her Ladyship expressed her displeasure."

"Don't be proper," Myriam says. "Alec's no stuffed shirt." Alec mouths the words *Very good!* at her, and she smiles. Though she approves of few people, Alec clearly passes muster.

"It's all right, really, Ned," I say. "If I need to go up there and be shouted at some more, tell me now."

Ned looks from me to Alec a couple of times, still unsure, then relaxes and becomes himself again. "Mad as a wet hen, like I said. It would be funny to watch, if she hadn't thrown her shoes. Hard to laugh when you have to duck."

I can't help giggling. "Tell me she hit Horne."

"Near as a touch! I wouldn't go up there for anything, if I were

146

you. Leave it till tomorrow; it'll be bad enough then." Ned takes a seat on the bench with us. "I've got an hour or so to myself, thought I'd check in on you. Layton took himself off with that Russian count friend of his."

Alec and I share a look. His hand briefly touches my arm, warding off the fear I should feel at the very thought of Mikhail.

*I will hurt someone you love.*

"What about you, Ned?" Alec says. "Will you leave service when you reach America? I imagine you'd be glad to see the last of the Lisles."

Alarm pierces me. I haven't told Ned yet; I know I should, but I don't want him to have to hide it any longer than necessary. Ned doesn't catch the meaning behind Alec's question, though—just thinks it's a bit odd. "I expect to stay in service all my life, sir—I mean, Alec. Not with the Lisles, though. I've got my reasons for remaining with them a while yet, but when the time comes, I'll find myself a better household. One with fewer flying shoes, at any rate."

"Forever, Ned?" I ask. That makes me sad. "You couldn't ever have your own house, or get married."

"I don't expect to get married," Ned replies.

Myriam folds her arms; the sea breeze makes her dark hair stream out behind her, vivid against the bright sky. "You want to have love affairs by the dozen?"

This is where Ned would usually launch into one of his jokes, but he's oddly serious now. "The way I see it, men and women oughtn't to get married just because. You should marry when you're

147

really truly in love, forever. When you've found the one girl you'd most want in the whole world. If you haven't got that, then best not to marry at all, I think."

"Perhaps you will find love yet," Myriam says, more gently.

Ned simply shakes his head. He casts a sidelong glance at Alec, uncertain no longer. "And what brings you down here? Get tired of all the caviar and brandy upstairs? Must get old."

"I came for the company," Alec says. His eyes meet mine, and I feel almost shy.

"It's like that, is it?" God bless Ned, he doesn't try to shoo Alec off or tell me I should know better. "Well, in for a penny, in for a pound—do you want to have tea down here? It's not as good as what you're used to, but honestly, it's not half bad. And sometimes people play the piano."

Would there be another impromptu dance? I like the thought of dancing with Alec.

His face falls, and I remember. I look at the sky, which is already slightly dimmer than before. Sunset is coming.

"We have to go," I say. "I'll be back directly, though."

"Nice to meet you both." Alec's voice is tight, but his smile is genuine. "Guard the prisoner, will you?" He points, and Myriam frowns in consternation to see the dolly beneath the bench. I realize that he truly likes both Myriam and Ned. It's so odd to think that these people I've come to know—the ones society puts in three different boxes—might all be friends if things were just a bit different.

And if Alec weren't cursed by a werewolf's bite.

Myriam and Ned say their good-byes as we head back within the ship. Happily we can remain on F deck. Alec's face betrays only a shade of the strain he must be feeling, but I can see it, now that I'm looking for it. Once we're in the hallway, again alone, he says, "I stayed longer than I should have."

When our eyes meet, I know why he stayed, and I feel that knowledge quiver down deep inside.

Together we walk back the way we came—from third class to first class, from laughter and sunshine to what he endures at night. I've thought about it ever since I learned his secret, but now I dare to ask him more. "Does it hurt?" I say quietly, as we go side by side through the corridors.

"Like being ripped apart." Alec is so matter-of-fact as he says this. It makes me shiver. "But I can't think about it much after I'm changed. So it's blurry."

"What do you mean, you can't think about it?"

"When I'm a wolf, my mind—it's not the same. As a human, I can't remember it very well." Of course; he was even surprised to see me yesterday morning in the Turkish bath. "I'm not sure how much humanity is in me then. If there's any humanity left."

"Don't say that."

"Don't deny what I am." His voice is sharper, edged with what I think is anger—but that's not it. The sun is near setting. The wolf is closer to the surface.

It frightens me to see the change in him. Yet it thrills me too.

Alec continues, more quietly, "Changing back hurts less—it feels like going back to the way things should be, at least—but that, I have to remember. Every second of it."

He stretches his back, rolls his shoulders. His movements grow freer, less confined. He's even walking faster, and I have to hurry to keep up. I don't mind it. Something in me wants to break into a run so that he will run with me. I want this mad energy between us released.

With my key, we slip through the door to first class and go toward the Turkish baths. Once again, they are closed for the evening, but Alec can let himself in. "How did you get the key to the bath?" I ask.

He shrugs. "My father requested it. They don't deny the first-class passengers many privileges. All you have to do is ask."

That's how I got my key too, thanks to the Lisles' eminent name. "Must be nice."

"It is in this case, anyway."

I glance around, remembering how we were brought together here the first time. "Mikhail wouldn't—"

"He left me alone here last night," Alec says. The hall lighting reddens his hair, deepens the shadows on his face. His breathing is more shallow now. Almost ragged. "He hasn't bothered you again, has he?"

"Just to scare me." I should have told Alec about the note, perhaps, but in the light of day, I feel sure it was meant to scare me, to haunt me. It couldn't be a real threat. "As long as he believes I'm too scared to betray him to the Lisles, I think—I think I'm all right."

"But you won't be alone." Alec's hands close around my arms, bringing me closer to him. His voice is rough, his eyes intense. "Promise me, Tess."

"I promise."

We are only inches apart. He whispers, "With you—with you

150

I feel almost human again." Slowly Alec leans toward me, and I close my eyes.

When his mouth closes over mine, the kiss isn't gentle. He's almost desperate, the way he clutches me to him, the way he devours me. *The wolf*, I think. *The wolf in him is close to the surface, so close.*

But then why am I kissing him back just as desperately?

When our lips part, I'm trembling all over, and his breath is shaky. "You have to go," he says.

"I know." But we don't let go of each other at first.

"Please, Tess." Alec pleads with me to have the strength of will that is failing him. "I won't be myself much longer."

I remember the red wolf—the terror I felt two nights ago—and while I cannot recapture that fear, just bringing it to mind gets me to step back. His grip on my arms breaks, and he makes a small, frustrated sound. We both want so much more.

"I'm going."

"All right." Alec pushes open the door, releasing soft clouds of steam. "I know that—for your own good—I shouldn't see you again. But I can't stand the thought of not seeing you again."

"I'll be with the Lisles the rest of the trip." My voice sounds very small.

He closes his eyes, struggling against something. "Damn it, damn it, give me another five minutes." He's talking to the wolf, which will not listen.

Alec's hand is sinew-tense against my cheek as he pulls me close and kisses me again, this time only for a single hungry instant. Then he walks into the bath, letting the door swing shut behind him. His only farewell is the clicking of the lock.

Half in a daze, I wander back into third class. I don't know whether to feel elated or devastated. All I can think about is the taste of Alec's kiss on my lips.

As I hug myself, I realize that his jacket is still draped over my shoulders. I could just give it to a steward to deliver to the Marlowe family suite. Maybe that's what I should do. But it's an excuse to see Alec again, if I want an excuse.

And I do.

I slip the jacket on over my dress. He is so broad-shouldered and muscular that his coat drapes easily around me, tall though I am. It feels like a trophy. Proud, still giddy from his kiss, I lift the collar so that I can breathe in the scent of Alec's skin. Then I tuck my hands into the pockets, so I can feel the warmth of his hands and remember them touching me.

In one pocket, I feel a crumpling of paper.

I pull it out to see a collector's tourist card with a bit of newsprint wrapped around it. Curiosity makes me look at the card, to see what Alec finds interesting—but when I see, my heart drops.

There, in silvery tones, is a picture postcard of a beautiful woman, clearly costumed for some sort of ballet or opera in Oriental-style dress. Her figure is perfect; her profile is as delicately sculpted as one of the Greek marbles in Moorcliffe's garden temple. The white lettering at the bottom proclaims this to be Gabrielle Dumont.

The actress from Paris. The same one Lady Regina gossiped about as being Alec's possible lover.

Lady Regina claimed that their romance had "ended badly,"

but he still carries her picture with him every day. Does that mean he's still in love with her? But if Alec is in love with this woman, how could he kiss me like that?

And he acted so guilty about breaking her heart.

The crumpled newsprint falls from my fingers, swaying slowly downward; I catch it before it hits the ground. I don't know what I expect it to say, but I know I don't expect this.

It's from the *Times*. It reports on the shocking death of the celebrated actress Gabrielle Dumont two weeks ago in Paris.

The most shocking detail is how she died. She was "torn to death by a pack of dogs," on the street outside her home, though she lived in the heart of Paris. Nobody saw the attack, but nobody could mistake the signs of what had happened to her.

Torn to death by a pack of dogs.

Or by a wolf.

Alec said he had to leave Paris in a hurry. He said he has to live in the woods, far away from any human contact, from now on. He carries a burden of guilt inside him that can well up and take him over at any moment. Only now do I realize why.

He murdered Gabrielle.

## CHAPTER 14

"YOU SURE YOU'RE ALL RIGHT?" NED SAYS THROUGH a mouthful of chicken.

"I'm fine."

"You don't sound fine. You sound like a dead woman walking."

"And what would that sound like?" Myriam demands. "You wouldn't know."

"All right, all right, don't bite my head off."

The hubbub of the third-class dining hall almost drowns her out. Or is it just me? The world beyond my own skin seems so far away.

The newspaper clipping and tourist card are still in the coat pocket; Alec's coat remains on my back. It still feels like his arms around me, but it doesn't feel like an embrace any longer. It feels imprisoning.

*Torn apart by wild dogs.*

The red wolf and the black, ripping each other apart in their eagerness to get at me.

As a group in the back begins singing "Shine On, Harvest

Moon," for their amusement more than for ours, Ned frowns and tries again. He means well but simply does not know when to stop. "Worrying about Lady Regina? She'll be a bear in the morning, but honestly, how much worse can she actually get? You'll hold up fine. Always do."

"I'm not worried about Lady Regina." I'd never have imagined what would have to happen for her to be the least of my problems.

Ned asks, "You seasick, maybe?"

"Maybe that's it." I would agree to anything if it will make Ned stop asking me questions. I know he means well, but I want to wall myself up in my own mind and try to come to terms with what I've just learned.

Myriam begins asking Ned about life in service, and I laugh on cue at his best anecdotes about Layton's drunken exploits, but I'm not paying attention. She isn't either, really; she's just distracting Ned for me. I can feel her watchful eyes on me throughout the meal.

Afterward, we decline to attend the evening's dance. While we walk back to our cabin, Myriam says only, "Did Alec say something to hurt you? He seemed nice to me, but—your face this evening—"

"No. I don't want to talk about it." I grab her hand, not wanting her to think that I'm shutting her out. "Just—don't leave me alone. All right?"

She nods slowly. "As you wish."

So we spend the evening in our cabin, and she tells me about her life in Lebanon. Some of it sounds deliciously exotic—olive trees and the seashore—yet most of it is familiar. Everywhere people shear sheep and spin wool. Everywhere mothers prepare big bowls of soup for dinner before calling the children indoors. Everywhere children hate to leave home and yet know that they must.

The elderly Norwegian women—whom we think are named Inga and Ilsa, though we're not sure which is which—stay at the dance until late and arrive home rather giggly. I suspect they've sampled the beer. Their earrings are exchanged for my felt purse with grateful smiles, but mostly I want to tuck the purse under my pillow. I feel the coins in my palm, as a lump beneath my head, the promise that I will be able to start over someday soon.

I try not to look at the door and wonder if Mikhail is on the other side. Mostly I succeed. I try not to think of what Alec is going through, or what Alec has done. That's harder. But this night, for the first time since I have been aboard the *Titanic*, I am able to fall into a deep, uninterrupted sleep.

*April 13, 1912*

The next morning, I put on my uniform feeling as though my gut is heavy as lead. I tell myself that Ned was right, that it can't get any worse—the Lisles have already docked my pay, and beyond that, little else matters. I intend to quit in just a few days. So what if Lady Regina is so angry about my adventures with Alec yesterday? Why should I care if she fires me?

But she's already said she won't fire me. I've already decided to work through the end of the voyage, because I don't want my pay docked any further. This means I'll just have to put up with her nastiness, and right now—while my heart still aches from learning that Alec is a killer—I don't know that I can bear it.

*I'll bear it*, I tell myself. *I have to.*

Lady Regina won't be the worst of it, though.

I practically tiptoe into the Lisles' cabin that morning, but most of the family isn't up. Beatrice is wailing, though, and I can hear Horne trying to comfort her. With the pink dress folded under one arm, I step into Irene's room.

Irene is awake. As usual, she's still wearing her nightgown, her straw-colored hair hanging lank around her face. Dark circles shadow her eyes, and for the first time ever, she doesn't smile the moment I walk in.

"Good morning, Tess," she says, as politely as usual, though she looks likely to burst into tears.

This is the worst of it—knowing I've hurt the only member of the Lisle family who's always been kind to me.

"Miss Irene, I'm so sorry," I say. "It wasn't meant to show you up. You know that, don't you?"

"Mr. Marlowe and I had no interest in each other." Her mouth quirks in something that's supposed to be a smile, but isn't quite. "I couldn't convince Mother of that, so I suppose it was up to you."

"There's nothing between me and Mr. Marlowe. You know that's not even possible. For me it was only a chance to be up on the boat deck for a day, and wear something pretty for a change. For him—I suppose it was a bit of fun for a rich man. Nothing more than that."

It was so much more than that, but I want to deny it, both to her and to myself.

Irene lays one hand on my arm. Her hands are truly beautiful—slim and long-fingered, as pearly white and soft-skinned as any noblewoman could hope for. "Don't let him take advantage of you, Tess. You deserve better than that."

I could cry. "You don't have to be nice to me! Not when I've made your mother angry with you."

"Mother's always angry with me, and she always will be." Irene leans her head against the wall, as though it were too heavy. She's more trapped than I've ever been, I realize; at least I can quit being a servant. Irene couldn't even walk out of her house and get a job if she wanted to, because they've made good and sure she's utterly useless. She's never washed a dish or mended a seam. I bet she's never even brushed her own hair. She plays the piano, and paints blurry watercolors, and speaks a little French, which even she says is very bad. There's nothing she's fit for but marrying someone, and she doesn't even get to pick the someone.

I hand her the pink dress. She sets it in her lap. "I'll keep this, because I suspect Mother will ask about it. But when we reach New York—Tess, I'm going to give the dress back to you."

"No, miss. You mustn't risk it."

"It's yours," she insists. "You shouldn't lose it because Mother's mean, and because you wanted to spend one day on deck." We look at each other, and the distance between gentlewoman and servant seems narrower than ever. I could almost believe we're friends. "I know what it's like to want just one day of freedom."

I nod, telling her that I understand. Irene's hand pats my arm again, and for a moment I think she might hug me. I wouldn't mind.

But that's when Lady Regina walks in.

"You," she says. "Get to work. What can you mean, the morning after such an outrageous performance, coming in here to loaf around?"

I scramble for the silver-backed hairbrush on Irene's dressing table, so I can get started on Miss Irene.

Lady Regina's words feel like lashes across my back: "You're just like your sister, aren't you? A tramp with no morals, no decency. Watch you don't end up in the same trap, my dear. Or is it already too late for you, as it is for so many others?"

My sister, the mother of her grandchild. Hot anger boils up inside me, and I think I won't be able to keep from screaming.

But it's Irene who screams.

"Irene?" Lady Regina stares at her. It must be as much noise as Irene's made since she squalled after being born. "What's gotten into you?"

"Leave Tess alone! Leave me alone! Get out of my room! I can't stand the sight of you!" Irene looks positively mad. She picks up a small mug of water near her bedside and actually throws it at Lady Regina. It bounces off the wall, but it splashes her mother thoroughly, deflating her poufy hair. If I were less astonished, I'd never stop applauding.

Lady Regina doesn't budge. "Tess, leave us," she commands. "Go help Horne. She's useless with Beatrice this morning." I do as she says, though I wish I could stay for every word.

After the door to Irene's room slams behind me, I start toward Beatrice's nursery, but someone stands in my way—Layton.

He looks worse than ever. His fair hair is slicked back, but in such a way that it fully reveals how much thinner it's become lately. Ned must have done that on purpose. But what really strikes me is the pallor of Layton's face, the faintly swollen look of him. He's always been a heavy drinker, but he must have spent virtually all of the past two days intoxicated. Thanks to Mikhail, I realize.

I'm not the only pawn in rich men's games.

Layton stares past me at the shut door to Irene's room. The argument between mother and daughter is audible, but muffled— but when they were screaming, he would have heard every word. I realize that he's upset by something, and I think I know what it is. I've got him at a weak moment, and in a few days I'll walk away and never see Layton Lisle again. If I'm ever going to say something to him about this, I must act now.

"It's too late for my sister, isn't it?" I say. *"Sir."*

This is his cue to sneer at me, or tell me I'm imagining things, or maybe go ahead and sack me. Right now I'm so angry I don't care if he does.

He leans toward me, and he still smells faintly of alcohol. Either last night's indulgence hasn't yet lifted, or he began drinking at breakfast. I'm guessing the latter. "It wasn't my intention to—to have, ah, matters turn out that way."

Wasn't his intention? He damned sure intended to do what got my sister pregnant in the first place. "You could've stood up for her."

"What, and taken her to wed? Have a big ceremony at Salisbury Cathedral with the bishop present?" Layton's sneering now, but his pale eyes are hollow. There's no pleasure in these taunts. "What

160

kind of simpleton are you, that you think something like that would ever be possible?"

"I know the way of the world, sir. But you could've taken better care of her. You could have done right by her instead of leaving her to starve."

He goes white so suddenly that I put out my hands, sure he's about to topple over. "Daisy—she—she can't have *starved*."

Good Lord. In some way, he actually cares. Just not enough. "No, she didn't, no thanks to you. She's married now to a good man, one who can look after her."

Layton breathes out in relief. Whatever measure of concern he feels doesn't extend as far as jealousy about her new love; the fact that Daisy's now married means he doesn't have to let guilt trouble him any longer. "That's all right then, isn't it?"

"She was hungry. She was cold and alone and afraid. People in the village laughed at her and called her names. My father will never speak to her again. You did that to her, with your selfishness."

"You forget your place, Tess!"

"You forgot yours, didn't you?"

Anger contorts his features, and yet he looks more handsome—more like the younger Layton—than I've seen him in years. It's the first time I've seen anything as strong as a real emotion in him since . . . since Daisy left. "Don't you start too. I heard enough about it from Mother and Father to last me a lifetime. I would've—but you can't understand what it means, to have family responsibilities."

I who shared a bed with my sister, who helped feed my sick

gran, who did more for the members of my family than Layton will ever do for his. But I hear what he didn't say. "You wanted to do better by her. You were going to give her a decent sum of money and support the child. But Lady Regina told you not to, and like a little lapdog, you obeyed her." The obedience cost him, I see now. Did Lady Regina realize that when she defeated her son about this, she broke his will forever? Even if she does, I'd bet she doesn't regret it.

The thought of Daisy, pregnant and alone, with only his golden pin to live on, and Layton abandoning her out of cowardice, fills me with an anger that crowds out rational thought. Before I can stop myself, I slap him—good God, I've struck a Lisle. It seems as if the earth should split in two. The blow didn't land hard, but he's off balance in his intoxication, so he grabs at my skirt as if to stop himself from falling on his rump.

I hear fabric tearing. The rip in my uniform is nothing, I think. Mostly I'm overcome with contempt for what a pathetic sight he is.

But then my felt purse tumbles to the floor, coins jangling, and Layton snatches it.

"What's this?" He pours the money into his hand, and a few of the coins tumble to the floor. I start to go for it, but he blocks my way with his other hand. "Quite a fortune for a ladies' maid. You can't have kept all this."

"I did. I saved it. It's mine." Although it's mostly true, I remember that pound note I found on the stairs. My doubt must shadow my expression, because Layton gives me a smile of pure triumph.

"I don't think so. We don't pay you nearly enough to put this

much aside. You call me a lapdog, but better that than a thief."
Anger has made him worse than the weak, drunken noodle he
usually is; it has made him cruel. He scoops the coins and bills
into his fist and stuffs them back into the bag, and puts it in his
own pocket. "Stealing around the household, Tess. Tsk-tsk. That's
a firing offense."

"That's my money. Give it back to me."

"Let's ask Mother whose money it is, why don't we? I'm pretty
sure we both know whom she'll believe."

Layton has stolen my money. All my savings, every cent I had
for my new life in America. If I quit when we reach New York City,
the pittance Lady Regina would give me as severance wouldn't even
rent a room for a week. How am I supposed to do this now?

And I know—Layton and I both know—that there's nobody
I can tell who will believe me. Yesterday I might have tried to get
Alec involved, but I know better now. I could ask Myriam to talk
to George, but he's infatuated with her, not me, and I never showed
Myriam the money, so even she couldn't swear to it.

It's so unfair that I want to cry. But then, that's what it means
to be a servant. To be ruled by people the world calls your betters.

Layton sways on his feet, still drunk.

I slap his face so hard it hurts my hand. His head whips around,
and I think for a moment he'll fall. But he rights himself and
clutches my arm.

"I hear you've run afoul of my new friend, Count Kalashnikov."
Layton leans closer to me, borrowing the power to frighten from
Mikhail. "He likes you, he said. But you won't favor him with

your attention. Stupid of you, to refuse the attentions of a wealthy man—or, as I hear, to chase one when another is far more eager for your company."

"Count Kalashnikov—he's using you," I say, but Layton ignores this.

"He'll be staying in the same hotel as our family when we reach New York. I'd like to be able to show him true hospitality. And look at it this way, Tess—you can earn your coins back one way or another. With him or with me?"

I rip my arm free and run for the door. I don't care if I'm abandoning my duty. I don't care what Lady Regina will do next. There's no way I'm going to be near Layton for one more minute.

"Where are you going?" Layton laughs. Then he starts coughing, so feeble that he's almost a joke. "On this ship, dear girl, there's nowhere to run."

# ⇥ CHAPTER 15 ⇤

WHAT AM I GOING TO DO?

I must leave the Lisles' service. But I've lost my money, so now I can't leave.

Layton probably doesn't mean half of what he just said. I'd made him good and angry, but in the end, he's too weak-willed to carry out that kind of threat. The last of what was good in him died when he abandoned Daisy; if he remembers his better self at all, no doubt he drowns the memories in wine. No, there's nothing to fear in him. But Mikhail—him I can't protect myself from. Maybe he's told Layton he desires me because he's trying to get Layton to leave us alone together. If that ever happens, he'll kill me just for the fun of it.

The only protection I had was Alec, and now I might need to be kept safe from him, too.

Where can I possibly turn? If only there were someone on the ship who knew the truth but was no danger to me—

Wait. There's someone. Exactly one person who knows about all of this.

I have no idea if he'll hear me out, but I must try. And at least I have an excuse for going to his rooms.

The ship's steward announces me. "Sir, the Lisles' ladies' maid is here to see you. Something about a coat left behind by your son?"

"Show her in," says Howard Marlowe.

As I walk in, I see him, seated in front of their fireplace. Mr. Marlowe wears pinstripes and a blue cravat, more like he's about to stride into a boardroom than enjoying himself at sea. He's as large a man as his son, less handsome but only because of his years. His eyes remain brilliantly green, and his jaw remains firm; he's not dulled with drink or fat the way so many older men are. Were it not for his gleaming bald head, he could almost be taken for Alec's elder brother rather than his father.

I say nothing to reveal my true purpose at first—not until I've gauged his temper. Instead I set Alec's jacket on the nearest table. "Alec left this with me yesterday evening, sir. I thought I ought to return it promptly."

"Thank you." He isn't friendly or unfriendly. I would call his mood . . . cautious. "Alec is unable to thank you himself. He's still sleeping."

Just after breakfast—I'd guessed as much. Alec must have dragged himself up from the Turkish baths, weak and ragged as I saw him before, to get what rest he could. Pitching my voice to be steady, I say, "This must be his best chance to sleep."

Mr. Marlowe doesn't take it as an insult or threat as I had feared he would. The expression on his face reveals only relief. "My son said you knew the truth."

"I'll tell no one." Whatever else Alec may be, I made him that promise and I intend to keep it. "You can count on that."

"Thank you for your discretion. It means a great deal to him, and to me."

"I need to talk to someone about this," I say. "Mikhail—Count Kalashnikov, I mean—he's causing trouble for me, and I don't know who to trust or what's true. You're the only one I can turn to."

He rises swiftly, and I think I must have overstepped my bounds. But instead of showing me the door, Mr. Marlowe guides me toward their private promenade deck. "We mustn't be overheard in the corridor," he murmurs as we sit in the woven wicker chairs. "And I don't want to waken Alec if we can help it. He needs what rest he can get. Do you want some coffee? Ah, but you're English. You'll want tea."

"I'm fine, sir." Mr. Marlowe is as unpretentious as his son. Though I can't say I feel at ease with him, given what I've come to speak about, I like him. It helps.

Mr. Marlowe says, "You must be cautious of Count Kalashnikov. The Brotherhood has no use for women."

"Alec told me, sir. And I already knew the count was a dangerous man. He's trying to make friends with my employers, and he's got them fooled."

"He'll kill you if he can." Mr. Marlowe says this as easily as if he were commenting on the weather. He's not making light of it; the facts are that obvious. "You should leave their employ if at all possible. Do you need a reference in the United States? I could provide one."

A reference from one of the wealthiest and most powerful men in the country would no doubt get me a job in the best households available. I sag back in my chair, relieved. "That would be so good of you, sir. Thank you."

He studies my face, not unkindly, and yet I see for the first time that he isn't merely a friendly, down-to-earth American, but a businessman with the ability to size up the person across the table. "You might have blackmailed us. Demanded money to keep Alec's secret."

"It never occurred to me, sir." What a nasty thing to do. Sounds like something Mikhail would try.

"You're a good girl, Tess. I know my son had no choice but to trust you, but—he could have found no one better to keep the secret."

Mr. Marlowe speaks of his son with such love. Can he maybe tell me that my worst fears about Alec aren't true?

"Please, sir, forgive me for mentioning it, but—I found this in Alec's pocket." I pull out the newspaper clipping and the tourist card of Gabrielle Dumont. "This isn't—tell me this isn't what it looks like."

Mr. Marlowe's shoulders sag, and something inside me tears apart.

"You're asking me if my son is a killer. I wish I had an answer for you."

"What happened to Miss Dumont?"

He doesn't reply immediately. Instead he stares out at the ocean, squinting against the brightening morning sun. I recognize his hesitation, because I've seen it sometimes in Irene—the last person in the world I would have expected Howard Marlowe to have anything in common with. He wants to talk, but he's afraid to.

"It's strange, isn't it?" he finally says. "What discovering the supernatural does to your mind. You question everything. Even your own memories."

"It does make things look strange all of a sudden, sir."

Mr. Marlowe nods as he pulls a cigar from his jacket and rolls it between his fingers. "So far as I knew, Alec and Gabrielle were only friends. My boy and I have always been close, but I was a young man once, and I certainly didn't tell my pop about every girl I—" He catches himself. "Every young lady I met. But I got the impression that she wanted more from Alec than he had to give."

I refuse to feel triumphant about this. The woman is dead, maybe at Alec's hand. What he felt or didn't feel for her is no prize for me to claim.

"A werewolf made a good friend for an actress. They were each busy every night, and therefore happy to meet during the day. Both of them adored the bohemian scene." Mr. Marlowe doesn't sound as though *he* adored it. "Going about with painters and composers, visiting those strange clubs with the posters of monstrous-looking women gone all green. Never could see the appeal myself. But I wanted him to enjoy himself as much as he could. So much of his life has been stolen from him. At least Alec could have this much of his youth."

Bohemian Paris sounds glamorous. I imagine women wearing the sort of sexy costumes Gabrielle Dumont wore in the photo, though that's ridiculous; I'm sure it's nothing that outlandish. Alec's long curls are now explained.

"I ought to have warned him not to spend so much time with her," Mr. Marlowe says. He withdraws a small pair of silver clippers and snips the end of his cigar. The sweet scent of tobacco lingers in the air. "For her sake, if not for his. I have no doubt their connection killed her."

My mouth is dry, and I grip the arms of the chair to anchor myself. "You mean—you think he did it. Alec murdered Gabrielle."

"A werewolf murdered her. Sometimes I tell myself it could have been anyone in the Brotherhood—they were pressuring both me and my son by then, and they would have resented any other sources of friendship he had. And as I said before, they have no use for women. They delight in killing them. Had they no mothers? No sisters, no sweethearts? I don't understand that. But then, I've never understood the Brotherhood." He sighs heavily. "I kept a basement cell in Paris. That was where Alec transformed each night, and I could keep him locked away for his safety, not to mention everyone else's. But the night of Gabrielle's death, the lock broke. I returned at dawn to find the door open and Alec missing. He awakened halfway across Paris with little memory of the night before. So he was free that night. He knew where Gabrielle lived. Alec could well have been the werewolf that killed her."

"But—it wouldn't have to have been him."

"Oh, I've tried to convince myself of that. I think I could, if it were not for one thing: Alec believes it himself."

It's true; even knowing him only a few days, I can't deny it. All the things he said to me yesterday afternoon—about the mistakes he made in Paris—the guilt that hangs on him as heavy and dark as a shroud—it's about Gabrielle. About Gabrielle's death.

Mr. Marlowe says, "Alec carries around the tourist card to remind himself of the danger he represents to anyone he cares about."

I look down at the image of Gabrielle Dumont. If Alec was her friend, then probably she was somebody I would have liked. She went down the same path I'm on—the one leading to the shadow world of the werewolves. And now she's dead.

"My advice is to stay as far away from this as you can," Mr. Marlowe says. "I hate to deprive my son of such a loyal friend. But for your own safety, walk away while you still can." He strikes a match to light his cigar. It flares blue, then orange, and I smell the smoke. "Take my calling card. I shall have a letter of recommendation sent to your cabin before we make dock, so that you can find employment as soon as you arrive in New York City."

"Thank you, sir. You've been very kind." I hesitate. "Alec's lucky to have you."

"Lucky. If only he were."

Mr. Marlowe's expression grows more distant; remembering this painful past has depressed him. Quickly I rise and excuse myself. The sooner I leave, the better.

But I don't move fast enough.

I'm halfway through the sitting room to the door when Alec steps out of his bedroom, still knotting the belt of his dark silk robe. His unruly chestnut hair is rumpled from sleep, and his face has the hard, ragged look of a man who has been through pain. When he sees me, his eyes widen and a weary smile appears. "Tess?"

"I was just going." Was it only last night that we kissed so passionately he made me weak? My heart beats faster when I look at him, but I no longer know whether it's from desire or fear. "I didn't mean to wake you."

"It's all right. I'm glad you're here." Alec's so *happy*. Why has he become so sure of me in the same moment that I've become more afraid of him? Energized again, he walks toward his father on the promenade deck. "Dad, have you and Tess gotten to know—"

His voice trails off, and I realize what Alec has seen on the table: the tourist card picture of Gabrielle Dumont.

When Alec turns back to me, the expression on his face rips through me: pure betrayal. Pure shame. He hates that I know what he's done. His hands clench, and his eyes narrow, and I can't tell if what I see there is pain or anger. I know only that I see the wolf within.

"Tess, go now," Mr. Marlowe says. "Go quickly."

Is he protecting his son or me? Either way, the hair on the back of my neck stands on end, and I turn and dash into the hallway. The door slams shut behind me. I don't know who slammed it, and I won't look back.

After wandering through the ship for nearly an hour, uncertain of what to do or where to turn, I walk out on the boat deck. Fresh air tugs at my golden curls beneath my white linen cap. With my hands on the railing, I look over at the water so far below. The

*Titanic*'s vast size means that I am peering down from the height of a church steeple. Around me, in each direction, the ocean stretches out to every horizon. Even aboard this enormous ship, I am one small speck in infinity—so entirely alone.

I glance behind one shoulder, thinking of Mikhail, but he isn't here. And murdering me on deck, when John Jacob Astor—the richest man in the whole world—might walk by at any moment, seems beyond even Mikhail's audacity.

But he will come after me. The Lisles must be dealt with. And Alec . . . I don't know what will happen between us from this point on, but I know we will meet again.

I've been looking for someone to rescue me since I first felt the hunter's stare on my back when I boarded this ship. Before that, I thought I was so strong and so smart, with my little felt purse of money to save me. Now I feel like I understood nothing about the world then—nothing about the true horrors it holds—except for one thing, one that I realize is more true than ever: Nobody else will ever be able to save me if I'm not fighting as hard as I can to save myself.

To do that, I have to decide who to trust. I have to decide what I believe.

I look toward the east, squinting my eyes toward the morning sun.

First things first: I have to return to the Lisles' cabin one last time.

Probably I'm already fired after I simply walked off duty without permission this morning. But I need to know for sure what terms I'm leaving on. If I'm not even going to have a penny to start with in New York City, I have to come up with another plan. Maybe I could ask to stay with Myriam's family just for a day or two; with Mr. Marlowe's recommendation, it shouldn't take me any longer than that to find work.

They wouldn't try to make me pay for my cabin, would they? I could never have enough money to buy even a third-class ticket on a ship such as this. But that would require the Lisles to air some of their dirty family laundry before the officials of the White Star Line—so I'm guessing not. Hoping not, in any case.

Lady Regina will demand the uniforms back, of course. I'll have to mend the pocket Layton tore, or else she'll make me pay for the damages. Well, she's welcome to this stupid cap.

Despite my resolve, I have to bite back my dread as I step into the Lisles' suite. Yet the explosion of scolding from Lady Regina I'm expecting doesn't happen. The only person in the front room is Horne, who snaps, "Took you long enough. Miss Irene's waiting." Which is what she says every day I'm not there at dawn.

I can only stand there and blink. I ran out on the job and the only punishment is . . . nothing?

Finally I return to Miss Irene's room. She's sitting exactly where I left her, cheeks still flushed, breath still fast. Although she doesn't look up from the floor when I come in, she recognizes me. "I told Mother I'd given you some errands to run. I didn't explain what. If she asks, make something up."

"Thank you, miss." I'm less relieved than dismayed. I'll do the work, in the hopes of getting the money, but I'm still in the center of this mess—and too close to Mikhail. The world's largest ocean liner suddenly seems far too small.

To set aside my own fears, I study Irene for a few moments, taking in how distressed she looks. She's always been thin, but I've had to take in the waistlines of her gowns two inches during the past month, and I have to tug her stays hard to get them tight enough for her corset not to hang loose on her body. For her to shout at Lady Regina as she did, something extraordinary must be wrong. As well as we get along, though, it's beyond the bounds of the servant-employer relationship for me to ask Irene about it directly.

I try, "Are you sure you're well, miss?"

"As well as can be expected." She sighs. "Come on, Tess. Make me pretty. Dress me up like a doll so Mother can parade me around."

An idea comes to me. It's both so radical and so obvious that it's startling. It will snarl Mikhail's plans in a way he won't discover until too late. It will give me some small measure of power in this terrifying mess.

But more than anything else—if I do this, I will help Alec. I will give him a chance to finally get the upper hand in his battle against the Brotherhood.

Is it worth committing a crime to help him? Worth risking my freedom, potentially even my life?

My practical nature says no. For the first time in a very long time, I ignore my practical side. What I feel for Alec—the depth of his desperation—moves me more than logic or caution or any thought of my own safety. Perhaps I should believe it has only made me insane, but down deep, I know: He has made me braver. Stronger. Someone who could do anything.

Someone who would do this.

Slowly, I say, "Shall I get you something fine from the great box, Miss Irene?"

"Sounds marvelous." Irene, hardly glancing in my direction, tosses me the key.

So I unlock the box and choose a nice strand of pearls.

And I steal the Initiation Blade.

## ⊰ CHAPTER 16 ⊱

IN THE FINAL HOUR BEFORE EVENING, I AM UNEX-
pectedly freed from my duties. Irene's dark mood this morning
had, perhaps, been a sign of impending illness; she takes to her bed
by late afternoon.

"Are you sure you won't want to dress for dinner, miss?" I pat
her foot to soothe her. Lord knows her mother won't.

"I won't." Her face is turned into the pillow, so her voice is
muffled. "I'll see you in the morning."

By rights I ought to check with Horne before I go, but she'll
tell me to wait and see what Lady Regina says. Lady Regina will
demand that Irene get ready for a formal dinner. But if I'm already
gone, her Ladyship can't make that demand. Leaving saves me and
Irene both.

I know immediately what I need to take care of first. It's what I
swore to myself to do the moment I stole the Initiation Blade, but I
hardly thought I'd get a chance so soon. But where do I go?

When I turn toward one of the portholes, I see the soft, pink light of the late afternoon. The final hour before sunset—the final hour of freedom. I know my destination.

I walk onto the first-class deck. In my uniform, I'm invisible among the glittering notables milling about. None of them would recognize me as the elegant girl from yesterday afternoon; some of the same ones who murmured admiring compliments my way now look straight through me. I move among them like the shadow amid the sunlight. The weight of the dagger in my pocket makes me feel strong, and I almost wish for Mikhail to challenge me. But he doesn't appear. He's still clinging to Layton like a leech, I suppose. I almost wish I could be there in New York when they open up that box and find the dagger missing, to see the smirk finally wiped off Mikhail's face.

Then I consider what would follow the smirk—homicidal rage. Let Layton deal with it.

As I walk toward the bow of the ship, where the sunlight is brightest, I see a long, lean figure silhouetted against the rail, unruly hair ruffled by the breeze. Alec. His suit is nighttime black, turning him into a kind of shadow himself. He is drinking in the sunlight, living his last hour of humanity to the fullest. Just as I knew he would be.

Slowly I step closer to him. Nobody is near us. Although I am silent, and my footsteps would surely be lost in the rushing of the wind, he hears me. Perhaps it is the wolf that hears me. "Tess," he says without even turning.

"Alec." I want to touch his shoulder, his back, but these final few inches between us feel like a distance I cannot yet cross.

"You asked my father if I was a murderer."

"He says you don't know if you are or not."

Alec's head droops. "No."

The sound of children's laughter makes us both look to the side, where a woman in a frothy white dress of lace is shepherding her three small daughters—all as lacy and beribboned as their mother—toward the railing, only a few steps away. I say, "Where can we speak?"

"Follow me."

Alec leads me back into the ship, into a room with white, elaborately decorated walls and fine carpets on the floor; the shelves of leather-bound books available tell me this is the ship's library. White Grecian columns give the room a kind of otherworldliness. The elegant, half-drawn drapes turn the late-day sunlight deeply golden. At this hour, so close to the evening entertainments, the library is deserted except for us. Alec and I are alone together again.

He paces the room, agitated, until he looks back at my face and stops himself. Perhaps he thinks he might frighten me. I slowly sit on the divan against the wall, gripping the damask-covered arm of the sofa with both hands.

"Gabrielle was the only true friend I had in Paris," Alec says. "Sometimes I thought of her as the sister I'd never had. The wild one, the one who could dare to take to the stage and keep bad company and do all the things that would shock my father, and yet remain good at heart." A rueful smile touches the corners of his mouth, as if he were thinking about an unruly little girl in pigtails instead of a sophisticated actress. "I used to think that if I could ever tell anyone besides Dad what had happened to me, it would be her. I wish I had. If I'd told Gabrielle the truth, she would have known to be afraid of me. She could have protected herself. She might still be alive."

"This is why you had to return to America in such a hurry. You were afraid you would be connected to Gabrielle's murder."

"If they guillotined me, it would be no more than I deserve. And sometimes I think it would be easier to die than to go on, knowing what I probably did to her. But the scandal, the grief— it would destroy my father. He's blameless in this. I keep finding new ways to ruin his life, and mine. All I could do was flee Paris, put aside our search for more information to use against the Brotherhood. All I could do was take myself away from humanity, as much as possible."

I lean forward and speak very carefully. It's important that I ask this in exactly the right way. "Do you remember killing her?"

Alec shakes his head no. "The wolf clouds my mind. I never remember much afterward."

"The Brotherhood could have—"

"Oh, Tess, do you think I haven't asked myself that? Yes, it's possible. But then why wouldn't they have told me, to show me their power? That's the kind of thing they do—lord it over you. It's just as possible that I did it, and—I'll never really know."

"*I* know. You didn't kill her."

Alec stares at me, almost disbelieving, and he sits heavily on a nearby chair as if this revelation has stolen his strength. I drop to my knees beside him and take one of his hands in mine.

"That was the Brotherhood. They did to her what they tried to do to me—use her to make you feel guilty and afraid. That's why they didn't tell you, to make you doubt yourself! Mikhail thinks that if you commit a murder, you'll need them to preserve your freedom, and you'll undergo the initiation to keep yourself from ever being in a position like that again. So they killed Gabrielle and made you think you'd done it. When that didn't work, they tried once more with me, and tried to make you kill me outright."

He's not convinced. "I can see your reasoning. But the fact remains, I was free. I could have killed her. I knew where she lived. And as a wolf, I'm no different than they are."

"Yes, you are! I keep thinking about that first night, when Mikhail threw me to you." The steam and the heat fill my memory, and I see the red wolf even more clearly than I did then. "I've turned it all over in my mind time and time again, and I'm convinced—you could have killed me if you wanted to. But you didn't. When I closed myself inside a door that could never have kept you out, you stood guard outside. When Mikhail changed into a wolf as well, and tried to attack me—Alec, you fought for *me*. I realize that now. Not as your prey; you fought to *protect* me. I believe you saved me that night. Had you been with Gabrielle on the evening when she died, I know in my heart that you would have saved her too."

"You can't be certain." Alec shakes his head. In his eyes, pain wars with hope.

"I can be, and I am. Maybe you don't remember who you are as a wolf—but as a wolf, you remember who you are as a man.

181

You're more than a beast." I grip his hands tighter, hold them to my heart, kiss the knuckles, clutch both hands beneath my chin. "Your humanity can't be taken away from you. Not by the Brotherhood or the curse or the moonlight. Your heart is stronger than all of that. Believe it. Because I do."

He takes my face in his hands and kisses me. Last night we were passionate, but this is different—more intense, and yet sweeter. As he opens my mouth with his own, I tilt my head back and slide my arms around his neck.

Alec pulls me up into the chair with him, almost in his lap. His embrace is warm. Through his suit I can feel the power in his muscles, sense the presence of the wolf beneath the surface, and yet I'm not afraid any longer. The wolf is part of the man. I accept them both. I want them both.

Against my cheek, Alec whispers, "I'm a danger to you. If not as a wolf, then—as long as the Brotherhood pursues me—"

"Mikhail's been after me since before you and I met, remember? That's *why* we met." I caress his cheek as we curl together in the chair. "And besides, if I wasn't in the thick of it before, I am now." From my pocket, I pull out the Initiation Blade.

Alec's eyes widen as he sees it. Shock swiftly turns to pride. "Tess, you're—you're—"

"Brave?"

"I was going to say audacious. But brave, and courageous, and wonderful." He kisses me, even deeper this time. The dagger is heavy in my hand; my body feels warm and weak throughout every joint, every bone. But I keep my grip. Jewels press into my skin, and the metal loses its chill against my skin.

When we can think again, I rest my forehead against his chest and we study the Blade together. "It looks medieval to me," he says. "Perhaps a thousand years old. How far back does the Brotherhood's power reach?"

"It hardly matters anymore, does it? Because they can't have your future." How has this not occurred to him before? "Alec, this is what they use for the initiations, isn't it? That means you can do it yourself. You can stop yourself from changing every night if you don't want to, without having anything to do with the Brotherhood."

The elation I expect doesn't come. Alec looks grave as he traces around the hilt of the dagger, the curves of my fingers as I hold it. "It's not that easy, Tess. The change requires more than a cut from the Blade. As I understand it, there's old magic involved—old magic I don't know."

I sag against him, crushed. "This doesn't help you at all?"

"What? No—this helps me enormously. More than anyone else has been able to help me since this insanity began." Alec lifts my chin with one crooked finger. "I don't know the magic, but there may be others outside the Brotherhood who do. There are rebel werewolves out there—former Brotherhood members who left, others who refused to join. I've even heard rumors of female werewolves who hide from them in secret packs. If I can find even one werewolf outside the Brotherhood who knows how to use this Initiation Blade, I can be free. I can free others." He smiles at last. "This blade means everything. This blade means hope."

We kiss again, but already my more practical side is kicking in. Alec's the one with the grander tragedies and aspirations; I'm the one who knows how to make a goal and a plan. "We have to be doubly cautious during the rest of the trip. Mikhail mustn't guess we've got it until after the *Titanic* makes dock. It's only two more days, but Lord knows our first four days have been eventful enough."

Alec weighs this carefully. "Will he look for it before then?"

"Layton said something about them making a deal once they were ashore. So it sounds like we have time." I take one of Alec's hands in mine and firmly place the Initiation Blade in his palm, then wrap his fingers around it. "You should be the one to keep it. Do you have a safe in your quarters, too?" He nods, but obviously wants to argue this part with me. My finger presses against his lips to silence his protest. "That makes your room a much safer place to keep this than mine. Besides, we already know Mikhail won't kill you or your father for it; it's the Marlowe Steele money and influence they want, isn't it? They need you alive for that."

"Yes. But Mikhail *would* kill you for it," Alec says. "And I'm not happy about the danger this leaves you in."

"That makes two of us, but what else is there to do? I've managed to remain around people or in safe areas so far, and Mikhail's backed off me the past day or so. As long as he thinks he can charm that dagger from Layton, that's where he'll focus his attention."

"Perhaps. Sometimes when he takes a step back, it's just a sign that he's biding his time. Changing his strategy." Alec's fingers comb through the few gold curls loose at the nape of my neck.

Have we been kissing each other all this time while I'm still wearing my stupid linen cap? Not exactly the romantic image I'd hoped for. But the light in Alec's eyes tells me that he thinks I'm beautiful, cap or no cap. "Listen. You're right about hiding this from Mikhail if we can. But if he confronts you—Tess, if he threatens you and you can't get to me or to my father—you must tell him you hid the Blade."

"And make him even angrier?"

"It will. But if he believes you're the only one who knows where it is, he'll leave you alive. And that gives me time to get to you." Alec frames my face in his hands. "No matter what, Tess, I promise you—if you're in danger, no matter what, I'll find you."

"I told you before," I whisper. "I believe in you."

The kiss that follows seems to last forever, and I never want to let go.

But sunset is coming.

When I walk Alec belowdecks for his confinement, we don't go to the Turkish bath. "Turns out they're being opened tonight at the request of one of the especially illustrious passengers," he says as we walk out of the elevator onto D deck. His thumb brushes against my knuckles; his little finger draws a shape on my palm. I'd never realized merely holding hands could be so intoxicating. "I'm not sure exactly who, but I'd wager on Benjamin Guggenheim."

When we reach our destination—the squash court, of all things—I see that Howard Marlowe is already standing at the door. Although I expect Alec to drop my hand, he doesn't. Instead he turns to explain—as though I were the one who had a right to an explanation, and his father was the newcomer. "This location isn't as secure as the Turkish bath. And Mikhail interfered with that once, so who knows what he might try here? Dad will keep guard tonight."

"Good evening." Mr. Marlowe says this as politely as he would to Lady Regina—perhaps even more politely, come to think of it. "Alec, I realize you've been pleasantly occupied elsewhere, but time is short."

"I know. I'm going." Alec gives me a look that makes me melt, but we're not alone any longer. To my surprise, he kisses me, right there in front of his father—just a quick touch of the lips, but so much more than I expected. "Good night, Tess."

"Good night." But what a ridiculous thing to say to someone who will spend the night in torment. I add, "Remember what I told you. About who you truly are."

About the beast retaining the goodness of the man. Alec's face lights in a smile. "I remember." Then he goes through the squash court door, and Mr. Marlowe and I are alone.

Mr. Marlowe doesn't immediately speak to me, and I realize from the dark circles beneath his eyes that he's exhausted. His son's changes take a toll on him, too. "You'll stay here all night, sir?"

"It's for the best," Mr. Marlowe says. "I had to get this key from a very senior officer, so I think not even Mikhail can enter. But we can't take any chances."

"If it would help you, sir, I could stay here for the first few hours. You could get a nap, and I could keep watch."

"Mikhail's too great a danger to you. He won't come after me."
This is a good point, and I nod, acknowledging it. Mr. Marlowe's
gaze becomes even more penetrating. "I worked hard to build a
business. A place for myself in society. A good life. I want that good
life for my son. The best."

A life that doesn't include a romance with a serving girl, no
doubt. Anger blazes up inside me, though I know he's saying nothing any rich man wouldn't say. Only years of service in the Lisle
household keep me silent.

And I'm glad they do, because the next thing Mr. Marlowe says
is, "Never in my wildest dreams did I think my son might meet a
woman who could accept what he's become."

"Mr. Marlowe. Sir. I—I don't know what to say."

"You needn't say anything. I just thought you should know.
The two of you have enough obstacles; I won't be one of them."

I feel like I might cry. Quickly I drop Mr. Marlowe a curtsy
and hurry away, back to third class.

At the doorway into the third-class section of F deck, I bump
into one of the only other people with a key to go between classes:
Ned, who's dressed in his valet's uniform and clearly headed back
to the Lisles'. "Lucky you. Poor Miss Irene's taken to her bed, and
you get a holiday at sea."

"Don't be nasty. Maybe you'll get lucky, and tomorrow Layton
will be seasick."

Ned snorts with laughter. "He'd deserve it. But like as not
he'll be too busy dallying around with his new Russian friend.
Loathsome, if you ask me. A real bounder."

"I don't like the looks of—of that Russian either. You be careful, Ned."

"Careful?" His freckled face looks puzzled. "What d'ya mean, careful? I was going to look in on Miss Irene—do you mean I shouldn't catch cold?"

"Never mind. I'll see you in the morning."

My evening free is spent eating an enormous amount at tea to make up for the food I didn't get earlier in the voyage, and a bedtime so early even the old Norwegian ladies look at me like I'm pathetic. See if I care. I finally feel safe on this ship, and I could use a solid night's rest. Besides, I'll dream about Alec all night long.

After I've napped a couple of hours, I'm awakened by the muffled sound of voices outside the door—one woman's, one man's. Although the words are indistinct, the tone is not; these people are very, very happy. When the door opens, I see Myriam, a giddy smile on her face, twirling one long lock of black hair between her fingers.

Which means the man's voice on the other side of the door can only have been George's.

"Well, well." I sit up in my bunk and prop myself on the pillow. "It's the middle of the night. Did you get home with *your* underwear?"

"George is a very decent and respectable man."

"That's not a yes."

Myriam sticks her tongue out at me, but we're both near laughter. Beneath me, I hear one of the old ladies murmuring happily to the other. Maybe they're reminiscing about when they were young and in love.

"You had a good evening, then?" I lie back down as Myriam changes into her nightgown.

"Wonderful. He told me all about his travels, and what I should expect in New York and—oh, everything." She bounds up to her mattress and flops on it, almost like a little girl eager to jump on the bed. Myriam's face is even more beautiful when she's this happy; there's a kind of glow about her, even in the dark of our cabin. "Tess, he promised me tonight—for his next job, he's signing onto a ship that will travel along the East Coast of the United States. So we will be able to see each other again soon, and often."

"Myriam, that's wonderful! You've both become so serious about each other, and so quickly."

"Romance at sea has its power." She folds her hands beneath her head. "As you should know."

I remember the way Alec and I kissed tonight. "I know."

George and Myriam have a future. What about me and Alec? Before today, I thought it was impossible, and for more reasons than I could count. But those reasons are falling like trees beneath the woodsman's ax. The Brotherhood may lose any chance of having power over him, now that he has the Initiation Blade. If Alec can find someone else who knows the initiation magic, then he will be free from the need to change every single night. His life will become almost normal, save for once every twenty-eight days. And his father—the wealthy, powerful man who might have stood between us—all but gave us his blessing tonight.

Or am I fooling myself? I know that Alec cares for me as I do for him. But what will love matter when we're back on land? Social boundaries aren't as strict in America, or so I hear, but there's no place on earth where millionaires marry servant girls. It's just not done. And surely the Brotherhood won't let him go so easily.

I want to be with Alec. But I can't let myself believe in the impossible.

Tightly I close my eyes, trying to blot out my knowledge of the future, my dreams for something I can't have.

That's when I hear the screams.

# ⊰ CHAPTER 17 ⊱

I BOLT UPRIGHT IN BED AS MYRIAM CRIES, "WHAT'S happening?"

The screams in the corridor multiply as something thuds heavily against the wall. Then there's another sound—deep and low.

Growling.

"Oh, God." I jump from my bunk and go to the door. Even as Myriam shouts for me to stop, I open it and look into the hallway. There are half a dozen people in their nightclothes sprawled on the floor or flattening themselves against the wall, all of them shrieking and scrambling in an effort to get away from the wolf. Even before I see the red fur, I know it's Alec.

Then he's there—enormous as I remembered, equally as feral. This is the first time I've seen his wolf self in full light, and it's shocking both how terrifying and how beautiful he is. His fangs are the size of knives, brilliant white; his fur gleams chestnut as it bristles along his long back. The four paws on the ground are as broad as dinner plates and tipped with curving claws.

The red wolf is half-mad, turning and twisting in the corridor, powerful jaws snapping. But I see what no one else can see—that the Alec within is fighting every animal instinct in an effort to harm no one. He's biting at himself, drawing droplets of blood and tufts of fur, torn between the ravenous hunger of the wolf and his human desire to keep everybody safe.

"Let him be!" I shout, but nobody pays me any attention, if anybody out here even understands English. When I hurry into the hallway, Myriam grabs my arm in an effort to hold me back, but I shake her off and run toward Alec.

If he sees me, he'll remember himself better. Maybe I can coax him into a quiet area somewhere, someplace no other passengers will be so that nobody will be endangered, and he'll face less temptation. It's worth a shot, anyway.

But someone else reaches him before I can—George, with three stewards behind him.

"No, don't!" I reach out one hand, futilely attempting to stop this from happening.

George doesn't hear, or doesn't listen. Why should he? He's a good officer, trying to protect the people aboard this ship from a threat he never imagined. George throws himself at the red wolf in an attempt to tackle him.

The red wolf doesn't bite George. But he does claw him, viciously, tearing ragged lines in his uniform and making George cry out in pain.

Oh, God, will he be a werewolf now? No, that's only a bite. But the clawing is bad enough to wound, and once the red wolf smells blood—

"George!" Myriam's behind me in the hallway now, drawn

there by her desire to protect either me or George. I try to push her back—the more people out here, the worse it is for everyone—but everything's happening too fast.

The stewards are after the red wolf now, pushing at him with chairs and some bit of wood—an oar or something, I can't see, I can't tell. As the wolf snarls, he steps back into a crouch, like he could leap forward at any moment. Every muscle is poised to pounce. Some of the people in the hallway take their chance to run, but others seem paralyzed by fear.

What happens if they catch him? What if they have him in a pen at dawn when he changes back into my Alec? His secret will be revealed, and I can't even imagine how terrible that would be.

But then I realize how much worse it might get when another steward rushes forward clutching something he must have grabbed from an emergency case: a large red ax.

"No!" I throw off Myriam's hands and run forward, leaping over one of the terrified people lying in the hall to hurl myself between the red wolf and the ax. With outstretched arms, I shout, "Don't hurt him! Leave him alone!"

"Crazy girl! Get out of the way!" The steward slams the ax handle into my side to push me clear. It knocks the breath out of me and sends me tumbling to my hands and knees.

The red wolf snarls ferociously, and I realize why: He thinks the steward is attacking me.

Alec remembers himself enough to protect me no matter what.

Even as I scream a warning, the red wolf leaps over me, taking the steward down to the ground. The ax clatters uselessly to the floor.

"Let me through!" a man's voice cries. I twist my head to see

Howard Marlowe running toward us, his suit askew and his bald head gleaming with sweat. In his hand is something small and silver; as he gets closer, I recognize it as a physician's hypodermic.

Next to me, the steward screams as the red wolf sinks his jaws into the man's throat. Blood spurts out, so hot it steams, and the steward's cry twists into a grotesque gargling noise. Worse still is when he stops screaming.

"No!" But I'm speaking to Alec now, the Alec inside who can hear me. I try to steady my voice, though I am shaking so hard I can't rise to my feet. "Come on, now. It's all right. Nobody has to get hurt."

The red wolf lifts his head from his prey and stares at me. Blood drips from his jaws. His green-gold gaze is that of an animal's—hard, reflecting light like a mirror.

If I could call him by name, it would help. But I can't. If there's any chance of keeping Alec's secret after this, I have to try to hold on to it.

Still on my knees, I crawl closer to him. The red wolf is barely inches from me now. He stands completely still, his massive body shaking from pent-up energy and hunger. I can feel his hot breath on my neck.

Behind me, I hear Mr. Marlowe edging closer. I keep my eyes focused on the wolf's, willing him to look only at me.

"Remember," I whisper. "Remember."

For one brief moment, the wolf's eyes appear human, and it is Alec looking back at me—

Mr. Marlowe stabs down with the hypodermic, plunging the

needle into the wolf's flesh. It howls, an eerie, terrible sound, as it slumps against the wall and collapses. I lean against Mr. Marlowe's leg, weak with relief.

"A tranquilizer," Mr. Marlowe says. He's breathing hard. "That will knock him out until well past sunrise. I keep it on hand for emergencies."

"What's the meaning of this?" demands George, who has picked himself up. Although he winces when he moves his scratched arm, he straightens his uniform and is again serving as an officer of the ship.

Mr. Marlowe attempts to smile, though that doesn't quite work. "It's all taken care of now, officer. You should look to the injured man. Leave the animal to me."

"Is this your dog, then?" George points at the sleeping form of the wolf. "You brought a dangerous dog onboard and didn't keep it in the kennel? That's against regulations, sir."

"I sincerely apologize," Mr. Marlowe says. "I will of course make restitution to anyone harmed. . . ." His voice trails off as he sees the other stewards around their fallen comrade. They're making no move to assist him—are they fools? That man needs to get to a doctor right away. Good God, Alec bit him, and that means he'll be a werewolf now, unless—

One of the stewards takes off his jacket and drapes it over the fallen man's face. He's dead.

Alec would rather have died than have done this to someone else, but it's too late now. This man has died because Alec tried to protect me. There's no restitution for that. He has become the killer he always feared he was.

Mr. Marlowe fumbles for words. "I—I realize the dog is my responsibility. I take full blame for this. I will of course pay any fine or civil judgment—"

"Are you trying to bribe me, sir?" George draws himself upright. "I may only be seventh officer aboard this ship, but I hope I'm honest."

"By no means! I only meant to put things right."

"This can never be put right, sir," George says. "Which is why we're throwing this vicious dog off the starboard stern."

"No!" I cry out. George stares at me, bewildered by my reaction. A few yards distant down the hallway, I see that Myriam is equally confused. "You can't. You—you just can't."

Mr. Marlowe says, "Why don't we take this up with the captain?" He stands taller, adjusts his suit until he looks more like the wealthy and powerful man he is. "The dog is mine and I wish to keep it."

Maybe George recognizes him then, but he doesn't back down. "Good God, do you care more about what's to become of your dog than the man who died here tonight?"

If they throw "the dog" overboard, two men will die tonight. The horror of the murder I witnessed doesn't take away from the fact that Alec has to be saved.

"I'm truly sorry." Mr. Marlowe's voice breaks on the word, and my heart hurts as I feel how much this pains him. He's a good man, one who would never fight George on this if the stakes were any less than his son's life. "But—I must insist on speaking to a higher authority before you do anything rash."

"Rash!" George looks furious, as well he might. "I'm not waking up Captain Smith; he'll have the lot of us thrown overboard. But there are other authorities aboard this ship. And we'll let them decide what's to become of the animal."

I look down again at the red wolf, deep in drugged sleep on the floor. He might be drowned before he wakes.

## ⊰ CHAPTER 18 ⊱

THEY TIE THE RED WOLF AS IF HE WERE A HOG FOR slaughter and throw him in a wooden crate.

"You won't touch him," Mr. Marlowe declares. "Not if you want your job on this liner in the morning."

George's temper is no better. "I follow the rules aboard this ship, unlike some. When we've heard from Mr. Andrews what to do, it'll be done. If he wants to give you your damned dog back, he can. But if he's sensible and wants it drowned before it can do any more harm, then that's the way it has to be, and all your money and influence won't change it."

I wince as the stewards roughly hoist the crate and take it—I don't know where. As badly as I want to follow him, to protect Alec, I know it's impossible. Shivering with cold and the aftermath of shock, I can only hold out one hand in useless protest as they take the crate through a passageway and the door swings shut behind them.

Mr. Marlowe removes his jacket and drapes it across my shoulders. Only then do I realize that I'm still in my nightgown, with my curls hanging loose past my shoulders. "You did your best," he murmurs.

I turn to him and see, for the first time, that there is a dark red shadow across his eye, which is beginning to swell. "Mikhail?" I whisper. He nods once.

Mikhail overpowered Mr. Marlowe at the door of the squash court and released Alec, in the hopes that he would kill someone. Alec had warned me that Mikhail's silence might mean a new plan, but I didn't suspect this.

"Come along then," George says stiffly. He bears his own wound without a flinch, even as he uses his injured arm to open the door. When I follow Mr. Marlowe, he stares at me. "Tess—I mean, Miss Davies, what has this to do with you? Shouldn't you go back to your cabin? It's been a devil of a night."

I stop short, uncertain how to answer.

Mr. Marlowe rescues me. "She has been considering taking employment with our family. I'm pleased to see such initiative in looking after our interests, Miss Davies. Please accompany us."

It's as good a lie as any. George frowns a bit, but he raises no further objection. I glance over at Mr. Marlowe, who gives me a nod. Really I ought to go back to my cabin, but there's no chance of my sleeping more now. When I do return, the first thing I'm going to have to contend with is an interrogation by Myriam, who is obviously aware that something's up. Facing the captain or first officer or whoever "Mr. Andrews" is seems easy by comparison.

Besides—I have to know, as soon as possible, what's going to become of Alec. If Mr. Marlowe can talk or bribe his way out of this, we can get the crate back, let him wake up in a bed for once, and look toward the future.

If Mr. Marlowe's fortune and influence fail him, Alec will either be drowned in his sleep or transform in the crate to be revealed as a monster before the whole world.

We walk out onto the deck in first class, headed somewhere I don't recognize. Is it just the strangeness of this night playing tricks on me, or is the air much colder than it was before? The rest of our trip has been pleasant and temperate, but suddenly the air has a bite. Maybe it's just fear playing tricks on me. Making me imagine what poor Alec would feel if they drop him off the ship, into the bitter chill of the north Atlantic, to die.

Our footsteps seem so loud in the hush of the night. On the dark, endless ocean before us, I glimpse a spur of white—a little ice, nothing more.

Mr. Marlowe isn't at all well, I realize. His gait is unsteady, his stare unfocused. I take his arm. "Are you all right, sir?"

"I've failed him." Mr. Marlowe closes his eyes for a moment, as if trying to block out the horrible truth, and I have to guide him along our way. I'm not sure whether the blows from Mikhail now blackening his eye have dazed him, or if he's simply numb with shock. The situation is dire enough on its own, but he may be hurt. We should ask for a doctor, but not now. We have to face the gravity of what has happened tonight, but not now. Now we have to fight for Alec's life.

"Where are we going?" I ask George. "Which officer is Mr. Andrews?"

George looks at me, somewhat awkwardly. We're friendly, and

yet we're caught on opposite sides now. The worst of it is that I can't blame him for what he's doing; knowing only what he knows, he can hardly do anything else but protect the passengers. "Mr. Andrews isn't an officer at all."

"You mean he's only a passenger?"

"Only a passenger! Hardly. Mr. Andrews is one of the senior designers for the White Star Line. He designed the ship we're sailing on now."

"That's quite impressive," I say, meaning it. "But why are we talking to the ship's designer, of all people?"

"First of all, he's the second most senior representative of the White Star Line aboard the *Titanic*. The most senior representative is J. Bruce Ismay himself, and if you think I'm waking up Mr. Ismay after midnight, you're mad." George touches his scratched arm— it's still bothering him. We might all be at the doctor together, afterward. "More than that, though, Mr. Andrews—he's sort of the person we all turn to. He settles arguments among the crew, deals with tricky situations. You can trust his judgment."

I hope that's true.

George is the one who knocks on Mr. Andrews's cabin door; by chance, he's still awake. When we walk in, he's wearing a brocade evening robe over pajamas, but he receives us as politely as though this were high tea. "Please, everyone, take a seat." Andrews has a light Irish brogue, and a broad, kindly face. When he smiles at me, I find myself smiling back despite everything. "I take it you've come for advice, Mr. Greene. Now, what's all this about?"

"Mr. Marlowe brought a dangerous dog aboard, and it got

loose tonight and killed one of the stewards. Bit a couple of other fellows, myself included," George says. This is untrue—George was clawed, not bitten, though I can see how he might be confused from the shock of the fight. Nor did Alec bite anyone else. But all that pales next to the fact that a man is dead. "It ought to have been restrained. Now I can't see keeping it aboard ship. Ought to be thrown overboard, if you ask me."

"It's my property," Mr. Marlowe says. "It's my responsibility. I've offered to pay all damages. The dog is mine, and I want it returned to me safe and sound. Tonight."

Mr. Andrews's eyes flicker over me, and I know he's wondering what on earth I have to do with this situation. I can't explain, but I say, "We oughtn't to kill it. Not if there's any other way. Should we, sir?"

"It is a deadly beast and must be put down. However, despite your commendable caution, Mr. Greene, we cannot throw it overboard," Mr. Andrews says. "The dog must be tested for rabies."

"Rabies?" George goes white. That would be the worst possible outcome of a dog bite—though he can little suspect how much worse it would've been had Alec actually bitten him. Then again, maybe not; rabies is fatal.

"I'm certain the dog's not rabid," Mr. Marlowe says.

Mr. Andrews says, somewhat tersely, "We must think of the injured men first. You realize the dog will have to be destroyed for the rabies test. I'm quite sorry, but that's all there is to it."

I think fast. The *Titanic* might contain nearly every luxury known to man, from steam baths to a squash court, but I'll bet anything there's no veterinarian on board. "We can't do the test until we reach New York City, though, can we, sir?"

"No, we can't." Mr. Andrews looks at me and Mr. Marlowe sympathetically, understanding that—however unlikely it might be—we are together in this. "Would it comfort you to keep the dog with you until we reach port?"

"It would, sir." Mr. Marlowe is already breathing easier, and I know why. When we reach New York, he will procure some stray and have it tested for rabies instead. "After the dog is tested in New York City, I will turn over the report to the White Star Line, and of course to the injured men directly."

"That seems reasonable," Mr. Andrews says. "Mr. Greene, do you agree?"

"Reasonable, aye, sir, but perhaps not sufficient." George shakes his head sadly as he looks at his torn sleeve.

"I think he scratched you," I venture. "Not bit."

"You might be right, and it's glad I am of it, but that's not much consolation." Now that the immediate rush of fear has passed, so has his anger—but not his resolve. "If that dog of yours broke out once, he could break out again. What if he were to bite someone else? I couldn't have it on my conscience, sir."

Mr. Andrews bows his head slightly, considering this. The argument is shifting against us, and Mr. Marlowe and I look at each other in alarm.

Just then, there is a knock at the door. I expect some other minor ship crisis, arriving on Mr. Andrews's doorstep to be resolved. I never expect Mikhail to walk in.

Although I manage to stifle my gasp, Mr. Marlowe goes quite pale. I clutch his hand. Mr. Andrews doesn't notice; he's too busy dealing with his new guest. "I beg your pardon, sir, but I don't believe I have the honor of your acquaintance."

"Count Mikhail Kalashnikov, at your service." Mikhail pulls out his card. "Though we have not been introduced, a few simple inquiries will confirm that I am the representative of a large organization. An organization that is a major shareholder in the White Star Line."

My God. Alec told me the Brotherhood had power, money, and influence, but I hadn't realized until now—they're part owners of the ship itself.

"I heard of this unpleasantness," Mikhail says silkily. His dark eyes rake over me, and I remember that I'm wearing no more than a thin nightgown and Mr. Marlowe's coat. "It is best if I take charge. My organization is prepared to make full restitution to the injured parties. A physician on board will be assigned to tranquilize the wild animal until we make port."

"You, take charge?" George doesn't like the sound of this. "I've never heard of you before."

Mikhail smiles his thin, unnerving smile. His teeth are too large for his mouth, too white amid the dark spear of his beard. "Then perhaps we should wake Captain Smith. I assure you—he has heard of my organization's role in the White Star Line. He will confirm my orders."

"I don't doubt it," mutters Mr. Andrews. "Mismanagement has plagued this project from the beginning."

"Shall I pass your concerns on to Mr. Ismay and the rest of the leaders of the White Star Line?" Mikhail says. "If they hear that one of their designers likes to slander them on transatlantic crossings, perhaps they will reconsider whom they employ in future."

This dismays Mr. Andrews not one whit. With spirit, he says, "If you think I could get no other work as a designer after building many of the finest and most elegant ships ever launched, you're sorely mistaken, Mr. Kalashnikov. And if you think I'm the only White Star employee who ever grumbled, this must be your very first day aboard a ship!"

Mikhail stares, clearly unaccustomed to having anybody stand up to him. I like Mr. Andrews as much as I've ever liked anyone on only five minutes' acquaintance.

Mr. Andrews continues, calm once more, "As it so happens, before your arrival, we had already reached an agreement that the dog must be tested for rabies, which can only be done ashore. So it remains onboard for the duration of our journey. If a physician can keep it tranquilized, and I have Mr. Marlowe's word as a gentleman that this will be done, then the dog may as well be kept alive for the rest of the voyage. It may in fact be better for the purposes of the test."

"That'll do," George says quickly. Though I can tell he still has doubts, he didn't really want to kill someone's dog in front of him, even if it did something terrible. Myriam has found a kind man.

"Entirely acceptable." Mr. Marlowe rises to his feet. His movements are stiff; his eye is blackening quickly. Mikhail must have hit him hard. "Thank you, Andrews. You dealt with this situation handsomely."

"Comes with designing a ship, sir. You take responsibility for all her operations—even the unexpected ones." A flash of humor brightens Mr. Andrews's face as he shakes his head, but then he frowns. "Quite a bruise you took there. In the struggle with the dog?"

"Yes," Mr. Marlowe says hurriedly. "That's it." I can almost feel Mikhail's smirk.

Mr. Andrews continues, "Now, if you'll excuse me, I'd like to get a bit of sleep tonight. If possible."

"Aye, sir. Thank you, sir. It's good to know we have you to turn to." George hurries out, with a nod in my direction.

Mikhail doesn't look nearly as pleased, as well he might not, but Mr. Andrews isn't the main focus of his attention. Mr. Marlowe is. I take Mr. Marlowe's arm again, unsure whether I want to protect him or want him to protect me. In any case, we all walk out on deck together.

George hesitates before leaving us. "Good God. Tess, I've got something for you." Stiff from his injury, he nonetheless fishes in his pocket and hands me a bit of crumpled paper. He leaves a bloody fingerprint on one corner. "A Marconigram. It's irregular for anybody in third class to get them, so I said I'd walk it down to you. Forgot in all the insanity."

"For me?" I don't know anyone wealthy enough to send me a Marconigram, at least not anyone who isn't on this ship. It must be a mistake, but I don't feel like sorting it out right now. Instead I ball it in my hand and nod at George, who tiredly walks off, no doubt headed to the ship's doctor.

As soon as we're alone, I say, "How could you do such a thing?

206

Hurt Mr. Marlowe, let Alec out without caring about the consequences?"

"How could I not?" Mikhail pulls out one of his cigars and smiles, as relaxed as if he were enjoying brandy with the other millionaires in the grand dining hall. "Mr. Marlowe, you and your son still fail to understand the risks of your situation. As long as Alec is not initiated into the Brotherhood, he must change every night. As long as he changes every night, he is a danger to himself and to others."

"Only because you turned him loose," Mr. Marlowe retorts. "We took precautions, dammit."

"Did you not take precautions the night of Gabrielle Dumont's death?" Mikhail replies.

I jump in. "Alec didn't kill Gabrielle. You did. You set him loose to make him think he killed her. You threw me at him to try to make him kill me."

Mikhail rolls his cigar between two fingers, leering at me as though every word I say pleases him. "And tonight he killed a man, did he not?"

Silence. Neither Mr. Marlowe nor I can answer. Alec would rather have died than done that.

"It's like they always say in English: The third time's the charm." Mikhail steps closer to Alec's father. It's as if I no longer exist. "If your son joins us, he regains control over his nature. Over his destiny. He will gain allies throughout the world who will never desert him. And for such a small price! All Alec needs to give us is the loyalty we would give him in return. Along with a percentage of

Marlowe Steel's profits, of course, and the use of your considerable personal influence. But is that too much to pay for your son's safety and happiness? Consider our offer, Mr. Marlowe. Talk to your son. Get him to see reason before it's too late."

With that, Mikhail saunters off into the night.

Mr. Marlowe walks silently with me back into the ship. Once we're alone again, I say, "You mustn't listen to Mikhail. You know they'd own Alec forever afterward."

"It's not my decision to make." His voice is hollow. "Alec alone must make that choice."

"But he listens to you—he loves you so much. Don't lead him astray." I want badly to tell Mr. Marlowe about the Initiation Blade, but if he breaks now—if he tells Mikhail about it and tries to bargain with it behind our backs—what little power it's given us will be lost. "Please, sir. You're hurt. You're shaken. Anyone would be. Go to sleep now and think on it in the morning."

"I'll sleep after they've brought Alec back to my cabin." He rouses himself from his stupor enough to pat my hand. "Thank you, Miss Davies. For everything. But now you—you had better get some rest."

"Sir—" But he's walking away from me now. I can influence him no more.

I hurry back to my cabin. The efficiency of the *Titanic* crew can't be denied; the blood has already been mopped from the floor of the corridor, and the walls have been washed back to a gleaming white. The poor dead steward is—where, I wonder? Down in the hold?

Already buried at sea? Tomorrow morning, half the people who witnessed this madness will think they merely had a bad dream.

Myriam is in the other half. As soon as I open the door, hoping to tiptoe in, she launches herself off the bunk and grabs my hand. "We have to talk," she whispers as she propels me down the hallway toward the women's toilet facilities. *"Now."*

The third-class women on this deck share washing facilities, with many WCs, many sinks, and an entire wall of shower stalls in one great white room. Dozens of us all use it together, which some seem to consider a hardship. At Moorcliffe, I've only got my chamber pot, so it seems nice enough to me. So late is the hour that Myriam and I are alone in the white-tiled space.

"Tell me what's going on," she says, crossing her arms in front of her. The hem of her nightshirt is too short for her statuesque frame, revealing quite a lot of leg. "And how it concerns you. No stories. Tell me."

I know I should lie, but I'm too exhausted to come up with anything. So I blurt it out—the whole truth, about Alec, the Brotherhood, Mikhail, Gabrielle, werewolves, everything. What does it matter if I say it out loud? It's not as though Myriam would ever believe me. The only danger is that she'll now believe I'm completely mad.

Once I've finished, Myriam blinks once, then says, "I believe you."

"What?" She's not even all that surprised. "Do they have legends about werewolves in Lebanon or something? Do you know about them?"

"There are stories, which I thought ridiculous until now," she

209

snaps. "But you are not imaginative enough to invent such details on your own."

I want to argue with her about my imagination, but if she believes me, I had better leave well enough alone. "Well, it's all true. Myriam, what are we going to do? How can Alec get out of this?"

She holds up one hand. "Alec is a good man, and I know you care for him. But this is his burden. Not yours, not unless you take it on yourself. Tess, walk away from this. At best you will be hurt when he leaves you—and you know he must, don't you? More now than ever before, now that this man has been killed. At worst, you could be the next one to die. Have nothing else to do with him."

"I can't. I know you're right, Myriam, but—I can't."

"You are a fool," she says, but almost tenderly.

"Tell no one." I put force into my words; this is important. "It's dangerous for you to know this."

"As if I would tell anyone this. I do not want my first stop in America to be the nearest lunatic asylum."

Exhausted and shaken, I want to wipe my eyes with my handkerchief, but that's not what's crumpled in my hand, is it? That's the Marconigram, the one that can't be for me. As Myriam watches me, equally puzzled, I unfold the bloodstained paper and see my name. Could there be another Tess Davies on board?

But as I read on, I realize this really is for me. A blade of pure terror shoves its way into my chest.

TESS I GOT CUT UP IN THE STREET TODAY. THESE MEN
GRABBED AT ME AND CUT A SHAPE IN MY PALM LIKE

A Y. IT BLED SOMETHING AWFUL BUT I'VE BANDAGED IT. THEN THEY GAVE ME MONEY AND SAID I WAS TO WIRE YOU. I'M MEANT TO TELL YOU THAT IF THE COUNT GIVES THE WORD, THEY'LL FIND ME AGAIN AND CUT MORE THAN MY HAND. WHAT DOES IT MEAN, TESS? ARTHUR IS TAKING MATTHEW AND ME TO HIS MUM'S NEVER FEAR. I AM SCARED FOR YOU AND WHATEVER YOU'RE MIXED UP IN GET OUT OF IT. WRITE ME AS SOON AS YOU GET THIS. I LOVE YOU. DAISY.

The Y shape must be the one I recognize from the Initiation Blade. The symbol of the Brotherhood.

# ❧ CHAPTER 19 ❧

*APRIL 14, 1912*

They found my sister. They could kill my sister, and they will if Mikhail says the word.

I try not to think about it, but that just brings up another horrible image: the dead steward last night, lying in a pool of his own blood. Alec must be in such pain right now; I know his father told him the truth.

"Ow," Irene whines as the hairbrush hits a tangle. "Sorry."

"You don't have to apologize to me when I pull your hair." I try to bring my mind back to what I'm doing. There's nothing I can do for Daisy now, nor for Alec, and I won't get a spare moment to see him or ask how we can help Daisy any sooner by dragging and daydreaming through my work.

Irene's "mystery illness" vanished last night after an enormous row between her and her mother; I wasn't here, but both Ned and Mrs. Horne have whispered the news to me. As Mrs. Horne tells it, Irene's an ungrateful girl who doesn't understand the opportunities

Lady Regina provides for her. As Ned tells it, Lady Regina's so cruel to Irene that it's all he can do to stick to his duty instead of telling the old cow off. I know which version I believe. Irene must not be able to bear the haranguing any longer, because she's up early today and prepared to look her best.

But she looks as pale and weak as if she truly were ill. Her eyes don't even focus on her reflection in the mirror. I venture, "Are you sure you're all right, miss?"

"No." She puts her head in one hand, and I realize she's about to cry.

"Oh, Miss Irene. Don't be sad." I sit next to her on the little bench and put an arm around her. Normally she pulls herself together quickly enough, but this time she rests her head on my shoulder, and I can feel hot tears soaking through the sleeve of my uniform.

"I've got to get married," she says, as if it were a death sentence. "Mother wants me married before the year is out. Soon as we can manage it."

"I'm sure you can. It's not the worst thing in the world, is it, miss? You might meet someone you like." I've wished for it, for her sake: maybe some bookish son of a wealthy family who would like her sweet, unassuming ways. He could be in New York City, or Boston.

"Mother doesn't care if I like him or not."

Time to be honest, I suppose. "Is it—is it about the money, Miss Irene? I don't mean to be impertinent, but downstairs we've all suspected that perhaps—the family finances—"

"Money?" Irene looks up at me, and to my astonishment, she starts to laugh. "Do you think they want to marry me off for the money?"

That's exactly what I've thought. I can't imagine what else it would be.

As I stare at her in consternation, Irene says, "You see, Tess, it's much worse than that. I'm . . . ruined."

I was only slightly more surprised when I saw Mikhail transform into a werewolf. "Ruined" is a polite euphemism; what it means is that the young lady in question—Irene—has lost her virginity before being married.

How could that be possible? She's been chaperoned about, hardly let out of the house except in "society," where the rules are generally obeyed. Some young girls find ways around that, I imagine, but *Irene*? She's so modest, so unlikely to run wild.

And how would Lady Regina know? The question is rhetorical at first, but then I think about it. "Miss Irene—please tell me—nobody hurt you, did they?"

"No. I wasn't mistreated." By mistreated, she means raped: Thank God for that much. Loose strands of pale brown hair hang over half her face; the other is already coiffed. It's like you could split her down the middle—the picture of the proper Edwardian girl and the real woman within. "I love him. I took the risk. And now I have to pay the price."

Oh, no. "You're not with child, are you?" But that can't be right. My job includes rinsing out all Irene's underthings; I know the schedule of her courses as well as my own. That's been clockwork the whole four months I've been with her.

214

She lifts her face to mine, and her smile is sad. "Not any longer."

Suddenly the past few months make sense. I was promoted to ladies' maid unexpectedly, and abruptly, when Irene's previous maid went to a new situation in Scotland. Downstairs we all talked about how odd it was for her to leave with almost no notice, and how strange that the Lisles gave her a glowing reference despite that. Now I understand. That maid would have known that Irene was pregnant; she would have noted the missed cycles and perhaps have seen her through the miscarriage. The Lisles would have wanted her gone to keep the rumor from spreading through the household, but they'd have taken good care of her to insure her silence.

"Mother doesn't know who the father is," Irene says. "It hurt her so deeply that I wouldn't tell her. I know you must loathe her, and I wouldn't deny that sometimes she behaves abominably, but you must understand, Tess. Mother married into the nobility. She's never felt as easy as her friends who have a title in their own right. Layton's been such a disappointment to her, and what I did—there's not a mother in England who wouldn't be angry with me, after I got with child by a man I refused to name." Irene takes a deep, shaky breath. "I think she has it in her head it's some wealthy young man I met at a cotillion, someone I could blackmail into marrying me if I were more 'practical.' So now she says she can't trust me not to go astray. She wants me married quickly, and I have to face it, even though I love someone else."

Not some wealthy young man. Someone who could spend some time with her. Someone she loves. Someone who probably loves her in return.

Before I can think better of it, I blurt out, "It's Ned, isn't it?"

215

Irene reels back, and I can't tell whether she's more shocked or relieved that someone finally knows. "Did he tell you?"

"Not that you were ever together! Nothing about the baby. He's not breathed a word, miss. But—well, he's always been sweet on you."

"And I've always been sweet on him." Irene's smile is wistful. "His father was in our service too, you know. I remember playing with Ned on the grounds as a child, before Mother caught me and scolded me for associating with my inferiors. Even then I knew there would never be anyone else for me."

Ned and Irene. There's never been anyone else for him, either; I feel sure of that now. A hundred separate incidents come together in my mind to form a delicate snowflake pattern—the two of them always searching for ways to be in each other's company. And the other evening, on the deck, he said he would never take a wife because there was no point in marrying anybody besides the one person in all the world you wanted most. He was thinking of Irene, a girl he can never have.

I know he must love her, but my Lord, how he has hurt her. "He shouldn't have put you in that position, miss. Ned's a good man, but it was—careless. Thoughtless. To let that happen to you."

"Oh, don't blame him! It was—once, only once, and we were both so carried away." There's color in her cheeks now, real happiness, if only in memory. "Last autumn, one day, I was meant to be at Penelope Chambers's tea party, but she fell ill in the middle of the afternoon and we had to go home. Father had the driver and nobody else was free to fetch me, so Ned came. And then there was that rainstorm—oh, Tess, do you remember that rain? It was like the sky had been split open."

I don't remember a thing about it. No doubt I spent that day scrubbing floors and never even got the chance to look at a window and notice it was raining.

Irene looks up into that long-ago sky, welcoming the storm. "We had to duck into the nearest shelter—this little barn—and wait. It was like we were all alone in the world. We hadn't really been alone together like that since we were children, and both of us knew we'd probably never have hours to ourselves again. The truth spilled out, and when I knew he loved me too—when we both knew it was our only chance—I don't care that I'm ruined. I don't care that Mother hates me. I would never take it back. I'd never change a thing." She looks beautiful now, more beautiful than I've ever seen her. Love illuminates her from within. "I think I was happier in those hours with Ned than most people ever are in their whole lives."

I nod. "Then I'm glad for you, miss. I'm only sorry Lady Regina ever had to find out."

"Ned doesn't know about the baby," she says. "I didn't tell him, and you mustn't either. It would hurt him so terribly. There was nothing Ned could have done, before I lost it or since."

That's true, of course. If the Lisles ever found out that Ned was the father of Irene's baby, he'd be fired at best, prosecuted for rape at worst, and Irene's willingness would count for nothing in a court of law compared to the fact that she's a fine young lady and he's a servant. Irene would never be allowed to marry him. They couldn't even run off together—Ned would be unemployable after such a scandal, and Irene's probably too delicate to work even if she knew how to do anything useful.

I still want to shake Ned for endangering her so, and a week ago, I would have. Now, though, I know what it means to care about someone so deeply. To want to steal a day with that person, even an hour, no matter what the cost might be.

And it was probably Ned's first time with a girl. Life in service doesn't allow for much romance. The two of them were probably completely ignorant about how to avoid a baby. I was too, before Daisy got herself in trouble; after that I made it a point to learn a few things.

Irene says, "I wonder, sometimes, what I'd have done if I hadn't lost the child. I was only just starting to believe I was truly going to have one when it ended." She puts one hand over her flat belly. "I would have given birth in June."

I can't imagine what the Lisles would have done with her. Bribed someone to marry her immediately, I suppose, and then the new child would have been welcomed as "premature"—the oldest fib there is. "I don't mean to be unkind, miss, but I don't know how well it would have gone for you or—or for the baby."

"I know. I do. Yet sometimes I imagine holding a little child with ginger hair." She straightens herself and takes a deep breath. "Mother made me swear never to breathe a word to another soul. But telling you has helped me, more than I ever realized it would. Thank you, Tess. For being someone I can trust."

"I'll never breathe a word of it. Not even to Ned."

She nods. "It's going to be hard for him, these next few months.

218

When the time comes, and I have to marry—you'll help him through it, won't you? I think it will be even harder for him to bear than it is for me."

I won't be in the Lisles' service any longer. Ned will truly be alone.

As long as Irene has told me her deepest secret, it seems like I should be able to tell her one of mine. But just as I begin to confess my plans to leave, we hear men's voices in the sitting room: Layton and Mikhail.

"Oh, God." Irene looks stricken. "They couldn't have overheard, could they? I don't even know if Mother and Father have told Layton."

"I think they just came in." I hop up from the bench and straighten Irene in front of the mirror. "You're all right, miss. Let's get you ready."

We fall silent as I lace her into her stays. Although I'm almost completely certain Layton didn't overhear, what about Mikhail? He has a wolf's senses, and a wolf's desire to rip out the jugular of anyone who gets in his way. If he overheard, if he has a secret to use against Irene, what might he do?

It's out of fear for her, rather than for myself, that I listen so intently to their conversation through the door.

Mikhail: "You're a chronic procrastinator, my friend. Already I know this about you. Always putting off until tomorrow what you could be enjoying today."

Layton: "Did I put off drinking that fine cognac last night? Or winning that first hand at cards? Lost the last one, of course, but if you ask me, Colonel Gracie cheats."

Mikhail: "You put off establishing yourself as a man of means. Establishing your family in the wealth and security you deserve. Why will you not do business with me now?"

*Oh, no. The Initiation Blade.* I thought we had until the ship reached New York City. But Mikhail's impatient—he wants it immediately.

Layton: "I told you, Father was most explicit in his instructions. We're to have everything appraised before sale."

Layton's already spilled everything to Mikhail about the family's finances—oh, maybe not everything, because it would hurt his pride, but enough for a manipulator like Mikhail to know the truth. At this point, he'll be lucky if Mikhail actually pays him for the Blade instead of blackmailing him for it.

Mikhail: "And I tell you now, the price I'm offering is more than generous. The appraisal may well be lower. These New World jewelers, what do they know of real quality? I've worked with Fabergé; no doubt I can give you a better estimate of the dagger's true worth than some colonial in a shop. Why not let me look at it, at least?"

Layton: "I suppose you might as well look."

They're going to the safe. They're going to ask Irene for the key, and they'll open the box. They'll realize the Initiation Blade is gone.

I'm about to get caught.

# ⚜ CHAPTER 20 ⚜

"IRENE?" LAYTON DRAWLS. HE SAUNTERS INTO HER
room without knocking, and she pulls her wrapper more tightly
around her. Though he glances at me briefly, he can't meet my eyes.
Ashamed of himself, is he? He should be. "Give me that key, would
you? To that big box in the safe."

"I can hear what you and that Russian are talking about. You
want to sell off Uncle Humphrey's things before we even get to
port. Why? So you can gamble the money away at billiards?"

"I say, Irene, you're out of line."

"No, you are." Maybe her confession has given her strength, or
maybe it's the memory of the brief time she had with Ned. Irene's
showing real spirit this morning. "What would Mother say, if she
knew you weren't following Father's instructions?"

"Mother would say you ought to listen to their son and heir!"
Layton's pale face looks even worse when he flushes; the fish-flesh
pink of his nostrils and cheeks makes his skin appear even pastier
by contrast. I can't laugh at him, though, not with Mikhail only a

room away, obviously hovering nearby. "Hand it over, Irene."

"And what if I don't?" She crosses her arms. Then, as if an afterthought, she says, "Tess, why don't you see if the ship's laundry has my lace collar done yet?"

I frown, ready to contradict her. Her laces are my responsibility and nobody else's. But her eyes flick toward Mikhail, and I realize she's picked up on his unhealthy interest in me—even if she can't possibly have guessed why that is. In order to protect me, she's sending me out at a time Mikhail won't follow.

"I'll go see, Miss Irene." I give her shoulder a grateful squeeze and hurry out.

Mikhail's dark eyes follow me across the Lisles' sitting room as I go, but he says nothing, and I manage not to look him directly in the face.

As soon as I'm out the door, I start running down the hallway. One of the ship's stewards from last night gives me a look—I must be gaining infamy among the staff for being in the thick of trouble. Let them gossip about me, as long as they don't guess Alec's secret.

When I reach the Marlowe cabin, I bang on the door. Nobody answers at first, and I wonder if they're still asleep. Then I remember the drugs Alec was given. Won't he still be tranquilized, unconscious? I wonder if he has to be awake to change back, whether he's still a wolf crated in his father's sitting room.

But it's Alec who opens the door. His robe is open, revealing the expanse of his chest and abdomen; his pajama bottoms are slung low enough for me to see the curve of bone above his pelvis.

Given the trouble we're in, this shouldn't have the power to distract me, but for one blissful moment, it does.

Then he says, his voice ragged, "*Tess*."

Alec pulls me into the suite and into his embrace. I close my eyes as I wrap my arms around his waist and revel in the warmth of his body and the scent of his skin. He pushes the door shut and then leans me against it. Yet I sense that he is the one who needs support.

"Dad told me," he whispers against my neck. "I know what I've done."

"You were only trying to protect me! The steward pushed me to the side; you thought I was in danger."

"It doesn't matter why." Alec's words are muffled. "I'm a murderer now. There's no denying it any longer."

"You didn't mean it, Alec. It wasn't murder. It was—a horrible accident."

"That's not good enough, Tess. If it happened once, it could happen again. And that dead man's family won't give a damn that it was an accident. He's just as dead."

"Only because of the Brotherhood."

"What does it matter who lets me out? As long as I can get out, as long as it's possible for me to do what I did last night, then I'm a monster."

He's tearing himself up over something he couldn't have helped. Isn't he in enough pain already? I silence his guilt the only way I know how, by kissing him.

It strikes a match between us. Lights a fuse. Alec kisses me back so urgently that I can hardly breathe. One hand is at the back of my neck, the other wrapped around my waist so that I can't pull away. But I don't want to pull away. I tug at the neck of his robe, wanting more of his bare skin to see, touch, kiss.

When our mouths part, I have to gasp for breath. His lips brush against my cheek, then my temple. "My sweet Tess. You deserve so much more than I can give you. So much better than a monster."

"You're not a monster."

"I am. Last night proved it." He pushes my curls back, passion already ebbing into tenderness. "You just refuse to see it, because of loyalty to me."

"Enough of this." I want to shake him. Or kiss him again. Both, really. But I can't forget what I came for. "Mikhail's on the verge of getting Layton to sell him the Blade. It could happen any minute now. Once they know it's missing, Mikhail will know I took it. And he'll tell them to hurt Daisy."

"What?"

I explain about the Marconigram, what they did to my sister, what they will do once they realize I've crossed Mikhail. My throat tightens, but I'll be damned if I'm going to break down crying like an idiot when every second counts.

Alec listens, but his alarm seems to diminish. When I'm done, he says only, "We'll take care of Daisy. I promise you."

How can he promise that? I know he means it, but I don't see how Alec plans to do it. Besides, he seems to have forgotten an even more pressing issue. "Mikhail's going to come after us."

"Let him come."

I stare up at Alec. His words aren't mere posturing; he doesn't seem threatened. He actually wants to confront Mikhail. Though I can't guess exactly why, I sense enough to become wary. "Alec, what are you going to do?"

"What I ought to have done months ago. While I still could have saved Gabrielle and spared that man last night." Although he's looking at me, he's looking *through* me—at some dark horizon I can't see. "I'm going to take care of everything."

"Alec—whatever you're planning—you mustn't—"

He interrupts my words with a soft hand over my lips, and stops my mind like a clock that's come unwound. In one tick, time stops and I can't speak or think.

Alec's eyes never leave my face as he caresses my hair. "Tess, until the last hour of my life, I'm going to wish we could have found each other in a different way. Before any of this happened to me. If I'd known you, if I'd had you to live for, maybe I wouldn't have made the stupid mistakes that led me here."

"Alec—"

"You're strong enough to stand up to anyone. Smart enough to do anything you want. Don't sell yourself short; don't be afraid of what your new life is going to offer. Because I know—if there's any justice in this world, good things are going to come to you. Better things than you ever dreamed."

This isn't only him telling me how he feels about me. This is Alec telling me good-bye.

"What are you doing? What are you planning?" Oh, God, he wouldn't kill himself, would he? If he thought it was the only way to save others from the danger he represents as a wolf, he might. "Don't you dare give up. Not on me and not on yourself!"

"I know what I have to do, Tess."

"I don't want to hear another word of this." I try to wrest myself from him, but he holds me too tightly and won't let go.

Alec says, "You have to understand. These past few days, when I was with you—I could dream about what it would be like, not to be a monster. I got to live as a man once more. You'll never know what it means."

"Do you think I don't know what it means? Maybe I'm not a monster, but I've never had anything in my life—never had anyone that I—that I—" A sob threatens to steal my breath, and then Alec kisses me so hard I truly get dizzy.

When our lips part, he whispers into my open mouth, "Say it, Tess. I want to hear you say it." But before I can speak, he kisses me again. It goes on and on, blotting out everything but the taste of him, until suddenly someone pounds on the door.

We jump, and in that first instant I know: It's Mikhail.

I cling to Alec, wishing there were someplace for us to run, but he doesn't seem alarmed. He carefully takes my hands in his, kisses them, and walks to the door to let Mikhail in. Despite his confidence, I put my hand on one of the heavy marble clocks on the mantel; if Mikhail comes after me, he'll get a smack on the head, as hard as I can swing.

Mikhail strolls in, but it's a parody of his usual calm. The anger he feels roils beneath the surface, too petty to reveal the wolf; this is purely human spite. "So. You realized that my interest in the Lisles had nothing to do with their pretty little housemaid. Well, almost nothing to do with her." His eyes sweep up and down along my body. "You've got quite a résumé now, Alexander Marlowe. Ivy Leaguer, heir to a vast fortune, would-be architect, werewolf . . . and jewel thief."

"I'm the one who took it," I insist. "He's no thief."

"But he's the one with the Blade, isn't he? You're not fool enough to keep it for yourself, are you, Tess?" Mikhail continues to circle Alec, who looks back without flinching. "Or is she, Alec? Shall I drag her down to her cabin, rip it apart—and rip her apart—to see if I can find what I seek?"

"You'll never find it," Alec says. "Unless you go to the bottom of the ocean and look there. I'm happy to throw you overboard after it, if you like."

Mikhail's eyes narrow. "You can't have been fool enough to destroy an Initiation Blade. It's your leverage, and hers."

"It's what you use to bring more people under your grasp. As late as yesterday, I thought that was an evil I had to stop in any way I could." Alec takes a deep breath. "But after what happened last night—"

"After you killed a man?" Mikhail says, so innocently, as though he weren't the one who hurt Mr. Marlowe and brought this to pass.

"Yes. After that. You may have caused it, but it could as easily have been an accident. My father could drug me every night, but then I'd be an addict, less than alive. As long as I transform every time the sun goes down, I'm taking a horrible risk—not only with my life, but also with the lives of others. It's irresponsible. Unconscionable. I can't go on this way."

Dread strikes like ice at the core of me, even as Mikhail begins to smile. "Have you finally come to see reason?"

"I've come to see the inevitable." Alec squares his shoulders. "I want to be initiated into the Brotherhood."

# ❧ CHAPTER 21 ❧

BETRAYAL CLAWS AT MY GUT. ALEC JOIN THE Brotherhood? It can't be possible.

Mikhail's face splits into his shark's grin. "I knew you would eventually see the advantages. A far finer life is about to be yours."

"I don't care about your money or your privileges or your smug belief that you rule the world," Alec says. Contempt for Mikhail is etched into the strong lines of his face. "This is about one thing, and one thing only. As long as I transform every night, I'm a danger to everyone—from strangers to the people I love most." He turns to me, just briefly, and I feel as though I will weep. "Last night I took a human life. After that—I have to be initiated, and soon. Conscience demands it. Any other desires I have aren't worth ruining other people's lives for."

The worst part of all of this is that I understand. I hate it, and yet I know Alec's right. No matter what precautions we take, how hard we try to make Alec's transformation into the wolf safe for everyone, the Brotherhood will undo them. It's unfair, and it's

229

sickening that this is happening just when we might have had a chance to keep Alec safe—but it's happening. We can't run from it. We're trapped with it in the center of the ocean.

But to sell himself into slavery to the Brotherhood—I can't bear it. "Alec, don't. You mustn't."

"I must. After what happened last night, there's no other choice for me."

After he killed a man, he means. So I reply, "The Brotherhood could turn you into a killer for their own purposes. How is that any better than what happened last night? If you ask me, it's worse."

"They could. But they won't," Alec says flatly.

Mikhail gives me a contemptuous look, as though I'm a silly child asking why the sky is blue. "Waste a man of Alec's wealth and station as a thug? We have better uses for him than that."

In response to all this talk about his "uses," Alec lifts his chin, using every one of the inches he has over Mikhail. "Besides, if I can't challenge the Brotherhood from the outside—maybe I can change it from within. There must be others like me, brought in against our will. What if there are more of us than there are of you?"

He can't believe in that fairy tale, can he? I want to shout him down, but I'm almost too upset to speak.

Mikhail merely laughs. "Sooner or later, you'll think the way I do, Alec. After you've learned the pleasure of the kill, the meaning of dominance—you'll understand everything." His face hardens into a mask that's almost a mockery of his handsome features. "And from the very beginning, you'll do as I command; I am your elder in the pack. Therefore, your mind will always belong to me."

At first I don't understand, but then I recall what Alec told me that dawn in the Turkish baths.

*If the Brotherhood can control me as completely as they claim, then he could order me to murder you, and I'd do it.*

They can control his mind. From this moment on, Alec will no longer belong to me. He was mine for hardly a second, and yet I feel like the loss will be with me the rest of my life.

"Don't listen to him," I say to Mikhail. "He's upset. He's not himself." Even I don't believe my own words, but I can't bear to remain silent. Quickly I step between Alec and Mikhail, so that the monster will have to look at me. I fascinate him in some way, do I? So terrified am I for Alec that I would even use that to distract him. "You can't hold him to anything he says here."

"You smell like . . . fear. And lust." Mikhail's smile sickens me. "A tantalizing combination."

The door swings open so hard it hits the wall with a thud, and we all jump—even Mikhail—but it's only Mr. Marlowe. "Get away from my son," he says, so savagely that even a werewolf might flinch from his anger.

Before Mikhail can respond, Alec says, "Dad, it's all right."

Mr. Marlowe realizes the truth, and it's as if he somehow shrinks into himself. His powerful frame weakens as he takes in Alec's resolve and Mikhail's presence, and draws the inevitable conclusion. "Alec. No. As hard as we've fought against this—"

"We fought well." Alec puts one hand on his father's shoulder, and I avert my eyes, because the love between them is too great and too painful to bear witnessing. His body trembles, as though telling Mr. Marlowe this caused him physical pain. "I can never repay everything you've done for me."

"You're my son. You never have to repay me. That's what it means, to have a child."

"But now you have to let go. You have to accept that you can't save me from this. We tried, Dad. We did our best."

Mr. Marlowe is on the verge of tears now, but he nods and steps back, surrendering to the inevitable.

Alec looks back at Mikhail. "Swear one thing to me. One small thing."

"You can't believe his promises!" I cry. "He's a liar. Don't you know that?"

"I will give you my word," Mikhail says. "Not as a gentleman—that's worthless. But as a wolf of the Brotherhood, to one who will soon join my pack, yes, I swear."

Weirdly, I think he might actually mean that. Being a werewolf is the only thing that man holds sacred.

Alec says, "Promise me that you will send a Marconigram telling the Brotherhood never again to harm or threaten Tess's sister."

Oh, God. He's not doing this only to protect some potential future people he might injure. Alec is selling himself to the Brotherhood—giving up everything he has, every hope of a decent life—so that Daisy will be safe. He's doing this for me.

"It shall be done," Mikhail says, and I know he'll do it. Maybe I should feel relieved. Later, for Daisy's sake, I will. Right now, all I can do is press my fist against my mouth to hold the sob inside.

Alec must do this, to save her. And I have to let him.

Mikhail shuts the door again, as bold and confident as he was before. "These people are unnecessary to us, Alec. Tell them to leave."

Oh, God, is it happening now? Right now? I would've thought they'd have to wait for a full moon or something. But no, this is immediate. It is inescapable.

"They're staying." Alec remains strong, resisting Mikhail as far—and for as long—as he can. "I have nothing to hide from them. Not even this."

"Very well." Mikhail shrugs. "Let them watch. It will be a pleasure to see their faces as they realize that you no longer belong to them. From this day on, you belong to me."

From his jacket, Mikhail withdraws the Initiation Blade—the one the Brotherhood already owns, one I've never seen before. This one has been polished with pride, and extensively used; the handle is crosshatched with use, and there are indentations in the metal from centuries of being held. Centuries of being used to force men to do the Brotherhood's bidding. Etched into its hilt is the Y symbol they cut into my sister's skin.

As Mikhail holds it aloft, he says, almost dreamily, "They say these were forged in Roman times. That the emperors were the first to master the wolves, and that this was part of their inexorable hold on power for almost a millennium." Light glints along the edge of the blade. "We have been one Brotherhood ever since. One unbroken line of power. Someday you will take pride in this, Alec. Someday you will understand what it means to be above the swill of mere humanity. How close being a wolf is to being a god."

Being a wolf doesn't seem anything like being a god to me, unless a god gets twitchy every full moon and is likely to have fleas. Or so I'd like to say to Mikhail now. But I must remain silent. The transformation fills Mikhail with a kind of pure wonder that is contagious, and despite myself, I wonder what it would mean to be able to change forms at will. To be both beast and woman. Not godlike, surely—but beyond anything I've ever experienced.

Mr. Marlowe puts his arm around my shoulders, and I sag against him as I might have done with my own father, if he were kind instead of harsh, or supportive instead of condemning. Together we watch, helpless, as the initiation begins.

Mikhail points the Blade at Alec. "To your knees."

Alec hesitates only for a moment before kneeling in front of Mikhail. Though he keeps his face still, his gaze strong, I can feel how this submission scorches his pride.

With the point of the dagger, Mikhail flicks one side of Alec's robe off his shoulder, then the other. The silk crumples to the richly carpeted floor. Alec wears only his low-slung pajama pants now, all but naked in front of us.

As Mikhail steps closer, he begins muttering something beneath his breath in a language I can't understand—Latin, perhaps. The room darkens, and at first I think the lights have gone out, or that the ship might be sailing into a storm. But this is a different kind of darkness, one that surrounds and confines us. One that denies the light we ought to see. I cling more tightly to Mr. Marlowe as Mikhail lifts the Blade to Alec's shoulder and digs the point in.

Alec grimaces, clearly biting back a shout. Blood begins to

trickle down the muscles of his arm, past his elbow, along his hand. Droplets from his fingers drip onto the carpet. Mikhail has only begun his work; clearly relishing Alec's pain as he slowly, deliberately carves the slightly asymmetrical Y shape into Alec's shoulder.

The room grows darker and darker. It's as if the cuts in Alec's flesh are what's stealing the light.

Mikhail's chant ends. He lifts the Blade to his lips and touches the tip of his tongue to the metal, to taste Alec's blood. The darkness flickers, and for a moment I can see both the wolves and the men—they are not changing, but it's as if they're both there, inseparable—

Alec falls backward as if stunned, and the light snaps back to normal. Mikhail sheaths the dagger at his waist. "It is done. He is ours."

"Get out." Mr. Marlowe's voice shakes. "You've done your worst. You've got what you wanted. Now leave us."

"Not until I show you what Alec has become capable of." Mikhail fixes me in his intense stare again, and my body seems to freeze. "You suggested that I would turn him into a killer. Perhaps I should take you up on that suggestion."

I want to bolt, but he's between me and the door.

"I could have Mr. Marlowe killed—but no. The father still has his uses. The girl . . . that's another matter," Mikhail says. He turns his attention toward Alec. "Women are weakness embodied, Alec. Your passion for her saps your strength. Prove your loyalty to us. Kill her."

"You're insane," Alec says, panting for breath. He's almost on all fours on the carpet, still unable to stand again.

"Find your strength. Listen to me." There's something uncanny about Mikhail's voice as he says it. The darkness seems to return again, but only to shroud Alec, whose eyes become unfocused.

*The mind control. He's taking over.*

"Stop this!" Mr. Marlowe demands, snapping whatever spell Mikhail was casting in two. He steps in front of me to serve as a shield. "Tess is to remain unharmed."

Mikhail sneers, "You no longer give the orders here, old man."

"I give *this* order—that is, if the Brotherhood ever wants a penny of my money."

"Your son—"

"Can be written out of my will and cut off from my accounts at a moment's notice. I could send a cable and be sure it was done before we even reach shore. And the Brotherhood doesn't only want my money, do they? You're gangsters, the lot of you; you want me to use my political influence for you as well. That's what you mean, by my 'uses.' I tell you now, if you hurt this girl, that will never happen." Mr. Marlowe straightens, some vestige of his pride restored. I'm so grateful I could hug him.

Mikhail backs down with no good grace. "Not worth having trouble over a female. But I warn you now, little girl—speak one word of this, and you'll be dead before dawn. As Mr. Marlowe wishes I shouldn't have Alec do the killing, I'll take care of it myself. Your death will last longer."

"I won't tell," I swear. "For Alec's sake, I'll never tell."

"He ought to have asked for your safety along with your sister's," Mikhail says. "Because your sister will have no more trouble from this day on. Maybe you won't either, Tess. You're hardly worth it, and besides—I have what I want."

Though still bloodied, Alec regains enough of his strength to rise to his feet. "Leave us. Please."

"Politeness at last. Perhaps you're beginning to learn." Mikhail's bow is exaggerated to mock us all. "Enjoy the first night you've known in two years, Alec. Say good-bye to the mere humans who have weighed you down for so long. Tomorrow at dawn—you belong to us. If you will excuse me, I have a Marconigram to send to my associates in New York. They were waiting for us all along, of course. How relieved they'll be to hear that they won't have to persuade you further, Alec. They'll be ready to bring you into the Brotherhood fully—and forever."

Mikhail saunters out. The moment the door shuts behind him, Alec sinks back to the floor, clutching at one ankle as though it hurts even more than the terrible cuts in his shoulder. Mr. Marlowe and I sink to his side to help him.

"You tried it, didn't you?" Mr. Marlowe says. He sounds weirdly excited, almost hopeful.

Alec pulls up the leg of his pajamas to reveal his ankle—which has a small chain wound around it, one that seems to have burned into his flesh. He gasps, "Tess, take it."

I peel it away from him as quickly as I can. The blisters it has left are so horrible, so blackened, that it takes me a moment to realize what it is I'm holding: his mother's locket.

"Silver," I whisper.

Already breathing easier, Alec says, "I was able to put it on when you confronted Mikhail, Tess. When you stepped between us. That distracted him just long enough; I'd have had to stall him until tomorrow, otherwise. Who knows if it works or not—but I had to try."

"Good for you. Both of you." Mr. Marlowe takes the locket from me to gaze down on the portrait of the long-dead woman inside the locket. "It seems only right that your mother could be the one to save you."

"But silver burns werewolves," I protest. "Alec, you're hurt. Why did you do that to yourself?"

Alec takes my hand. "We never found the people who knew what we most wanted to learn in Europe. That doesn't mean we didn't learn *anything*."

Mr. Marlowe adds, "One ancient book we studied said that the touch of silver could prevent the Brotherhood's magic from fully taking hold during the initiation. Pray God it's true!"

Relieved, I squeeze Alec's fingers in mine. "You mean, Mikhail can't control your mind?"

"I hope not," Alec says. He doesn't share in his father's elation.

"Did you feel that he was controlling you, before, at the end of the initiation? Something was happening." I remember again that terrible darkness that swirled around us.

"I'm not sure. I felt weak, but I was in so much pain from the silver and the ritual itself—it's hard to know." Alec grimaces as he looks down at the burns. "Maybe it kept their magic from working on me that much. On the other hand, it could mean the initiation didn't work at all—and I might change tonight, the same as I always have. We won't find out whether this worked until I'm truly tested. It was a book of legends, no more. Legends can lie."

"The Brotherhood will try to hold sway over us, regardless," Mr. Marlowe says.

"I know, Dad. I'm sorry you got dragged even deeper into this."

"Any sacrifice is worth it for my son."

I'm trying to parse out how much of what I just saw was truth, and how much was false. "You weren't fool enough to chuck the Initiation Blade overboard, were you?"

Despite everything, Alec laughs. "That's what I love about you, Tess. Practical to the end."

The word "love" makes me quiver, but I press on. "You didn't, did you?"

"Of course not," Alec says. He tries to adjust his seat on the floor but winces; Mr. Marlowe pulls out his handkerchief, and I take it from him to hold against Alec's cuts and staunch the flow of blood. "There are only a few Initiation Blades in the world. Having two of them aboard this ship is extraordinary. If the silver didn't work—if Mikhail can fog my mind, control me—then we can use the Blade as a bargaining chip later. It's some measure of safety for all of us. We have to keep it."

"Good." I dab at his arm and grimace as I see how much blood is scattered across the carpet. "You poor thing, you've bled everywhere. It spattered all the way across the room."

Alec sees what I see—a few droplets near the door—and frowns. "That's not my blood."

"What?" I don't understand. "But you were the only one cut. How can you tell?"

"Have you somehow managed to forget I'm a werewolf? I can

smell blood well enough to know the difference between some-one else's and my own. Mikhail smelled strongly of blood when he came in here. He—he must have attacked someone."

I gasp, sick with horror.

Mikhail came here after discovering the Initiation Blade wasn't in the Lisles' safe. He would have been angry, so angry, when he discovered it was gone—

Baby Bea.

Ned.

Miss Irene.

He could have killed them all.

## ⤝ CHAPTER 22 ⤞

LEAVING THE WOUNDED ALEC AND HIS FATHER behind, I dash back through the corridors as fast as I can. A stitch in my side stabs with every breath, and by now the stewards must assume I'm a madwoman, but I don't care.

The door to the Lisles' suite is closed but unlocked. I burst through to see chaos. The fine sofa and chairs have been tipped over, and the cut-glass water jug is shattered into dozens of glittering shards. One of the draperies is torn, and in Lady Regina's room, I hear little Beatrice wailing.

When I rush in the door, I see Layton sprawled on the bed. Blood oozes from cuts on his hands and face, and his nose is crumpled and puffy. Mrs. Horne stands next to the bed, bandages in hand, but she's not fixing him up; she's in a kind of stupor. I can't imagine what she must have seen, or what Mikhail might have threatened to do to her. Beatrice stands on her cot, shrieking in terror and neglect.

As I go to the little girl, Layton's head lolls to one side while he turns to me. One of his eyes has already swollen shut. "You," he says thickly. His lips and tongue must be cut. "Count Kalashnikov said it was you."

"You need a doctor," I say, trying to settle the child on my hip and cuddle her.

"Ned's making himself useful and fetching one," Layton snaps, then winces—no doubt that hurt his split lip. "And you've made yourself useful too, haven't you? Stealing from the family coffers."

My heart sinks. The denial rises to my lips, but it's such a bald-faced lie that I can't get it out.

"He would have paid us a hundred pounds for that worthless old knife." Layton pushes himself up on his elbows, though he grimaces as he does it. "More money than you'll see in your entire life, unless of course you steal for it. Did you do it to pay me back for Daisy? Because it was more than she's worth. More than the two of you are worth put together."

The insult to my sister pushes me past the brink. "You lied to Daisy. You made her think you cared about her, and you left her on her own when she needed you the most. Don't you dare insult her. She's worth a hundred of you."

Layton snaps, "I don't give a tinker's damn about your wretched sister. What I care about is the welfare of this family." Hypocrite. He's none too worried about the other family he abandoned, my sister and his son, and half the Lisles' debt must come from his endless gambling. But my self-righteousness withers as he continues, "You stole from us. If you think any member of the family will ever forgive that, you're mad. I shall have Ned fetch a steward.

You'll be kept under lock and key until we reach New York City. And if you don't tell me precisely where you're keeping the dagger, and any other baubles you might have stolen, I'll have you thrown in prison."

Prison. Anything but that. The very thought terrifies me. What kind of a life would I ever have afterward? And yet Layton has me now. I can't present him with the dagger again. Though I know Alec would return it in an instant to spare me this, giving the Blade back to Layton is the same as handing it to Mikhail. Doing that gives Mikhail even more power over Alec than he may have already.

Layton's battered, blood-spattered body is a sign of what can happen when the Brotherhood's power is defied. Mikhail would do this to Alec. He'd do even worse to me.

"What's he saying?" Mrs. Horne says in the same sort of unknowing, wondering tone more often used by children. Witnessing the beating took something out of her—imagine crusty old Horne being completely undone. "You—you took something of the family's? You're dismissed immediately. And you're to give it back at once."

At this point, being fired is the least of my worries. "You can have my uniform back at day's end, but I haven't got the dagger. I swear. You can search my cabin if you don't believe me."

"Who else could have taken it?" Layton coughs, a racking sound, and I see to my alarm that he's spat blood onto one of the pillowcases. Maybe it's just from his cut mouth, but if his ribs are broken, that can cause bleeding inside—it happened to one of the grooms last year, and his health still isn't right. "We persuaded the staff to give all of you keys to pass throughout the ship as you pleased. It looks like Tess has abused that privilege."

"If Mikhail had that knife, he'd like as not have used it on you!" My shout makes Beatrice start wailing again, and I cuddle her closer, trying to soothe her. "Sir, you've got to listen to me. Mikhail—I mean, Count Kalashnikov's a dangerous man. How can you not understand that, after what he's done to you?"

Layton pauses. Though he says nothing, I see what's behind his reluctance. Of course he realizes how malevolent the count truly is; his bruised and bloody skin tells that tale. But Mikhail scares him badly—maybe even worse than Mikhail scares me. He's lashing out at me because he's too weak to stand up to the real enemy.

"Think," I say more urgently. "Report this to the captain. There's no way he can ignore it." Probably the Brotherhood can make sure Mikhail walks away free at the end, but surely he'd at least be guarded for the remainder of the voyage. A report from a member of the English nobility would mean something. "You have a chance to protect all of us, sir. Yourself included."

Just as I believe I might be getting through to Layton, though, we're interrupted. Ned rushes in, almost skidding to a stop on the carpet. "The physician's with someone dire sick right now, sir, but he promises to come along as fast as he can." A few steps behind him is Irene, her hair still half-done; she rushed out hardly dressed, so eager was she to help her brother—and, perhaps, to remain near Ned.

"Blast and damn these doctors! They don't know what's

important. Did you offer him more money to come right away?" Layton asks.

Ned frowns. "Ah—no, sir. Sorry, sir, but it never occurred to me. I think the lady he's with is really quite ill—"

"You'll go back and offer him whatever he wants," Layton declares. "And then you're to fetch a ship's officer to have Tess arrested for theft."

Damn. He's too scared to think clearly. Instead of striking back, he's tucking tail and doing whatever Mikhail wants.

"Tess arrested?" Ned looks from Layton to me and back again, utterly bewildered. "That can't be right, can it, sir? You've taken a knock to the head. Maybe you're not thinking clearly."

Layton straightens himself as regally as he can, with his clothes rumpled and his face a bloody mess. "She's stolen the dagger. She's going to jail for it—and if she doesn't hand the dagger back this instant, I intend to see to it that she stays in jail for the next several years."

Irene steps forward and says, "Tess didn't steal the dagger. I took it."

Everybody in the room stares at her. I'm so astonished by her lie that I nearly drop Beatrice. With arms turning to jelly with shock, I manage to put the quieted child back in her cot.

"You?" Layton flops back onto the pillows. "Whatever would you take some old dagger for?"

"I wanted some money of my own. Mother and Father give me nothing, you know that."

"Mikhail—Mikhail said that Tess—"

"He must have found out something about it." Irene fibs so

smoothly you'd think she was a master criminal, instead of telling just about the first falsehood of her whole life. But that's what she does, isn't it? She defends other people when she can. "You see, I had her pawn the dagger for me in Southampton the night before we set sail. So she did have it—and it was good of you not to tell anyone, Tess. But you needn't pretend any longer just to protect me."

"Yes, miss." I drop her a curtsy, as I've done several times a day for the past few years of my life, but this is the first one I ever really meant as a sign of respect.

Layton sputters in helpless rage. "Well, it was ridiculous of you. Ridiculous, Irene. Mother and Father don't give you money because you're irresponsible, and don't ask me how it is we both know that."

So, they told him about the miscarriage. Irene's face flushes—and I'm uncomfortably aware of Ned, standing close to her but unknowing. Yet she doesn't back down. "They don't give me money because we haven't got much money left. The family's virtually penniless."

Layton looks even sicker than he did when I first walked into the room, and we servants can hardly do more than stare. It's not as if we didn't know. We've made jokes about the Lisles joining us downstairs to wash dishes, gags like that. But hearing Irene admit it—and admit that it's as bad as "penniless"—still feels like watching a cathedral crumble. The great ancient family of the Lisles is poor. The world I was raised in has turned upside down. Even little Beatrice stares.

"You should all get new positions as soon as possible." Though Irene seems to be speaking to all three servants in the room, her eyes are only on Ned. She wants him to leave more than the rest of us—to spare him the sight of her married to a man she doesn't love. "We might have to sell the house within the year, assuming anybody wants such a drafty old place. When they think I can't hear, Mother and Father talk about moving into a town house in London."

"Be quiet!" Layton coughs again, his face contorting in pain, but the shame of their poverty outweighs even the beating he just received. "Irene, you shouldn't talk about matters you don't understand. None of you are to pay her any mind."

"You should find better places while you still can. While our references still mean something," Irene repeats. Ned shakes his head, a silent *no*—I understand without any other sign that there's no other place for him than where she is.

Mrs. Horne has been wobbling back and forth all this time, like a child's toy sent spinning. In that same broken voice, she says, "Lady Regina will be very cross when she returns from morning tea."

I can't take any more of this. "Well, I was just let go. I take it I'll receive no leaving wages. I'll have my uniform sent up to you later this afternoon."

Ned grabs at my arm. "You're leaving just like that? Come on— it's been a strange day, and we're none of us ourselves."

"I'm leaving." The words catch in my throat. Funny, how I thought about all the bigger changes that would happen in my life when I left the Lisles' service, but I never once realized it would hurt to leave one of the few friends I've ever had. I clasp his hand in mine. "Be happy, Ned. Do whatever it takes. Don't let anything stand in your way." Then to Irene I say only, "Thank you. For everything."

And that's it. I walk out of the Lisles' suite for what promises to be the very last time. When I daydreamed about this, I thought it would feel like victory; instead, it's scary. But there's no way left for me to go but ahead.

"Tess!" I glance back to see Irene hurrying after. When she falls into step beside me, I realize that her demeanor has subtly altered; we are no longer mistress and servant, but two friends walking side by side. "You should have this."

She presses something into my hand; I look down and realize, to my astonishment, that it's two ten-pound notes. More money than I've seen in one place in my life—and far more than I'd saved to start over in New York.

"I don't deserve this," I say. I'm not about to admit to stealing the Initiation Blade, but surely Irene knows.

"You're owed something—you and your family. Send it to Daisy, if you think that's best. I sent her a little when I could."

Irene always knew about baby Matthew. It shouldn't surprise me so much, and yet—downstairs we know so much about them, and they seem to be so blind to us. But Irene's never been as blind as the others, has she? I ought to have known it wasn't Layton who helped look after Daisy in those first awful months. "I will, miss."

"Call me Irene," she says. "Where will you go?"

"New York City's as good a place to start over as any." We face each other in the hallway. "I expect I'll find work quickly enough."

"I've half a mind to join you." Her eyes are sad. "But I'd go west. Where the cowboys are. Can ladies be cowboys? Riding's the only thing I know how to do."

We're both smiling through tears now at her little joke. "You'd look a sight in one of those ten-gallon hats."

"I would at that." Irene holds out her hand, and I shake it. Perhaps it's oddly formal, given how close we've been these past few years, but it's nice to part like friends. Then she turns and goes back to her wrecked cabin, her wrecked life.

My first instinct is to return to Alec and sink into his arms, but that's wrong. He's been through so much last night and this morning; he's exhausted and heartsore, and I don't need to expect him to support me right now. I'm in no condition to support him, either. The nights on end without adequate sleep have taken their toll, and though it's early, this morning has been enough to make me certain this will prove to be one of the most tumultuous days of my life.

I return to third class and my cabin. The only person there is Myriam, who glances up from her book, takes one look at me, and says, "Good God, how could it have gotten any worse?"

"I quit my job. Or they fired me. I'm not sure which. Either way, I don't work for the Lisles any longer."

She hops off the bunk to study me more carefully. "Is that all?"

"No. But it's all I can say." Revealing more about the Brotherhood to Myriam than she already knows would only endanger her. "I'm so tired."

Myriam hesitates, and I know she wants to interrogate me

in-depth about what's taken place this morning. Instead she takes my elbow and guides me to the other bunk, helping me climb to my bed.

I shake the pins in my hair loose and toss away my linen servant's cap, which I've worn for the last time. Irene's ten-pound notes remain clenched in my hand. They're the one part of my uncertain future that's real.

Through the haze of exhaustion, I sense Myriam pulling a blanket over me. I want to thank her, but sleep claims me faster than I can speak.

When I open my eyes again, the light in the room has changed. I sit up, groggy and unsure of the hour. Myriam's still there, curled up on her own bunk and considerably farther along in her book.

"I was beginning to think you'd sleep straight through until tomorrow morning," she says.

"What time is it?" My voice is a croak. I run my fingers through my hair; golden curls are spilling out in every direction. I'm going to have to pay more attention to my hairstyle from now on, since I won't have the cap to hide beneath.

"Late afternoon. I saved you some food from dinner." She points toward the one small table in the room, which holds a napkin with some rolls and cheese. Next to it is one folded sheet of notepaper. Myriam, perhaps seeing me notice it, says, "That letter came for you."

It could be from Lady Regina, demanding that I return to service or at least send my uniform up immediately. But I know it's not. I clamber down from the bunk, still blinking sleep from my eyes, and take up the notepaper.

*Tess,*

*Lady Regina appeared at luncheon, saying that Layton was "ill." I could see from Irene's expression that there was more to the story, but obviously he's alive; Mikhail didn't do his worst. I'm grateful for that, for the family's sake at least.*

*She also announced that you'd been let go. I imagine that was quite a scene. She obviously thought I should know that there are penalties for defying her efforts at matchmaking. But I hope you are enjoying having another afternoon at liberty, the first of many days when you'll choose your own path.*

*If you have more free time at dusk, will you join me in my cabin? Even though I know you understand——you more than anyone——there are things we need to say.*

*Alec*

"Alec wants me to come to his room just before sunset," I say.

Myriam frowns. "This doesn't strike me as the wisest time to visit a werewolf."

"Tonight he won't change. At least—we think he won't change." When she gives me a look, I sigh. "I promise, you don't want to know."

"Are you going to him?" She is serious now, more kindly than

I've ever seen her. "I know you care for him, but—you know what he is. That there is no hope. Being with Alec Marlowe can only cause you pain."

"I know. He knows that too." The paper trembles in my unsteady hands. As short and kind as Alec's note is, I understand perfectly why he's asked me to his cabin. We as much as said good-bye before Mikhail arrived and the initiation ceremony began. But neither of us can let go yet. Not while we might be able to steal one more night.

## ╼ C H A P T E R  2 3 ╾

WHEN I KNOCK ON THE DOOR OF THE MARLOWES'
cabin in the late afternoon, nobody answers at first. Then Alec
calls, "Come in."

Despite my need to see him, I hesitate before walking inside.
His voice is ragged, tense—the way I remember it in the hours just
after the change, or just before.

It's not long before sunset. Did the touch of silver during his
initiation undo all the ancient magic? Will Alec transform into a
wolf as always?

But then I remember how the red wolf fought to keep himself
from hurting me that first night, and how he attacked to defend me
when he thought I was in danger. I'm safe with Alec—safer than I
am anywhere else.

As I walk inside, Alec is standing at the open door to their private
promenade deck. His father is nowhere to be seen. A fire flickers in
the fireplace, which surprises me until I realize the breeze blowing in
is chillier than it has been before on this journey.

Alec holds out one hand to me. "Watch the sunset with me."

I close and lock the door behind us, then go to him. He wears trousers and his white shirt, but the sleeves are rolled up and the collar unfastened. In fact, the shirt is unbuttoned halfway down his chest. It would be shockingly improper if we hadn't had our fourth conversation while he was in the nude. "We've done everything out of order, haven't we?"

"What do you mean?"

"Told each other our deepest secrets almost before we met. Saw each other in our skivvies before we first kept company." I look down at his long-fingered hand in mine as the cold wind from the ocean tugs at my gold curls. Pushing the strands back from my face, I finish, "Fell for each other before we could stop ourselves."

"Tess." He kisses me tenderly, cupping my face with one palm. "You look beautiful tonight."

"Wore my best for you." This dress is one I was making for Miss Irene before Lady Regina declared it was too "decided" a shade. It's dark red, the color of wine in candlelight. Though I wasn't able to afford the trimmings I would have sewn on for Irene, I finished it nicely; the soft fabric drapes well and outlines my figure while remaining modest enough for most occasions. Though there's nothing modest about the way Alec is looking at me, or how I feel when he does.

And yet there is sadness in his gaze, too.

"I need you to make me a promise, Tess." Alec weaves his hands into my hair, holding me fast. He's as serious now as on the day we met. "Promise me on your soul."

"Not until you tell me what I'm promising."

"You won't like it."

"People usually don't make people promise on their soul to do things they'd like to do." I take a deep breath. "You know I'd do anything for you. But don't make me swear without knowing what I'm swearing to. Trust me. Tell me the truth first. I want to know."

Alec nods slowly. Then he drops one hand from my face and reaches toward the table. His fingers close around a broad, sharp knife.

As he presses the handle into my hand, he says, "If I begin to change at sunset—I want you to kill me."

*"What?"*

"Touching silver during the Initiation might have prevented the Brotherhood from gaining control of my mind. But it might have disrupted the Initiation so completely that it had no effect. I might still be the werewolf I was before, condemned to change every night." Alec grimaces in such a way that I know he's thinking of last night, when a man died because of him. "If that's true, then I have to end this. I won't live as a slave, or as a murderer. Death would be my only freedom."

*No*, I think, but I don't say it. Didn't I tell Alec I'd do anything for him? And I understand why he's asking. This isn't a melodramatic gesture: This is Alec saying he'd rather die than be a danger to others. It is the most principled choice he could make. And yet I cannot curl my fingers around the knife.

"I was going to ask my father." Alec's words come in a rush. "But I can't ask him to kill his own child. Down deep he's a gentle soul. Doing that would destroy him, forever. I know it wouldn't be easy for you either, but—you're strong, Tess. Stronger than I think even you know. I don't think there's anything you couldn't bear if you had to."

"So you're asking me to bear this."

The cool air musses his chestnut curls. "You know I hate to ask you. Almost as much as I hate to die. But if the only choice left for my life is be a killer or become the Brotherhood's slave, then that's worse than no life at all."

When I set out on this voyage, I knew I could no longer live as the servant of the Lisles; if the initiation has not set Alec free, then he, too, is looking at a life of servitude—beyond liberty, beyond justice. Though I planned for a way out, what if there had been no way out for me? Would I have lived the rest of my years as a slave, or would I have chosen to end it?

Surely I can give Alec no less mercy than I would have wanted for myself.

Calling on all my strength, I slowly fold my fingers around the handle of the knife until I can pull it away from Alec. I look into his eyes. Though it burns me from the inside out, I say, "Yes. I'll do it."

Alec breathes out, relief overriding what must be his terror in the face of death. "Thank you."

"Did you leave a note for your father? Explaining this?" I gulp back a sob. "If I've got to kill you, I'll do it, but I won't be hanged for it."

"Ever practical." The shadow of a smile flickers across Alec's handsome face. "I left a note. Two notes, actually, for him to see when he comes back after his late-night brandies with Colonel Gracie. One explains everything, and tells him what I need him to do. The other is a false suicide note. It says that I can't get over Gabrielle's death and I'm planning to jump into the ocean. To drown myself."

Meaning that it would be left to me and Mr. Marlowe to hurl his body overboard and complete the illusion. Surely his body would never be found. It's as neat a solution as we could ask. And yet it devastates me, thinking of anyone as vital and alive as Alec being nothing more than a corpse, only deadweight to be thrown into the vast, depthless sea. Tears prick at my eyes, but I grip the knife harder.

Alec helps guide my hand until the point of the knife rests just beneath his breastbone—mere inches from his heart. "I'm sorry, Tess. I hate to ask you."

"Don't hate asking me to do what has to be done." I'm strong enough to bear it. I don't know if I believed that before Alec said it to me, but now I understand it's true.

The sun has begun dipping below the horizon—a sliver of orange-gold light sliced by the dark line of the ocean. I shiver as the cold wind whips around us, and for a moment I can no longer bear to meet Alec's dark eyes. I stare out at the water instead, and see a few spurs of ice—far more than I've seen at any other time during our voyage. "It's become so cold," I whisper. "Are we going farther north? Did we change course?"

"It's the sea that's changed." Alec's voice is uneven. Courageous as he is, he cannot disguise his emotions in the face of death. "I remember, when we traveled to Europe, the whole ocean was studded with ice. The ship had to stop half a dozen times. It seemed to take forever, and I was so afraid of what I'd become, so impatient to get where we were going—" He falls silent, and I know what he's thinking: He would give anything for those days back again in this moment when he may have only minutes left.

Overhead the sky is deepening its shades—still bright blue close to the setting sun, but beyond that periwinkle, and above that, sweeping around us and down to the east, a deeper navy that will soon darken to black.

I look at the point of the knife. It gleams in the dim light, and it feels so heavy in my hand. Alec's unbuttoned shirt lets me angle the blade against his bare skin. How hard will I have to push to break through skin and bone and heart?

"How do you feel?" Desperation chokes my voice. "Can you feel it coming on? Or not coming on?"

"I hardly know. My heart is beating fast, and I'm sweating—that's what happens before the change—"

*Oh, God.*

"—but I'm nervous. It could be only that." Alec is obviously struggling hard for control. "I can't tell the difference anymore."

He's so scared. My heart goes out to him, and in that moment I feel his pain more sharply than my own.

"It's all right," I say, keeping my voice even. "I won't let you change. You won't hurt me. You won't hurt anyone else. I've got you." It's as if I were holding on to him above an abyss, instead of being the one who might hurl him into it.

Our eyes meet again. The rosy sunset light paints our faces. I grip the knife harder, my heartbeat quickening.

The sun goes lower, and lower—only a thin line of light now——and then it's gone. It's night.

And Alec remains human.

My body seems to go limp. I let the knife fall from my hand as I stagger backward; Alec catches me and holds me in his strong arms, though he is almost as undone as I am. "Tess," he whispers into my hair. "I'm free."

"You're free forever," I repeat. "You have a chance, Alec. You have to have hope."

"My brave Tess." His mouth brushes against my cheekbone, the corner of my mouth. I pull him close and kiss him, then harder, until his lips open and his tongue brushes against mine.

The wind whips around us, colder and harsher than ever, and Alec pulls me inside, away from the coming chill. We stumble against the heavy carved chair in the sitting room—perhaps this is why I sink to my knees, pulling Alec down with me. Why he slides his arms around my waist as he leans me back onto the carpet in front of the fire.

Though I know better, and so does he.

"I can say it at last," he murmurs as we embrace, our bodies close together. "I love you."

"And I love you." It doesn't feel like a revelation. It feels like something I've known since the moment I met him.

"Tess." Alec's breath is warm against my throat. We're tangled up in each other now. I pull his shirt open, baring his broad

259

shoulders. His body covers mine. "I can't offer you anything."

Marriage, he means. A future. Everything his bondage to the Brotherhood denies us. All those things that seem so important in the bright light of day but are so meaningless now.

"You can offer me tonight." I arch my body under his until he groans. In the last moment before his mouth covers mine again, I whisper, "That's enough."

Hours later, I lie in Alec's bed, clad only in soft white sheets. Alec lies next to me, still tracing the lines of my body with his fingers, his expression one of wonder. "You're so beautiful. More beautiful than I ever imagined."

"I could say the same to you." I can't resist an impish smile. "If I hadn't already seen how beautiful you were in the Turkish bath."

He grins and kisses me, and we fall back on the bed giggling, as if this were only our first night together instead of our last. This is how I always imagined a girl would feel on her honeymoon: cherished, loved, womanly, and fulfilled. I don't know what all those old ladies were whispering about, claiming that it hurts the first time. Didn't hurt me a bit, not even at first, and after that first—oh, I understand so much more now. Why people make mistakes for this. Why people risk everything.

We risked little; I know how to be careful. Alec does too, and he took care of me without my having to ask. Neither of us wants a baby. That's for the best, I know, and yet I wish somehow I could carry something of him with me always.

What I'm really wishing is that I didn't have to tell him good-bye.

The smile fades from my face, and his too, as he watches. We've hidden from the hard truth as long as possible. Time to face reality.

"You know you have to go," he says. "For your good, not mine."

"I know. Mikhail and the Brotherhood won't allow a woman in your life. Least of all one who knows their secrets."

"And there's still no saying whether or not they can control my will. Despite the silver, the initiation worked enough to make me free to change or not, on any night except the full moon. It may have worked enough to make them control me. And if they commanded me to hurt you—"

"You would." I sit up, holding the sheet to my chest. "I know we have to part, Alec. You made that clear before I ever came here."

Alec hesitates. "This is a hell of a thing to say after we—don't misunderstand why I'm asking—Tess, if you need money to start over in New York, we can give it to you."

He's worried that he'll make me feel like a whore, as though I couldn't tell the difference between that and what happened between us tonight. It's for his sake that I'm glad to tell him, "I don't need it. Irene gave me two years' salary as leaving pay; Lady Regina will be furious when she finds out. I'm well set."

Alec nods, though he looks uncertain. Two years' salary to me is probably less than the cost of one of his polo ponies. But it will suit me fine. "Is there nothing I can do for you?"

"Your father offered me a letter of recommendation. I wouldn't mind that. Would you have him send it to my cabin before we make dock? I expect he'll do it in any case, but—a lot has happened. So remind him, maybe." I don't know, now, whether I will return to service in America, or whether I'll look for some other line of work. Irene's generosity gives me time to consider the possibilities. The letter serves as insurance, though, that I will always have that option open to me.

"Of course." Alec speaks so quietly. For the first time, I let myself wonder what things might have been like for us if he were free—if the Brotherhood hadn't sunk their claws so deeply into him. Would he have wanted to see me in the United States? Courted me like a proper young lady? Even asked me to marry him?

Those romantic notions don't burn very brightly in my commonsense mind. Millionaires don't marry ladies' maids. And if Alec were not a werewolf, and suffering under that curse, we'd hardly have met. I would have known him only as a young man Lady Regina thought suitable for her daughter.

And yet I can't dismiss the idea entirely. I want him so badly. It feels so unfair that this can never come to pass for either of us.

Now that sadness has crept into our time together, I know the time has come to leave. We've had a joyful night, and I don't want to be the one to ruin it with tears. "I have to go."

Alec opens his mouth to protest, but he says nothing. He knows why I have to leave—knows my thoughts almost as soon as I think them. I put my red dress back on, plait my hair back into some semblance of propriety. Behind me, I hear Alec pulling on his robe. When we face each other again, we are no longer joyful young lovers. We are people being parted forever.

He kisses me even more passionately than he did when we

made love. Again and again our lips meet, until I am almost unable to catch my breath. All this and yet I know we are saying good-bye.

When at last we pull apart, Alec reaches into the pocket of the robe. From there he pulls out his fine linen handkerchief; sparkling within the folds of linen is his mother's locket. He still can't touch it.

"I want you to have this," Alec says. "Whatever my mother could do for me is done. The protection she wanted to give me—the love this holds—it belongs to you now, Tess."

Blinking fast, I take the locket from him and fold it in my palm. "I'll keep it forever," I promise.

"If you ever need help, you know how to find my father. And my father will know how to find me."

"If I ever need help." Though I mean to need no one's help. I don't want to become a burden to Alec, convincing myself I must rely on him as a subterfuge to bring us together over and over. That will only cause us pain. "Now you have to be the one to make me a promise."

"Anything," Alec says.

"Watch the sunrise this morning. You can finally see that again too, and that will remind you to—to have hope. No matter what you've lost, no matter what you've been through, there's hope."

We kiss again, but now tears are swimming in my eyes and neither of us can bear it. I break away from him and walk out of the cabin without saying good-bye.

Alec doesn't make me hear his farewell. He just shuts the door behind me, one barrier that stands for all the others that keep us apart.

I head back down into the belly of the ship, only half paying attention to where I'm going. By now I know the path well. Maybe I should look around a bit more, as I'll have no other reason to return to first class and its grandeur. No doubt a steward has already gone to my cabin, hoping to collect the precious key between first and third class; now that I'm no longer in the Lisles' service, I have no excuse to keep it. But my awareness is drawn inward, as though my entire world were outlined by my skin.

My heartbeat is still quick, and underneath my clothes I imagine I can still feel Alec's touch, his kiss. I close my hand around the silver locket that belonged to his mother, then put it in my pocket for safe-keeping. This is the one thing I can keep forever.

Tonight I know I'll cry myself to sleep. Then there will be one more day of the voyage to endure. I'll ask Myriam to walk with me on deck. Go to a dance in the third-class hall. Maybe talk a bit more with Ned and say a better farewell to him, when he's off duty in the evenings. It won't be so bad.

Back on F deck, I walk past the squash court—empty now—down the silent hallway. It must be quite late now. What does it matter? Tomorrow I can sleep late if I like—something I haven't been able to do once in all the years I've worked for the Lisles. I unlock and step through the door between first and third class almost absentmindedly. Just as I start to shut it behind me, a hand slips through and grabs me about the waist, pulling me backward. Too startled even to scream, I look behind me and see Mikhail.

His smile is a scimitar blade within his dark beard. "You can't have thought I was done with you."

## ⊰ CHAPTER 24 ⊱

THE DOOR TO THIRD CLASS SWINGS SHUT, TRAP-
ping me alone with Mikhail. I twist out of his grip, and for a
moment I feel relief—but then I realize that he let me go. He has
me cornered, and he enjoys it.

"You told Mr. Marlowe you would leave me alone," I say.

He holds up one finger, close to my lips, as though he would
silence me, or kiss me, whichever I'd hate more. "I made one solemn
promise—for your sister's safety, not yours. I owe Mr. Marlowe nothing. Only the Brotherhood holds my loyalty; only the Brotherhood
deserves it. Alexander Marlowe will understand this, given time."

I want to tell Mikhail what he can do with the Brotherhood,
that they will never own Alec, but I hold my tongue. They mustn't
guess what he did with the silver, that he has a chance to obey his
own will instead of theirs.

He studies my face, clearly liking what he sees. "Tearstains.
How poignant. Has Alec already finished with you?" I turn my
head from him. Mikhail chuckles. "It's already begun, then.

His understanding that mere humans—especially women—are beneath the notice of gods."

It stings. Though I know in my heart the truth between me and Alec, Mikhail's version of events is too close to Daisy's story and to my own worst fears: that rich men use poor girls and throw them away. Even if that's not what happened to me, I hate that Mikhail can even think such a thing—and that I have to let him believe it.

That doesn't mean I have to play along with everything that man says.

"You're no god," I retort. "You walk on all fours and you smell like a dog. That's not what I worship in church."

"You're so ignorant that you don't even know what a god is." Mikhail steps closer to me, his heavily muscled frame making him like another kind of wall I can't get through. I glance from side to side, hoping someone will emerge and force him to back off, but this area of first class has no cabins, only luxuries like the squash court. "You only see the form of the wolf. You don't know the reality of it. The agony of the change, and the glory of knowing that your body and your mind are capable of becoming other than human. More than human. We defy death. We defy the prisons of our mortal bodies. We defy everything that governs pathetic humanity like you."

"But you've got nothing better to do with your time than harass us, do you?" I fold my arms. Though I'm terrified of him, I'll be damned if I'll let him see it. "Go back to ruling the universe from Mount Olympus or whatever else it is you mongrels do. You've got

266

nothing to gain from hurting me and everything to lose."

I feel very good about this defiance until Mikhail coolly replies, "I have one very important thing to gain. The other Initiation Blade."

"Alec—he threw it overboard—"

"I'm not surprised a stupid little girl like you thinks I would believe such a ridiculous tale. Now, Alec should have known better."

Damn. He knows. What leverage the Blade can give me has to be used now. "I gave the Blade to Alec. That's all I know, beyond what he's said. But if he's still got it, and you kill me—he'll toss it overboard for sure."

Mikhail doesn't back off. He doesn't even stop smiling. "No doubt young Mr. Marlowe would react poorly if I were to kill you. But I don't mean to kill you. I mean to hurt you. That can last so much longer."

My whole body goes cold.

"What might Alec do to save you from pain?" Mikhail tilts his head, narrows his eyes. I see the wolf in him so strongly now, more strongly than I did when he had fur and fangs. "Handing over the Initiation Blade would be only the beginning."

That's the moment when I become so afraid that I go beyond fear. Within the space of one blink, I'm suddenly consumed by white-hot rage. Mikhail wants to hurt me? I'll show him hurt.

I slam my hand into his face as hard as I can, so hard the bones of my arm ache. In that first instant, surprise is on my side, and Mikhail's only able to stumble backward. I use that moment to go after his eyes with my fingernails. He shouts out in pain, and it's the sweetest sound I've ever heard.

But then my advantage is lost. Mikhail recovers and grabs my arm, twisting it savagely behind me until I'm afraid the bone will break. I scream again and again, but there's no one to hear. Mikhail's other hand claps across my mouth anyway, less to silence me and more as if to smother me.

He pulls me against him, his chest to my back. Surely he can feel the terrified pounding of my heart. "You'll pay for that," he mutters into my ear, his voice silky. This one enjoys fear—drinks it the way others do champagne.

His hand tightens against my face, and I think he might forget his plans for manipulating Alec and kill me just for the fun of it. But that's when the ship begins to shake.

It's the strangest sound—like a thousand marbles being spilled across a stone floor, though deeper and larger than that. The vibration of it ripples up through our feet, and there's another kind of motion too. A shudder. As though the ship herself were as afraid as I am. And it's so close. . . .

We stand still for a moment, Mikhail as startled as I am. Perhaps he's trying to figure out what happened. I've got more immediate concerns.

I drive my elbow backward into his gut hard enough to make him retch. His grip loosens enough for me to pull free. I run away from him as fast as I can, but not fast enough—Mikhail's inhuman speed means he's on me again in a second. He slams into me, driving us both down to the floor. His fists clutch my hair, and I cry out in pain. Though I try to roll over and free myself, I can't.

If only I had that Initiation Blade now, I'd stab him through the heart—but I think of something better.

With my one free hand, I reach into my pocket and close my fingers around Alec's mother's locket. Her *silver* locket.

With the locket in my palm, I smack my hand against the side of Mikhail's face, and there's no sweeter sound than his howl of pain. As he recoils, clutching his injured cheek, I roll over and get myself free. Stumbling to my feet, I start running for the door to third class. People will be there, friends and strangers alike. Surely Mikhail wouldn't hurt me in front of a crowd of witnesses.

Just as I grab the doorknob, though, Mikhail clutches me by the waist and pulls me backward so hard I lose my balance. My sweaty fingers lose their grip on the locket, and I shriek as it falls to the floor. Then he slings me over his shoulder as though I were a rolled-up carpet.

"You'll pay for all of that," he says through gritted teeth as I pound helplessly against his back. "You have no idea how much you'll pay. Before I'm done, Alec will have to beg for your scraps."

He pulls open a door—the squash court, I think—and drags me inside. When he flings me down, I stumble backward, and I expect to see him turn into the wolf at any moment.

Instead, he just stands there. Mikhail's not even looking at me. He's staring at the far corner of the room.

Slowly I turn my head in that direction, and that's when I see the water.

One corner of the room is bubbling with dark water. It's like the spring near the duck pond on the Moorcliffe grounds, almost

269

silent but constant. The puddle in the corner broadens by the second, doubling in size within the time it takes me to recognize what it is. Did a pipe burst? Is the swimming pool overflowing? I don't understand why the squash court would be flooding in the dead of night.

"*Bozhe moy,*" Mikhail says. "We're taking on water."

"You mean—the ship?" That sound we heard—the shudder that passed through the entire *Titanic*—it led to this?

Mikhail doesn't answer me. It's as if the mere sight of the water has all but erased me from his mind. I wonder if I could slip out the door; maybe he wouldn't even notice.

But then he backhands me so roughly that my head slams into the wall. Everything goes dim—not black but gray—and I swoon so that I almost can't stand. Then I feel his hands on my shoulders as he bodily throws me across the room.

I know that I fall, though I can't feel the impact. I hear the door slam shut, and the turning of a lock, but I don't care.

Everything fades away, like a photograph that's been left near the sun too long. It would be restful if my head hurt less. Sometimes the pain stops, but then, time stops too. Although I am here, I'm not here. I wonder if this is the place between life and death. It doesn't matter to me if it is.

Nothing matters to me at all—until the moment cold water touches my hand.

# ⊰ CHAPTER 25 ⊱

*APRIL 15, 1912*

The frigid touch of water wakes me from my stupor. Groggily, I shove myself up on my elbows, forcing myself to remember what just happened as I scoot back from the cold damp. My head is thick with dull, deafening hurt. Only when I really see what's happening do I return to myself.

Dark, freezing-cold water is rushing into the squash court. Already it stretches the entire length of the room and nearly halfway to the door; on the far wall, where it began flooding first, it's already more than two feet deep.

Once again I remember the terrible sound that shook the entire *Titanic*. Though it seems impossible that anything could go wrong on a ship this new and splendid, there's no denying the evidence in front of my eyes. I can't imagine what could happen to a transatlantic steamer this far out in the ocean—we couldn't run aground, not out here. But whatever it is, it's happened, and it's bad. This room looks like it might be worst of all.

Bruised head swimming, I run to the door, but it's locked. Mikhail made sure of that before he left. And he was frightened enough of whatever happened to the ship to forget all about me, Alec, and the Initiation Blade. That's almost as scary as the dark water rising behind me—but not quite.

I throw my weight against the door once, twice, again. My shoulder aches, but the door doesn't budge. "Can anyone hear me?" I shout. My throat is sore from screaming, and yelling makes my head hurt worse. "Someone, anyone! Help!"

There's no telling if anyone answers me or not. It's getting hard to hear over the gurgling of the water, which is becoming louder as the water gets deeper. If anything, it's rushing in faster now.

My stomach drops as I realize that this entire room with its high ceilings could fill with water, and soon—and if I'm still locked inside, I'll drown in the squash court.

I need something to break open the door. Floating atop the water are a few pieces of abandoned athletic equipment—squash racquets, obviously. They're better than nothing. I hoist up my dark red skirts and wade into the water —

—and scream.

My God, the cold. It feels like being on fire. My flesh seems to freeze instantly, and my bones ache; the water is chilling my marrow. I leap back and try to fish one of the racquets out with my hand, and I snag the net, but the water hurts my fingers just as much. My hands are nearly numb by the time I get the racquet, and it's hard to hold on to the handle. But I smash it against the door as hard as I can, as many times as I can, because the water's nearly covering the floor now. I don't want to feel that terrible cold again, but within moments it will have me.

I slam the racquet against the door one more time, and it swings open. In that first instant, I stupidly think I've knocked it loose from the hinges—but there's a steward standing there, one of a small group. Though they look surprised to see me, nobody asks what I'm doing in the squash court; they're too horrified at seeing the water.

"Bloody hell," says one of them.

"What's happened?" I ask.

"We hit a berg," another man says, and I realize he must mean an iceberg. "Tell the captain she's taking on water fast!"

I push my way into the hallway, and the stewards and I are instantly running from the seeping water. My numb feet make me clumsy, and I nearly tumble before catching myself against the wall. Something shimmers on the ground: Alec's mother's locket. With trembling fingers I grab it, then begin running again. At first I hardly know where I'm going—just away from there—but then I make myself think.

The stewards knew about the accident with the iceberg.

They were inspecting the ship for damage.

They were very alarmed by the damage they found, enough to run back to the captain.

No matter how bad I thought this was before, it's worse.

I need answers, but who can tell me? My first thought is of kindly Mr. Andrews, but no doubt he's busy now, and unlikely to accept a call from the third-class girl who showed up in the middle of the night with a crisis about a dog. My second thought is better: George. If Myriam can find him, she can get more information about what's really going on. That means I have to find Myriam.

Though I feel weak from the cold and dizzy from the blow to my head, I dash into the third-class area, back toward my cabin. The hallways are more crowded than I'd expect around midnight; several people are up and around, no doubt roused by the sound of the ship hitting the iceberg. But nobody seems to understand the danger—they mostly seem annoyed, muttering in half a dozen languages about being jarred awake so late. Is it possible that this isn't as serious as it looked to me before?

But when I reach my cabin, I realize it must be that serious or worse. Because I haven't got to convince Myriam to find George—he's already here.

"Tess, thank God you've come." Myriam clutches at my arm. "George says we must go on deck and get into the lifeboats."

"Lifeboats? Are we—we couldn't be—" The word almost won't come out. "Are we sinking?"

"I don't know," George says. He looks pale and drawn. "We're still assessing the damage. But Captain Smith has said we should get people on deck and put ladies and children into the boats as a precautionary measure. He's no alarmist—the most solid captain on the White Star Line. If he says you should board the lifeboats then you should go." His eyes are locked on Myriam's. "Just to be on the safe side, my darling."

"We'll go." Myriam turns toward our open cabin door and says to the elderly Norwegian ladies, "Come on! We have to go to the lifeboats!" They stare at her in incomprehension. "Lifeboats!" Myriam yells louder, as though this will suddenly make them able to understand English.

Maybe the ship is sinking, George says. It's a possibility. Not a certainty. That's what he told us, and what I think he sincerely believes—honesty shines from his blue eyes. But even though he is an officer on the ship, I know something he doesn't. I've seen that room filling with water. I heard the curses from the seamen who saw the damage and rushed to tell the captain.

All of that tells me—the *Titanic* is sinking. Not maybe. Definitely. Now.

## ❧ CHAPTER 26 ❧

"WHAT ON EARTH HAPPENED TO YOU?" GEORGE takes a hard look at me, and I realize I must be a sight—hair mussed, dress ripped and water-spotted, shoes squelching and creating a puddle on the floor.

"I'm all right." That's as much as I plan to get into it. My mind is racing. Will Alec know of the danger? Will he and his father be safe?

Then a white life jacket hits me in the side, and I catch it by reflex. "Put it on!" Myriam says. Hers is already around her neck. "If we must take to the ocean in those tiny lifeboats, I want this with me. Come, grandmothers, put yours on as well." Then she says something in Lebanese, probably the exact same thing, but they know no more of her language than they do English. She pats the white life jacket, trying to encourage the Norwegian ladies, but they just pull the blankets up tighter around them. Surely they understand what a life jacket means?

But they don't believe the ship is sinking. What could sink the mighty *Titanic*? I wouldn't believe it myself if I hadn't seen

276

the water. Even the third-class passengers who understand English aren't paying George's suggestion much mind. They think it's no more than a drill.

As I put my life jacket on, George says, "If they actually want you to get into the lifeboat, to lower it into the water, promise me you'll go. I know it's scary—"

"I will be happy to go," Myriam says. "I haven't been comfortable on this ship since learning about the werewolves."

George frowns. "Beg pardon?" Then he shakes it off, no doubt assuming he misheard. "I must return to duty. I'll try to find you again." Quickly he kisses Myriam, then hurries back above decks.

Once he's gone, Myriam says, "What really happened to you?"

"Mikhail." No more explanation is necessary. "Myriam, I've seen the water in the squash court. It's rising fast."

She sucks in a sharp breath but remains calm. "Then let's get to the lifeboats." Quickly she glances over her shoulder at our roommates, who refuse to budge. "The others will follow shortly, when they realize the truth. Won't they?"

"Surely." It can't be long before water spills free of the squash court and other rooms on F deck; soon it will be running through this hallway as though it were a river. But above decks, it will take them longer to accept the truth. No doubt the stewards are taking better care of the first-class passengers—but the stubborn will still be slow to see. "Myriam, go up on deck without me. I'll be right behind you."

"What are you doing?" Myriam frowns.

"Alec," I say. "I can't go until I know he's safe."

\* \* \*

I run back up the many flights of stairs to first class. (The lifts might still be working, but I'll be damned if I run the chance of getting trapped in one while on a sinking ship.) Alec has to get off the ship too; he has to be safe. I trust his judgment, and his father's. They would heed the warnings and move promptly. But I have to know he's been warned.

Once I hesitate, midstep, recalling George's exact words: He said they were putting "ladies and children" into the lifeboats. But that was when they thought the sinking only a possibility. Surely the crew will let everyone off the ship, including the men, as soon as they see the real danger.

The only thing that could keep Alec from safety is if he tries to take care of me.

Despite my throbbing head and the dizziness that still washes through me in waves, I redouble my speed. I've got to get to Alec, and soon.

When I reach A deck and burst into first class, I stop short in pure astonishment. The scene around me is—almost completely ordinary.

The group clustered in the lounge might be the same genteel gathering from all the nights before, except that people's dress is more eccentric: Some are in their finest evening clothes, some in nightgowns and robes. Several of them are wearing their life jackets, though others simply have them tucked under an arm and many people still haven't bothered to find theirs. They're laughing at one another's jokes, and even as I look through the lounge to the grand staircase and the entry to the deck—where the lifeboats must surely be—I don't see a crowd. People are treating this as a lark, nothing more than an interruption in their grand voyage, a good story to tell at parties once they get home. In the distance, perhaps outside or in another lounge area, the band is playing "By the Light of the Silvery Moon."

Good God. They haven't even told the *rich people* this ship is sinking. Do they mean to keep it from us until the water closes over our heads?

As I weave through the group, heading toward the first-class passenger cabins, I spy one familiar figure among the few on deck: Irene.

I run to her. When I go through the doors, I gasp; it's markedly colder outside than it ever has been before on this voyage. No wonder we hit ice. My wet boots chill so quickly it makes me shake, but I don't stop running. Nearby, I see a lifeboat being lowered, filled with society ladies in furs and hats—but with so many empty seats they could easily bring their luggage along.

Irene glances away from the spectacle and sees me within moments. "Tess!"

"Miss Irene!" The old honorific slips out. "Thank goodness you're up here."

"Mother and Layton said it was a lot of foolishness, but I thought we ought to do as the steward said. Though I'm in no hurry to go down to the sea in one of those tiny boats." Her hair hangs loose around her face. She's wearing her sea-green robe with the gold tassels—and, I realize, she's not on her own. Ned stands a few feet away in his uniform, by her side as always. Probably they came up here mostly to be alone together; it hardly matters as long as they're within reach of the lifeboats. Irene adds, "Tess, are you certain you're all right? How did you get so wet?"

"The ship is sinking." No point in softening the blow. "On the lower decks, the water's already filling the rooms. I can't think for the life of me why they haven't told people the truth flat out, but the next time they load a lifeboat, the two of you had best get inside."

Irene's eyes go wide. Ned, I can tell, doesn't believe me. He says, "How can you be sure?"

I point at my water-stained dress. "I'm sure, Ned! Believe me, you'll be sure too soon enough."

"Mother. Baby Bea." Irene clutches Ned's arm. "They think it's nothing, merely a White Star drill. We have to go to them."

"Of course." Ned covers her hand with his own, daring for one moment to show what he feels. "We'll get them safe."

She turns to me. "Tess, will you come with us? I'm afraid they won't believe me unless you tell them what you've seen." Behind her, an officer calls for people to fill a lifeboat, but even knowing what she now knows, Irene never looks back, and Ned never looks away from her. "Besides, you need a bandage for your head. I think it's bleeding."

Though I'm wild with impatience to reach Alec, the Lisles' cabin is on the way to his, and besides—it's for Irene. "Let's hurry," I say. "In fact, let's run."

Nobody pays us any mind as we tear down the hallways, my waterlogged boots leaving dark marks on the expensive carpets. A few befuddled passengers are stumbling out, including one grande dame in a satin peignoir set and life jacket who has put her tiara on her head for safekeeping. The stewards are telling people, I realize, but politely, rapping on doors and asking if people wouldn't perhaps mind coming to the deck. That never knocked the fear of God into anybody.

Irene bursts through the door of her family's cabin, Ned and I in her wake. "Mother! Layton! Come, now, we've got to go quickly."

"Not the lifeboat drill again," Layton mutters. His voice is still thick, lips swollen from the beating Mikhail gave him. He's draped across one of the sofas near the fireplace (complete with blazing fire) and has a full brandy snifter in one hand. When he sees me, he sneers, "What, you brought your little partner in crime back for a visit?"

"The *Titanic* is sinking," I say to him. "There's already deep water belowdecks."

Lady Regina, in her frilly lace nightgown and robe, stares at me with distaste. "Still more lies. Now that you can no longer help Irene steal from the family, you've stooped to practical jokes? How pitiful."

"It's no joke." Though it's difficult to keep my temper, I try for Irene's sake. "Look at me, would you? I'm half soaked through. Water's rising fast down in third class."

Mrs. Horne stands in the far corner of the room, rocking back and forth on her heels. "The water," she says brokenly. "All that water." Her nightmare has come true, and she knows it, and it's frozen her in place as though she were a statue.

"Mother, please." Irene steps closer, thin hands clasped together. "If there's any chance of danger, we ought to go up on deck, don't you think? Better safe than sorry."

Lady Regina's scorn only deepens. "To be seen in our night-clothes? Hair uncombed? I knew before this that you had no sense of propriety, Irene, but I thought you understood that your brother and I have higher standards."

"Besides," Layton says, "what point is there in it? They can hardly complete the drill. A few unlucky fools will be lowered into the water to catch colds and feel seasick, but there's no way they can load everyone on. Not enough lifeboats."

It's as though I've been dunked in the cold floodwaters all over again. "What do you mean? This ship is—it's enormous, it's got everything imaginable, surely it has lifeboats for everyone."

Layton swirls his brandy as though its amber shade were more important than the fate of the *Titanic*. "Some of the chaps were talking about it over cards the first night. More lifeboats than virtually any other ship on the seas, but they took some of them out to make more room for the private promenade decks. Only sensible, really. And it quite relieves us the need to take part in their safety drill."

Not enough lifeboats. Not everyone on this ship can be saved.

The feeling that consumes me isn't fear. It's worse than that. Fear would be wondering if something terrible might happen. What sickens my gut and thins my pulse is the knowledge that something terrible will happen. None of us can prevent it.

All I can do is try to save the people I care about.

"Irene, you must go," I say, and Ned nods in agreement.

She doesn't budge. "Mother, please! Just for me, just this once, please listen."

Lady Regina isn't even looking at her. She's staring at me. "Your audacity knows no bounds, does it? My daughter may choose to be friendly with you, but this is my cabin, and you're not welcome here. Leave."

As if she could still give me orders! For Irene's sake, I think fast. "All the notables are up on deck. I'm sure I saw Lady Duff Gordon. The Countess of Rothes, too. They're laughing and telling jokes. This will be the talk of the voyage if—when the ship reaches New York. You don't want to be left out."

That sparks her interest. An avaricious gleam lights Lady Regina's eyes, and I think I've saved the worthless members of the Lisle family, not that they'll ever thank me.

But at that moment, Irene turns to Ned, smiling in relief. The emotion of the moment makes her expression a little too open, her movements a little too free. And Ned brightens to think that she will be safe. Surely they've exchanged such glances before, even while the other Lisles were in the room, but not right in front of Lady Regina's face. Ned realizes the mistake even as I do—even as Lady Regina's face crumples into a horror too deep for rage.

She's figured it out.

"You." Her voice shakes as she rises to her feet, staring straight at Ned. "You ruined my daughter. You've taken advantage of her."

Neither Ned nor Irene can speak. If any of us could come up with some kind of denial or alternate story right this moment, maybe we could convince her, but the moment passes. It's already too late. She knows what she's seen. Lady Regina might not be pleasant, but she's not stupid either.

"Mother, please," Irene begins, but Lady Regina lifts a hand to silence her. She looks less outraged than hurt, and in the narrow, foolish world of the nobility, it makes sense. Irene's virginity was a material possession of the family, one she threw away on her brother's valet.

"A servant? My servant?" Layton's bruised face contorts in a grimace. "My word, Irene, you might at least have had better taste. Ned, get out. Send your uniform back by ship's steward."

"You can't send him away!" Irene cries, the words torn from her. Lady Regina slaps her face, the sound ugly in the small room.

And then Ned slaps Lady Regina.

As she stares at him, he says, "I don't like to strike a lady, but if you ever—if you ever lay one hand on Miss Irene again, I won't be responsible for my actions." Despite the fat tears rolling down Irene's cheeks, I can see what it's meant to her, to have someone, just once, back her up.

On one hand I want to cheer for Ned; on the other, we have bigger problems. "You have to set this aside," I say. "We have to get to the lifeboats."

But none of them can hear me any longer. Layton's on his feet, shouting at Ned for hitting Lady Regina. Lady Regina is screaming at Irene for sleeping with a violent, untrustworthy man. Ned's telling them what he thinks of them, and he's got a lot to tell. Irene's crying and pleading on Ned's behalf. Mrs. Horne stands like a statue in the corner, useless.

This ship is sinking. There aren't enough lifeboats. I have

to get them up top again—Irene and Ned, if nobody else. What can I do?

It comes to me quick as anything. I dash into Lady Regina's room, where the crib is kept. I lean over and lift Beatrice out, struggling to balance the heavy, drowsy child against my hip. The dizziness from my injuries sweeps over me again, and my stomach clenches hard. If the situation were any less dire, I'd want to find a doctor around now.

When I walk back into the next room—and the argument, which has only become louder—I shout, "I'm taking Bea to the lifeboats. You have to come too."

While Ned and Irene look in my direction, Lady Regina simply snaps, "I'll have you arrested for kidnapping."

Let her try. I shout, "Ned, Irene, please, come with me!" I want this to end. I have to find Alec. And yet I still can't abandon them—these people I planned to leave for so long.

Irene still doesn't move. "I can't leave Mother and Layton. Ned, you should—go with Tess."

"I'm not leaving you," he says quietly. Their eyes meet, and the love between them is so obvious that I can't believe I never saw it before.

Irene's kindness has always been her greatest virtue, but now it's like a stone roped around her neck, weighing her down in rough waters. She is too good to leave her worthless mother and brother, even though it means risking her life. And Ned loves her too much to save himself without her.

Layton snaps, "Charming. I suppose you'll claim that taking

a young girl's virtue was a chivalrous act too, instead of something you ought to be hanged for." And the argument begins anew.

My bluff has been called. Frustration brings me close to tears, not least because taking responsibility for Beatrice means it will take me even longer to reach Alec. I want Alec to live even more than I want it for myself, and believe me, I'm in no hurry to die.

But putting Beatrice back means condemning the child to death. I can't do it.

"I'll put her on the next lifeboat," I shout to them all. "You'd best be right behind me."

Nobody pays any attention—not even Ned and Irene. They're trapped fighting their own battle now, when they need to be fighting for their lives.

Hoisting little Beatrice on my hip, I storm out through the sitting room. Lady Regina calls, "Get her back here!"

I just keep going; if Lady Regina only follows to chase me down as a kidnapper, at least it will get her, and by extension Irene, closer to the lifeboats. But nobody stops me.

God, the stairs—how many flights have I climbed tonight? And my head still pounds from where Mikhail hit me. Panting, I say, "Bea, wouldn't you like to walk?"

"No," she murmurs sleepily against my shoulder. Forget it; she'd only slow us down.

A few people pass me on the stairwell, all going back up to the main boat deck, all of them moving faster than me. Nobody's laughing now. It must be more than an hour and a half since I heard the iceberg strike the ship; the water must have risen far enough to convince more doubters.

Sure enough, when I return to the boat deck, the scene has changed. Laughter has turned to fear. The band's still playing (something romantic, almost sweet—maybe "I Wonder Who's Kissing Her Now"), but it's not calming anyone down any longer. Fewer people linger in the lounges, and these all seem to be men; the deck is packed, and women are shouting and crying. I realize that not all of my dizziness is entirely a matter of the blow I took to the head; the deck really has tilted underfoot. The front of the ship is lower than the back.

There's no longer any mistaking that the ship is sinking. I grip Beatrice tighter, prepared to fight my way through the horde—but as soon as I reach the deck, people begin to part and let me pass.

"There's a woman with a child!" someone shouts. "Bring them forward." Hands at my back push me closer to a lifeboat, and I'm stunned to realize that all these people are willing to delay their own chance so Beatrice will get aboard.

As I reach the side, just at the bow of the lifeboat, I get a look over the edge and feel dizzy. The surface of the water is much closer than it used to be, but it's still terrifyingly far. And the lifeboat is so small, packed with perhaps as many as fifty women and children.

The officer holds a hand out. "Come on, love, we'll get you and the little girl aboard. More room in these things than it looks." He might be offering me a sandwich at a picnic, save for the tension in his body.

"I can't—I've got to find Alec." And Irene. And Ned. And Myriam. And the old Norwegian ladies. I can't leave not knowing how they are. Yet I've got to save Bea. I look at the woman in the lifeboat who is nearest me, a dowager who looks grander and snobbier than Lady Regina does in her fanciest dreams. Any port in a storm: I foist Beatrice on her. "Please, please, take the little girl? Keep her safe?"

The woman looks at me, and it's as though the world goes silent. When her eyes meet mine, there's no such thing as her being rich or me being poor. It couldn't matter less that we've not even met. She knows I'm giving her a sacred responsibility, and she accepts it. I feel a shudder down in my soul as I realize that this woman would die before she'd let anything happen to Beatrice.

"I promise," she says, in a cultured American accent. "I'll look after her as though she were my own."

I run a hand over Beatrice's hair; the little girl's eyes have begun to well with tears. She knows something's wrong, just not what. "God bless you, ma'am."

"And you," the woman says, just as the officer gives the cry. The lifeboat begins to drop, and for a moment I feel like an idiot not being in it with them. But I know what I have to do.

I shove through the crowd back toward the doors. My balance shifts beneath me, and I stumble—or was that the ship? People cry out, and the mood around us grows yet more desperate. Woozily, I clutch a pole, feeling my exhaustion and my aching head anew. I wish I had more of my strength for this. I wish so many things were different. But I've got to keep going. If I stop now, it's the death of me.

A voice calls above the din, "Tess!"

No matter how badly I'm hurting, no matter how great the clamor around us, there's no way I could ever fail to recognize that voice. *"Alec!"*

I peer through the crowd and see him—chestnut curls mussed, a gray overcoat beneath his life jacket, as he pushes his way toward me. Summoning what feels like the last of my strength, I run to him, knocking into people, stumbling over my own numb feet, until I fall into his arms.

Alec crushes me to his chest, and for one perfect second, I feel the comforting illusion of safety sweep over me.

But only for a second.

"There aren't enough lifeboats," I whisper into his ear.

"I know." Alec just keeps holding me, pressing his lips to my forehead and my cheek. "I've been trying to find you. To save you."

"I've been trying to save you."

But as I look past him and realize there are no more lifeboats close by, I wonder if we've found each other too late.

# ⚔ CHAPTER 27 ⚔

"WHAT ARE WE GOING TO DO?" I CLING TO ALEC, SO tightly it must hurt him. "That can't be all the lifeboats. Surely." The decks are packed with people now—hundreds of us. Layton said there weren't enough boats for everyone, but they wouldn't even let a ship go to sea if they couldn't save more people than this. Would they?

"We won't find them waiting here," he says. Alec pulls me closer and kisses my forehead. As his fingers brush my bruised temple, I wince. "Tess, you're bleeding. What happened?"

"Mikhail came after me. He abandoned me once the ship hit the iceberg."

"To come after me," Alec says darkly. I realize that the corner of his left eye is puffy and shadowed; he'll have a shiner tomorrow. "Really, to come after the Initiation Blade. He came in—wild, worse than wild. I only got away from him because he was more interested in ransacking our cabin for the Blade." He holds open the heavy gray coat he's wearing over rumpled trousers and shirt to reveal the Blade's hilt glinting within an inner pocket. Mikhail will be looking for quite a while.

I take some satisfaction from the fact that Mikhail's cruelty and greed will doom him to death, but there's not much time for anything but the one most important fact I know: "We have to get off this ship."

"Let's keep moving along. It can only help our chances."

I know from the way Alec says it that he, too, knows not everyone on board will have a chance to live. Unless— "Is help coming? They would have called for help on the wireless."

"I don't know. We won't know unless we see the other ship actually coming to rescue us."

Both of us look toward the dark horizon, but there's nothing out there. Only a gleaming field of stars overhead and spars of ice in the water below.

Despair wells up within me, as cold and merciless as the water rushing into the *Titanic*. The countless hours I worked so hard, went without good food or decent shoes so that I could save money for a new life in America—they all seem to taunt me now. Only Alec's embrace is warm, real, here. I kept thinking he was a diversion from my goals, that what I've felt for him could stop me from getting what I wanted. That there was no way a man like him would ever belong to a servant girl like me. Too late I realize that he was the only thing I ever wanted that I could truly have.

I hug him even closer to me, as close as I can with the life jackets around our necks. It's as though the terrible danger surrounding us goes black—it doesn't go away, it's all around us, but it's hidden the same way nighttime hides the shapes that are so clear by day. Right now there's nothing but Alec's warmth and his love. I want to believe that nothing matters as long as we're together.

But that's not true. That's shock talking—making me numb, dragging us down with the ship. Even now I can feel the tilt of the deck increasing; the *Titanic* dips even lower in the front than in the back. Is the prow below water now? I can't see. Around us, people are beginning to shout and cry as they realize what I've known almost from the moment the cold water touched my hand. The ship is doomed.

Alec and I have only minutes to save our lives.

Alec begins pulling me toward the stern of the ship—slightly up the slope. "Not all the boats are gone yet," he says. "We can get you in one if we hurry."

"Not without you!"

"Tess—it's women and children first."

"But after—" My throat closes around the words. There will be no "after" the women and children are loaded aboard the lifeboats. Not enough room.

Alec's going to die.

Then a familiar face appears amid the throng: George, harried but still kind as he moves through the crowds, urging them to stay calm. His expression changes as he sees me, somehow becoming yet more desperate. "Tess! Why on earth are you still aboard? They told me Myriam was aboard one of the first lifeboats off; why weren't you with her?"

"I was trying to get the Lisles to the boat deck. Have you seen them?" George shakes his head. Please, please, let Irene have gotten out at least. At least Myriam is safe. "And Alec—here, Alec, this is Myriam's George. George, this is Alec. Is there no lifeboat for him?"

Alec looks both exasperated and fond. "I told her what 'women and children first' means, but she won't listen."

George hesitates only for the space of a breath. "There are a few extra lifeboats."

My heart leaps with unexpected hope. "You mean—"

Stepping closer to us both, George whispers, "They're collapsibles—emergency use only, so they ought to be launching them any moment. Can't announce it—we'd cause a stampede, and besides, who the hell can hear over this din any longer—forgive my language, Tess. Both of you, get over there." He points the way we should go, toward the collapsible lifeboats.

I give Alec a look that means he had better not choose this moment to get noble and self-sacrificing. Although I can see that he's reluctant to take this chance not everyone will have, he, too, wants to live. He turns to George. "Are you coming with us? To make a try for it?"

"No. It's my duty to remain aboard until the last—and I shall." George's voice remains steady and sure, even as he faces his death.

Fighting back tears, I stand on tiptoe to kiss George on the cheek. His answering smile is uneven. "Won't you tell Myriam— I'm sorry not to have had more time with her."

"Of course I will."

Alec and George shake hands, and though they only just met,

I see in the glance that passes between them that they might have been friends given the chance. But George is all out of chances.

Then Alec pulls me away toward the other side of the ship and our best shot at survival. Within moments, George is lost in the thickening crowd.

I can still hear the band playing—it's "The Blue Danube" now, I think—but the crowd has become larger and louder. Third-class passengers have finally found their way up en masse, but most of them don't speak English or still don't understand what to do. Most everyone has their life jackets on now. Although some people are still laughing, the sound of it has become shrill, and there's crying mixed in too. The chill of the night grows harsher with every minute; the brilliant, cloudless field of stars overhead almost seems to be mocking us in its perfection and serenity. As the slope of the deck deepens, people are increasingly likely to grab onto a railing or another person for support.

It haunts me, the people I see. The Strauses, sitting side by side in deck chairs and holding hands, apparently willing to die as long as they're together. A frightened little girl, sobbing for her mommy—in the moment before I can stop to help her, a kindly red-haired woman does so, promising to help the child find her mother, though by now she must realize how difficult this will be, if it is even possible. Boys no more than twelve or thirteen, trying to look brave as they stand by their fathers' sides, apparently already judged too much "men" to be boarded onto lifeboats as children.

Worse are the people I don't see: the elderly Norwegian ladies from my room. Ned. Irene.

We pass through the ship—running into the first-class lounge, where men in tuxedos continue playing cards, mostly out of bravado. The group in there has become a more motley crew: Women are now smoking cigars, and at least one uniformed waiter for the first-class dining room has donned a top hat he found from somewhere. People are behaving strangely—laughing in the face of death.

The sight of it shakes Alec too, but he doesn't slow down. "We have to get you to a lifeboat."

"We both have to get to the lifeboats," I correct him.

"I can't do it," Alec says, though he keeps leading me. "I can't get on a lifeboat when children are still here dying."

"Your life isn't worth less than anyone else's!" When Alec glances over his shoulder at me, his mournful eyes tell me he doesn't believe that's true. Will his guilt for the steward's death keep him from attempting to survive now? So I try again: "Alec, I need you with me. We're going to be in a tiny boat on the ocean in the cold, in the dead of night—God only knows when or if help is coming. Don't make me do it alone!"

Alec doesn't reply, but he grips my hand more tightly and pulls me in another direction. I hope it's a good sign.

We make our way past the magnificent grand staircase; one of the cast-iron cupids at the bottom is so tilted now that he seems to have taken flight. The angle of the ship makes running treacherous, but we keep going. As I glance back I see the first rivulets of water begin to trickle over the tile floor below.

Then I remember someone else I haven't seen. "Your father! We have to go after him."

"No. Dad's already chosen to go down with the ship. He said

he'd be ashamed to take a seat that could go to a lady." He hesitates, and I know he's fighting back a sob, though I can't think it unmanly to cry when facing the death of a beloved father. "Dad said I should go after you. We—we said our good-byes."

"Oh, Alec—we can't leave him—"

"Don't, Tess. I can't go through it again. He won't change his mind. You're the only one left for me to save."

My head whirls so that I nearly go into a faint, and I feel as though I might be sick. Is it just fear? Or is it Mikhail's attack? That seems as though it happened in another lifetime, not mere hours ago.

I simply tighten my fingers around Alec's. He's with me. We'll get aboard a lifeboat. Nothing after that will matter, because we'll be together.

We burst through the doors farther down the deck. It's far less crowded here, hardly anybody around but the crew. An officer stands near one of the lifeboat davits, and Alec calls to him, breath gray as fog in the cold air, "We need to get this girl into a lifeboat!"

"Both of us!" I shout, correcting him again.

It doesn't matter, because the officer shakes his head, and my heart plummets. "The last boat just launched! Hardly seconds ago!"

Oh, God. We run to the side of the ship, as if the man might have lied to us, but of course he told the truth: The last lifeboat within sight is being lowered down and is already a couple of dozen feet below us. The water is closer to the deck—too close now. We're trapped.

We're going to die.

Alec and I look at each other, stricken. Then I fling my arms around his neck. As he holds me close, I choke out the words, "I love you."

"I love you too."

"And I'm proud to stand by your side—no matter what comes." Tears blurring my vision, I look up at Alec's face. The tenderness of his expression melts my heart.

He frames my face with his hands as he says, "Tess. Only you could be brave enough to die with me. But I want you to live for me."

We kiss, as desperate as though we were drowning.

When our lips part, Alec says, "Forgive me."

Then he picks me up—inhuman strength lifting me from the deck as if I were half flying—and flings me over the railing of the ship, toward water, toward darkness, away from him forever.

# ⊰ CHAPTER 28 ⊱

IT FEELS LIKE I FALL FOREVER.

Time slows down, dragging out the horror of every fraction of a second that I tumble through the cold dark. What I see is a mixed-up kaleidoscope of images, each horrifying in its own way: the sleek white side of the ship banging into me as I thud against it on the way down, the small lifeboat as a light-colored teardrop against the dark ocean, Alec's face above me looking down. I want to reach out to him—I want to catch myself, climb back up, refuse to leave him—but there's no stopping the fall.

I land hard. Board and bone and oar slam into my back, and my already-whirling head strikes something that makes the world go dim. Cold water sloshes over the side, further soaking my dress, and the chill is so deep and so strong that my marrow aches.

"Watch it, you!" a woman cries as hands shove me roughly against the side of the lifeboat, my back against the canvas. "You like to have drowned us all."

"Stupid girl!"

"Lay off her, I'd have jumped too if it was me."

And other cries in languages I don't know. I try to tell them that I didn't jump, I was thrown, but the breath's been knocked out of me. As I try to focus, I see the lifeboat's mostly filled with women—third-class women like me, to judge from their humble shawls and tatty nightgowns. There are men too, though: a couple of sailors, and one wealthy-looking fellow with a handlebar mustache and a dull, dead look on his face.

But it all fades away too quickly.

When the lifeboat tips precariously to one side, I rouse myself—and only then realize that I blacked out for a moment. I've been repeatedly struck and doused with cold water, and while I kept myself going for so long, I can't go much longer. Nausea overwhelms me—the whacks to my head? Seasickness? I don't know. But I manage to push myself up on my arms to look around, and what I see makes me cry out in shock.

The *Titanic* is rising from the waters—the back end of it, I mean. Its lights are still burning despite everything, and so we can see the horror silhouetted against the starry sky. The gigantic propellers are surfacing as the prow of the ship dips down beneath the waves. Though we're farther from it than I would've thought—people onboard are rowing the lifeboat vigorously away from the ship—we're close enough that I think I can still see Alec, hanging on to the guardrail as the deck slopes out from beneath him.

"Go back!" I shout—or I try to shout. My voice is hardly a croak. "We have to go back for Alec."

"We've got to get clear, miss," one of the sailors replies. He never stops rowing. "When she goes under, the suction will drag down anything close to her. We'd be pulled down sure as anything."

I'm shivering so hard that my teeth chatter, and groggily I realize that there are a few inches of near-freezing water in the lifeboat. I'm getting more soaked by the second, and colder, but that doesn't seem as important as the fact that the lifeboat is apparently sinking too.

Someone else sees it and cries, "We're taking on water fast!"

"This is a collapsible," the sailor replies, like that ought to answer everything. Maybe it does. Maybe the lifeboat will eventually collapse and we'll be dunked into the water to freeze to death, or drown, whichever comes first.

There's a place just past terror where it turns into calm. I can do nothing to save myself, nothing to save Alec or the others. And least of all can I turn from the terrible sight before my eyes.

The *Titanic* tilts farther forward, its nose sinking forever beneath the water as the ship rises to stand almost on end. And there's this tremendous, unearthly sound—the crash of everything and everyone on board sliding forward at once. I imagine the grand first-class lounge with its carved wooden chairs and its crystal chandeliers, all of them falling from place and smashing into so many splinters and shards. My cabin with its humble bunk beds and my bag with all the few possessions I had in the world. That damned lockbox the Lisles made me carry. All of it is crashing down.

"My God," whispers someone in the lifeboat. None of the rest of us can speak.

The ship's lights flicker, shining on the still ocean for one moment more. I can see portholes of light underwater. Then they go out. The darkness around us is almost complete.

Then comes the most terrifying roar I've ever heard or will

ever hear. It's metal tearing apart. It's an earthquake. It's nothing that seems to belong to this world. Vibration ripples through the water, through my body, as the dark silhouette of the *Titanic* against the stars suddenly changes direction. The back of the ship crashes down, propellers slicing back down into the water, as the front vanishes forever. For a moment it seems as though the rear of the *Titanic* can float on its own, but within seconds it, too, is going down.

"Did it break in two?" I whisper. "How could it?"

"That's impossible," snaps the man with the handlebar mustache. "White Star vessels do not break in two."

Whatever argument we might've had about it is silenced that moment, because that's when we hear the screaming.

One person screaming is a horrible noise, but this is hundreds of people. Maybe a thousand people, all of them screaming at once, screaming for their lives, though there is no way to save them. We're already more than a quarter of a mile off, but the screaming is so loud that it surrounds us. The women on the boat cover their ears, grimace, and cry. Yet the sailors never stop rowing farther away.

"Stop." My voice is no more than a whisper now. I hardly have the strength to speak. "Please stop." There's no stopping. No saving them. No hiding from what's happening.

They're all dying. If they didn't get out at the last moment, if they never boarded lifeboats—Mrs. Horne. Lady Regina. George. Ned. Layton. Irene.

Alec.

There's a strange sound beneath the screaming, like the tide coming in. I think it must be the last of the ship sinking underwater.

But I can't tell anymore. I can't see. I can't even sit up. It's as if I am dying too.

Everything after that is strange and distant. I hear someone say, "She's in shock," and something stiff is wrapped around me—sailcloth, perhaps, the closest thing to a blanket onboard. As I'm lying in a few inches of cold water, this does little to warm me.

The screaming stops after forever, and yet too quickly.

The only sound is women sobbing and the lifeboat oars slapping into and out of the water in a steady rhythm, over and over.

My head hurts. I look up at the stars and imagine Alec's face among the constellations. Or is that a dream? I can't tell dreams from reality any longer.

"She won't last the night," someone says. "No telling how many will freeze to death before help comes."

"How long will that be?"

"No one knows."

The words don't seem to have anything to do with me. I don't feel cold any longer. I'm not shivering. The sensation that fills and numbs me is a sort of second cousin to heat—not warm and yet equally as comforting.

I think, *This must be death.*

*Live for me*, Alec said. So I can't die, not yet. I remember how much he wanted to see the sun rise again, and so I make a deal with myself. I will hold on until daylight. I will watch the sunrise for him. Then I can let go, and we'll be together again.

There's more darkness, more crying. Some surprise in the night as new people are discovered in the lifeboat—Chinamen who have

302

been hiding under the seats. The sailors say they're stowaways, but I recognize one of them from down below. His eyes meet mine briefly, and with a clarity that seems to be part of dying, I understand immediately what happened: They realized the ship was sinking, suspected nobody would let a Chinaman onboard a lifeboat, and hid to save their own lives. I think they did right. I wish Alec had done the same.

The others are angry. Then they're quiet. Still the rowing. My head feels too heavy for my body. Pain sometimes shoots through me, but as a pale, distant echo of itself. It hardly matters.

Finally, some endless time later, I see the horizon turning faintly pink. Dawn has come. It can end now.

But even as I lift my head for the sunrise, I hear someone shout, "A ship! It's a ship! We're saved!"

I feel nothing. It doesn't seem real, not even when we row up next to it, not even when they begin lifting us out in slings, one by one. I can't hold on to the sling, so they tie me in. Then it's like I'm floating, banging up along the side of a ship, like my fall from *Titanic* in reverse. I wonder if I will find Alec again on the deck waiting for me. Maybe none of it was true; maybe I've been trapped in some kind of nightmare.

Instead I fall onto a wood plank deck, and worried faces crowd around. One of them is Myriam's. When she takes my hand, I know it's all been real—all of it—and the horror is even more powerful than the fact that I've survived.

## ≈ CHAPTER 29 ≈

AS OUR RESCUE SHIP, THE *CARPATHIA*, ARRIVES IN New York harbor on the night of April 18, we are greeted by such throngs of people as I've never seen or imagined in my life. Rain pours from the skies in a deluge, but that is not enough to deter the thousands of curiosity seekers who have come to see the survivors of the sinking of the *Titanic*. The ones with the cameras are no doubt reporters. One of those even jumps into the water, trying to get hauled onboard and thus nab the exclusive story.

Myriam and I watch the bedlam from our vantage point, a porthole a couple of decks below. We're in a nice cabin, one turned over to us by kindly *Carpathia* passengers. Though the doctors weren't very optimistic about me when they hauled me up from the lifeboat, Myriam bundled me in blankets and made me drink mug after mug of hot soup until I finally asked her if she was trying to feed me to death. At that point Myriam proudly told the doctors that if I was strong enough to be rude, I was strong enough to live. While I still feel wretched, I can walk around a bit now, so I guess she was right.

"Let's go," I say to her. "We can press through the crush if we have to. I don't want to be on a ship again as long as I live."

"Soon. The first- and second-class passengers have to leave before we can."

"Of course."

We watch our fellow survivors walk out silhouetted by flash-bulbs, many of them in the fur coats that represent the only things they saved from the *Titanic*. Mostly they're women, but more first-class men than you'd think got away. A few of them even got their dogs on lifeboats; one lady struts out with her pet Pekingese in her arms. There's a young girl, my age, who helped Myriam with me on deck and who turns out to be the newly made widow of John Jacob Astor. There's Margaret Brown, the tough-talking American woman who apparently had to save her lifeboat from the ineptitude of the sailor who was supposed to run it. And there's Beatrice Lisle in the arms of the kind woman I handed her to on the night of the sinking. We were able to talk this morning; she sent a Marconigram to Viscount Lisle, who will come to Boston to collect his lone sur-viving child as soon as he can. I watch little Bea vanish into the crowd, the last link to everything in my life that came before.

*At least I saved her*, I think. *At least I did that.*

But that's only one life, one rescue. Yesterday as I tossed and turned in my borrowed bunk, passing between hallucination and dream, it seemed to me as if I had to watch all the others die.

I saw Mrs. Horne cowering in a corner of the Lisles' cabin, refusing to face the water even as it rose to cover the elegant carpets and the furniture, to swallow her whole.

I saw Lady Regina and Layton in one of the corridors, staring at the onrushing tide almost in outrage that the water could dare to interrupt their journey.

I saw Howard Marlowe smoking a final cigar on his private promenade deck, taking what comfort he could in the memories of the wife he'd lost and his pride in the son he believed he'd saved.

I saw George on the bridge with the captain, shouting orders to the last, hoping that by doing his duty he might save a few others.

Worst of all, I saw Irene and Ned already beneath the waves and beyond any hope, her dress and hair flowing out around her as the two of them reached toward each other. As the water closed deeper and deeper over Irene and Ned, they floated into a kind of embrace, the last one they could ever share.

This morning I walked the length of the deck, leaning feebly on the doctor's arm. He said it would do me good to walk. But what I was really doing was looking for them—all the ones I lost, the ones whose deaths I had dreamed. I wanted the visions to be only dreams.

But none of them were there. They're all gone, forever.

I never saw Alec, either in my dreaming or on the *Carpathia*. I can't bear to think about what happened to him. Perhaps my mind spared me that vision because the sight of his death would kill me. And as awful as I feel—as close as I came to the end—my heart stubbornly keeps beating.

*Live for me*, Alec said, and it appears I must.

They gave me a new dress, a gray frock donated by some

*Carpathia* passenger with better manners than taste in clothes, and tossed out the red one ruined the night of the sinking. Before they did, though, I collected the two things I needed from my pocket. The first is the two ten-pound notes Irene gave me, crumpled and still damp; it doesn't seem like money now, more like a farewell present. The second is even more precious. I take it into my palm now: the silver locket Alec gave me at the end of the one night we had together. He said it would protect me; maybe it did.

The face of Alec's mother looks up at me. Her husband and son are with her now. Should I take comfort in that? I can't.

Myriam makes a small sound in the back of her throat, and I focus again on the gangplank to see some of the *Titanic*'s surviving officers departing. They all stayed aboard until the last, just as George did, and went down with the ship. But some of them were able to climb atop an overturned lifeboat and save themselves. George wasn't among them. She must be tormented by the idea of him thrashing in that frigid water, trying to save himself and coming so close, but failing just the same.

I know better than to say kind words she'd see as pity. Instead I put my arms around her and rest my head against her back. Myriam rubs my hands and says only, "Still cold."

"Yes." It seems like I'll never really be warm again.

Once all the first- and second-class passengers are gone, those of us from third class are allowed to leave. The reporters left already; poor people's versions of events are apparently not newsworthy. But a few family members are there waiting for their loved ones. Myriam helps guide me down the gangplank, supporting me against her shoulder, until she walks into the embrace of her cousins. I stand back, awkward and unknown, thousands of miles from anyone besides Myriam who cares about me or even knows my name.

I glance over my shoulder at the *Carpathia*. From one of the porthole windows, I can see the Chinese men from my lifeboat peering out. America has a Chinese Exclusion Act, it seems—alone among the survivors, they aren't allowed to come ashore. They are even more unwanted than I am. It's no comfort.

### April 25, 1912

I sit by the window of the Nahas family's tenement apartment, looking down at Orchard Street. Once upon a time, I suppose there was an orchard here, impossible as that is to believe now. New York City is larger and brasher than I ever imagined, and if there is a louder part of it than the street below us, I never want to hear it. Hundreds of people mill through every moment: Children, dogs, workmen, young mothers, peddlers, pushcarts, and once, I swear, a monkey on someone's shoulder.

"How are you so quick?" Myriam says. She winces as her needle pricks her skin again, and sucks her thumb once to clear the sting. "You're almost done already."

My piecework for the pink dresses her cousin's garment business makes is folded next to me, save for the final bit in my hands. "I sewed part of almost every day for the past two years. Practice makes fast fingers."

"You could get a job in a proper shop, sewing like that."

"I will soon," I promise. "But I wanted to help out here a bit first. To repay you all for taking me in."

Myriam huffs. "You know you may stay as long as you like. I meant only that you are quite skilled with a needle and thread." She scowls at the crumpled sewing in her lap. "And I am not."

I laugh—it's not much, but the best I've managed since the night of the sinking.

As much as I've come to like the Nahas family, and as good as they've been to let me recover my strength here, I know I can't intrude on them much longer. This four-room apartment is a kitchen, a dining and work room, the room with the sewing machine, and a single bedroom. Seven people live here, including me, and when the two children go out to play in the streets in the morning, they are instantly replaced by two other seamstresses who work for the family business. The dress dummy is only a few feet from the sink. There's a water closet, which is nice, but it's three floors downstairs, and we share it with apparently half the population of the city. As soon as I had my strength back, I went to work sewing for their business to earn my board and repay them for their generosity, but I'm a burden already and would soon be a nuisance.

"I can't decide where to go," I say.

Myriam pulls her needle through, not looking up at me. "In such a hurry. You don't like it here?"

"You know that's not true."

"I know." We are better friends than two weeks' acquaintance should make us, but together we lived through an experience nobody else could ever imagine. And we share our wordless grief for the men we loved too briefly. It won't be easy to leave Myriam, and her brusque words mean only that she won't find it easy to watch me go.

"We have options now," I point out. This means what it always really means: We have money.

The entire world seems to be horrorstruck at the fate of the *Titanic*; every newspaper headline has screamed about the ship's sinking since we arrived in New York. Apparently the thing to do in polite society is to form a relief committee, because already there are dozens. Two ladies in fancy hats and coats arrived last night, as shocked by the scene on Orchard Street as I was at first, and proudly presented us with gifts of money. It's no fortune, but combined with Irene's ten-pound notes, it's more than enough to start over with. Some I'll give to the Nahas family to thank them for taking me in, but what will I do with the rest?

Myriam says, "You could set up some sort of a shop."

"Perhaps." But what would I sell? I think again of poor Irene, and how badly she wanted a new life of her own. "Maybe we should go out West and become cowboys."

"I don't care for horses."

Below us, a newsboy appears with the afternoon edition, and I set aside my last bit of sewing. I don't want to hear anything else about the *Titanic*—not about the hearings or the fact that Bruce Ismay, the head of the White Star Line, saved himself while others died, not about any of it. Just as my hands settle on the windowsill to close it and shut out the din, though, I hear, "Bodies from the *Titanic* found!"

I freeze. Beside me, Myriam takes a deep breath, as if steadying herself.

"Extra, extra!" The newsboy's high voice pipes over the crowd. "The ship *Mackay-Bennett* recovers dozens of bodies from the sinking of the *Titanic*! John Jacob Astor said to be among them! First-class passengers being taken to Nova Scotia for identification of the remains! Others buried at sea!"

Myriam and I look at each other, stricken. "Alec," I say. "And George."

"Not George," she says, though I can tell it costs her. "First-class passengers, they said. If they found George, they—they put him back in the water."

How horrible, to think of George being drawn out of the cold Atlantic only to be sunk into it again. It would be better if they never found him at all.

"How would they even know who was first class and who wasn't?" I ask, but I answer myself just as quickly. "The clothes, of course." Even in death, it matters whether your dress had been trimmed with lace, or whether your shoes were polished oxfords instead of worn brogues. It's the difference between a grave your loved ones can visit and being dropped into the water in a sack with stones at your feet.

But Alec was in first class, and the good coat he wore would have told them that.

Dozens of bodies, the newsboy said. They report now that fifteen hundred people died that night. That means there's no guarantee Alec's body was among them.

But there's no one else left to identify him—to see that he's buried as he ought to be.

When I look over at Myriam again, she says what seems like the last line of a conversation, not the first: "Yes, of course you must go."

I embrace her tightly. If this is the last thing I can do for Alec, then I mean to do it.

*May 2, 1912*

Halifax is a town on the coastline of Nova Scotia, and as I step off the train a few days later in my new clothes and warm coat, I think I might as well start over here as anywhere else. Smaller than New York, but larger than the village I was born in, and there's a softness to the late afternoon sky that I like. Like someone poured cream into the blue.

But Halifax is on a harbor, and I don't know if I want to see the ocean every day of my life. I'm not sure I ever want to see it again.

My hand slips into my pocket, where I feel the cool links of silver against my palm. If I find Alec here, before he's buried, I intend to put the locket around his neck. It's a way of symbolizing that he's with his mother again—and silver can't hurt him any longer.

I expect it will be difficult to find the place I seek, but as soon as I tell the man at the train station that I want to identify a body from the *Titanic*, everyone's at my service. A driver with a horse and cart is only too happy to take me to a hotel so I can go view the dead first thing in the morning.

"I can't wait until morning," I say. Putting this off any longer would be torture. The recovery ship arrived two days ago, but I wasn't able to get up here any faster. Thinking of Alec lying here, unknown and alone, has tormented me all that time. "I have to look for him now."

They pity me so much that this works.

I am taken to the makeshift morgue—in a curling rink, of all places, though I see the need to keep dead bodies near ice. The caretaker meant to lock up for the night but lets me in immediately. "We'll all wait outside," he says. "Give you your privacy. If you find the fellow you're looking for—"

"I'll come get you."

Then I will have to bury Alec. As horrible as that sounds, I must hope for it, because the alternative is that he is still sinking down into the Atlantic, never to be found again. It will rip my heart out to see him dead, but I want to see him. Even like this.

But when I walk into the rink, my resolve falters. The sight is more horrible than I ever imagined. Dozens of dead bodies, shrouded in white sheets, all of them laid out on ice. The few lights left on in the rink seem to shine blue upon the ice, as if the bodies were still floating on water. My shadow is long and watery.

Stupid, to be afraid of dead bodies. I force myself to step forward. My shoes slip against the ice, and I have to be careful of my balance.

The dead lie in long rows. I realize I will have to pull back the cloth and look on the face of each one, except for those few too short, fat or obviously female to be Alec. I will have to confront each of the dead and remember them screaming their last in the water.

If that's the price of finding Alec, I'll pay it.

I screw up my courage and pull back the first cloth. Too young, a boy of hardly sixteen. He had freckles.

This one is too old, too dark. He died with his evening suit on. I remember how some of them played cards and drank brandy in the lounge until the end.

This one turns out to be a thin woman—and I gasp as I realize who it is. One of the elderly Norwegian ladies from my cabin lies there, hands curled up by her chest as if she were still trying to huddle under her red-and-white blanket.

I sink to my knees by her side. Tears well in my eyes as I stroke her snowy hair, but I don't begin to sob until I realize why she's here—why the salvage crew mistook her for a first-class passenger. In her ears are the beautiful pearl earrings she so prized, the ones she lent to me in an act of unselfish kindness. She must have put them on as she left her cabin, finally, too late, convinced of the danger, hoping to save the one heirloom possession she valued most. She did.

I cry until I feel like it's impossible for me to cry any more. One of my hands closes over hers, the only good-bye I can give her. I never even knew whether she was Inga or Ilsa. Then I gently cover her with the cloth, wishing it could keep her warm.

Stiffly I rise and walk to the next body. Then the next. And the next. I think I am almost numb to the horror of it, that I can bear anything, until I pull back one more cloth and see who lies there.

Mikhail.

He lies there as perfect as a statue; his slicked-back dark hair and Vandyke beard aren't even mussed. The man might as easily be sleeping. Mikhail looks like he had a peaceful death, and his body is here for his loved ones to bury, assuming he loved anyone. There's no saying which emotion is stronger: my outrage at the fact that his worthless body was recovered when so many others weren't, or my relief that at least he's dead.

But I tell myself that's no way to think. Being glad Mikhail died on the *Titanic* means being glad the *Titanic* went down.

I can't grieve for Mikhail, but I can cover him up decently, I suppose. So I lift the cover again to pull it over his head—

—and his icy-cold hand clamps around my wrist.

I gasp. Mikhail's eyes snap open, as focused and malevolent as ever.

He's alive.

# ⊰ CHAPTER 30 ⊱

THIS CAN'T BE HAPPENING. AND YET IT IS. AS I GAPE down at Mikhail, his hand tightens around my wrist, and a shadow of his old mocking grin appears on his face.

I scramble away from him; his fingers lose their grip. But I stumble against another body and it paralyzes me for an instant. Mikhail pushes himself into a sitting position, then manages to stand. He's still weak, but he's definitely alive.

He *can't* be.

"This is a bad dream," I whisper. "Only a nightmare."

Mikhail rasps, "I told you we were gods." His voice sounds like that of a dead thing.

I look wildly around the shadowy blue rink, as if this will make the driver and attendant magically appear by my side. Our only witnesses are the dead.

"Last night—must have been—the full moon," he says. "In times of great danger—great cold—the initiated go into a place beyond the laws mere mortals are prey to. Then the moon awakens us. Restores us to life." Mikhail grins. "Do you see now how magnificent we are?"

I can't speak. I can't think. A dead man is talking to me.

"Night is falling. I can feel it." Mikhail's eyes close for a moment in satisfaction. "Soon my strength will return. Then I can change. I can be restored." His eyes open, and he focuses again on me. "I can eat."

I run for the door. Mikhail's on my heels, our footsteps echoing in the space. "Help me!" I cry out, but apparently the men waiting outside can't hear. There's only my voice echoing, *Help, help, help, help*, throughout the icy morgue.

He's not as fast as he was before—still weakened from enduring the sinking and his long, mysterious sleep—and I think for a moment I'll make it out. Then I feel Mikhail's hand grasp the sleeve of my coat and spin me around.

I stagger back and manage to twist out of his grasp once more. As he snarls in frustration, I realize that we're more or less evenly matched now. I stand a chance. If he wants a fight, he can by God have one.

My fingers curl into a fist—thumb on the outside so you don't break it, Ned told me once as a joke—and I smash that fist into the side of Mikhail's face. It hurts my hand, but it hurts Mikhail too; he shouts in real pain, and that feels so good the aching in my fingers means nothing.

I kick him in the shins. Again. Then I aim my kick higher, and Mikhail doubles over in pain.

"That's for Irene," I pant, "and how you tried to trick her family.

And that"—I shove him back hard, so that he hits the wall—"that's for Ned." Another kick, and another. "And that's for Mr. Marlowe, who only wanted you to leave his son alone. And that's for Alec—oh, God damn you for what you did to Alec—"

Mikhail's hand shoots out and grabs my ankle as I kick; the yank forward is so sharp that it sends me tumbling to the floor, and something in my knee cracks. Pain shoots up through my leg, down to my toes, and tears spring to my eyes.

"You have had your turn," he rasps, looming over me. "Now I shall have mine. Blow by blow. Pain for pain."

Evenly matched meant he still had an even chance, and right now it looks like that is turning against me. I fumble for my pocket, hoping to pull out the silver chain and locket to burn him again, but my coat's in the way.

Mikhail reaches down as though he's going to grab me by the hair—

—and another hand grabs him, stopping him in place.

"It's my turn," Alec says.

"Alec!" I cry out. Of course, of course—the Brotherhood initiated him. That means the same magic that protected Mikhail protected him too. When the salvage crew found their bodies and brought them onboard, they waited here, in a sleep just like death, until the full moon awakened them.

My Alec is alive.

"Tess," he says, but he never looks away from Mikhail. They face each other, equally disheveled, equally pale. Anyone would believe they truly had been brought back from the dead.

Mikhail says, "We saved you."

Alec answers, "You wanted to enslave me. You failed."

It's impossible to say which of them attacks the other first. They match each other punch for punch, shove for shove, and I can see the battle of the red and black wolves about to begin. Perhaps they're still too weak to change, but not for long.

In a flash, something shifts, and Mikhail seems to have the upper hand as he forces Alec back against a long, low metal table—perhaps a place where the bodies were examined. But I have my hand on the locket now, and I slap it against Mikhail's other cheek so he'll have matching scars. As he howls from the burn, Alec and I both push him back. It's two against one now. I prefer these odds.

Then Mikhail's head snaps up, and his eyes gleam gold like the wolf's as he stares at Alec. "You are initiated," he says. "You belong to the Brotherhood."

Alec stops. He becomes as still as if he were carved of stone. His eyes seem to dim and die as that mysterious darkness fills the rink. Only the ice seems to hold any remnant of its former light, an eerie blue that outlines the bodies too sharply.

Oh, no. The Brotherhood's mind control. The silver didn't protect him during the initiation.

"You are ours," Mikhail whispers, in the obvious thrill of triumph. He straightens, once again the gentleman in his dinner suit despite the burn scars on his cheeks. "You will do as I command."

Alec's hands go slack, unfolding from fists to hang at his sides.

Mikhail looks at me, and it's hard to say what he enjoys more: bending Alec to his will or making me witness it.

319

Then he says, "Kill the girl."

I can't run—my back is to the wall, and they're between me and the door. Alec turns to me, with his flat predator's gaze; the only thing more horrible than knowing I'm going to die is knowing that it will be at his hand.

Or can I kill Alec instead? He's not at his full strength. I have a chance. But that murder would haunt me forever.

I lift my hands, balling them into uncertain fists. Alec's mother's locket still dangles from my fingers. In case these will be the last words I say to him—perhaps the last words I will ever say, I whisper, "Alec, I love you."

Alec blinks. His eyes refocus. It is no longer a monster looking at me—it's Alec, my Alec.

He turns back to Mikhail and pulls something from the inner pocket of his water-stained coat: The Initiation Blade, just where he left it. At first, Mikhail can only look at the dagger with pure greed so overpowering that he doesn't even suspect what's coming when Alec lunges forward. The Blade punches between Mikhail's ribs, and Mikhail gasps, mouth wide in shock and pain, as blood begins to drip onto the floor.

I watch in horrified fascination as Mikhail pulls himself free of the Blade, which gleams wetly with his blood; between streaks of red, I can see the gleaming gold. Alec looks as if he can hardly believe he stabbed a man, but his grip on the hilt remains sure.

"Only—a wound," Mikhail gasps. "You will need more than that to kill me."

Alec swallows hard. "I know. I'll need silver."

With that he takes the Blade and swipes it, hard, against the sharp metal edge of the nearby table. Gold flakes away in ribbons, and when Alec holds the dagger up again, I can see the exposed silver core.

Mikhail presses his hands harder against his gut, as if he could hold the blood in that way, as if it were not already too late. "You won't do it, Alec. You always said you never wanted to be a killer."

"I don't," Alec says. "I'm doing this to save lives, Mikhail. To save Tess, and countless others."

"And to save yourself," Mikhail sneers.

Alec simply considers that before saying, "Yes." Then he plunges the Initiation Blade into Mikhail's heart.

The next moment is terrible. Mikhail groans—a sound that is in its way almost as haunting as the screams of the drowning on the night of April 15. It, too, is the sound of dying. Alec looks stricken, and I embrace him from behind, one arm along the length of his arm, so that the blame for the fatal blow he struck is mine as well.

Then Mikhail falls to the ground, as dead as any other corpse in the room. Alec somehow turns in my arms to embrace me too, and for a long time we can only hold on to each other, unable to believe we have triumphed over the Brotherhood. Over the ice. Over death.

A few hours later, I lie in the bed of a Halifax boardinghouse with flickering light from the fireplace playing over my bare skin, and Alec's.

After defeating Mikhail, we slipped out the back of the rink; I hope the poor men who were waiting out front will forgive me. Mikhail's blood has been mopped up, and he has taken his old place among the corpses. Ragged as Alec looked, we were able to tidy him up enough to pass through the streets of Halifax unnoticed. We found this boardinghouse and took a room—together, though this required a bit of subterfuge.

"Mr. and Mrs. Marlowe," Alec says, as though he read my mind. He lazily traces one finger along my shoulder. "Perhaps soon we can make that come true."

It doesn't surprise me at all; I knew almost from the beginning that something would tie us together forever. But it makes me smile. "Only right that you make an honest woman out of me."

"You're the most honest woman I know. Almost too honest."

"Just because I said you looked like death warmed over when we were trying to clean you up."

"That's one example, yes." But his bare chest shakes with suppressed laughter.

I kiss him, and that silences all laughter for a while.

When at last we part, breathing hard and smiling even more broadly than we were when we began, he says, "I thought I'd have to persuade you."

"To stay with you?"

"The danger hasn't ended because Mikhail's dead." Alec looks grave again. "Sooner or later, the Brotherhood will come after me again. Probably they'll be in Halifax within days, to see if Mikhail survived. They won't appreciate my defiance, or your interference. And I know you well enough to be sure you'll interfere." He means it as a tribute.

"You don't have to persuade me, for the same reason I don't

have to persuade you any longer." I put my hand over his heart. "When the ship was going down—when we thought we had no more time left—I knew how foolish we'd been to hurt ourselves by saying good-bye one moment before we had to. Now the miracle's happened. I have you back again. I won't walk away this time, Alec."

"The same reason." He smiles softly. "It would take more than the Brotherhood to separate me from you again."

I snuggle close to him so that we're pressed together from temple to toe. "Where will we go?"

"I wish we could just stay here. In this room, in this bed, forever." The firelight paints Alec's wild curls a deeper chestnut, almost red. "But you want me to be practical, don't you, Tess? We should go back to Chicago, at least at first. My father's affairs need to be settled. I don't want to take over Marlowe Steel, but I have to decide who I can trust to do it for me. And—I know we can't bury him, but I'd like to have a gravestone for Dad. Something to remember him by."

I squeeze his hand, acknowledging that need, but I have to ask, "Won't people be surprised that you're, well—*alive*?"

"Yes, but it's going to be easy enough to explain. You said the newspaper reports about the *Titanic* come two or three times a day and still contradict each other half the time. We can easily say I was left off the survivor rolls by accident, that I was injured and unable to send a Marconigram until now."

That makes sense. And I like the way Alec says "we," how perfectly understood it is between us that no matter what happens next, we'll be together. Flattening my hand against the broad muscles of his chest, I whisper, "And you're free."

"We might still have to go into hiding." Though his noble guilt no longer forces him to push me away, Alec still feels he must warn me. "The Brotherhood won't let me go easily, even if I walk away from Marlowe Steele. We should do it now, maybe, when they know nothing, but . . . I can't do it to my grandparents, my cousins."

Pretending to be dead is Alec's smartest course, but also the cruelest. He would never take that path. I envision the little cabin on the frontier he once spoke of, but snug and cozy now, not an outpost but a true home with smoke rising from the chimney and curtains on the windows. A garden with vegetables for us and flowers for me—amazing, to think of having my own bit of earth to plant flowers. Alec will no longer live as a wealthy man; I will no longer live as a servant. We'll be equals. Together. "As long as we're together, we'll be all right. You know that, don't you?"

"Except on the night of the full moon."

"One night a month. We can manage that, I know it."

"I hope we can." Though Alec still has doubts—and given all that has happened, he's right to—I don't see the same fatalism in him that I did before. He finally believes he has a chance at a good life. With me.

I say, "Free from the Brotherhood's control, too. We know that now. Mikhail tried it, but it didn't really work. The silver you touched during the initiation saved you."

"It didn't."

I prop myself up on one elbow to stare at Alec. He looks utterly serious, but not dismayed—in fact, the only word for the expression on his face now is joy.

"Mikhail had me," he says. "He had me under his control until the moment he commanded me to kill you—and that was something I could never do. My love for you is what keeps me human, Tess. And it always will."

# *FATEFUL* AUTHOR'S NOTES

ALTHOUGH I RESEARCHED THE *TITANIC* WHILE
conceiving and writing this book, on some points I chose drama
over accuracy. For instance, Myriam would almost certainly have
boarded the ship at Cherbourg rather than Southampton; servants
traveling in third class was so unheard-of that I'm sure Tess's handy
key was unheard-of too; and the *Titanic* had no "seventh officer."
Rather than fictionalize the life of an actual officer aboard the ship,
I chose to invent George Greene and his position onboard. In fact,
I worked around real individuals on the ship as much as possible.
Writing a big paranormal romance set amid a real disaster would
have felt disrespectful if that story were not firmly and totally a fan-
tasy, one that didn't make claims about the behavior, motives, and
culpability of anyone actually onboard. Among the few real-life
passengers named in *Fateful*, only designer Thomas Andrews has
more than a cameo, and that because he really did serve as a kind of
unofficial advisor on White Star journeys due to the trust everyone
had in him, something I wished were better known.

There were some historical points that, despite my research, I could never clarify. Who knew that there were running debates over the placement of the *Titanic*'s kennel—or that I could ever need that information? Where I couldn't find a solid answer, I made my best guess.

Moorcliffe and the Lisles are fictional, but Tess's life as a servant is not exaggerated. Everything from her bad mattress and the frozen water in her morning basin to the lack of electricity and plumbing in the servants' quarters is historically accurate—thanks to my friend Tara O'Shea and her extensive collection of books on life in service in the early twentieth century. My interest in the subject came from the classic TV series *Upstairs, Downstairs*. Sharp-eyed fans of the show will find that the ill-fated Lady Marjorie Bellamy has a brief appearance in *Fateful*.

Among the *Titanic* books I relied upon most were the classic *A Night to Remember* by Walter Lord and *1912 Facts About Titanic* by Lee W. Merideth. I also found invaluable the archives and message boards of the website www.encyclopediatitanica.com, where enthusiasts and survivors' family members have assembled a trove of information about the ship, the wreck, the aftermath, and the era. Any extraordinary bit of accurate detail should be rightly attributed to the research of the enthusiasts who have kept the stories of the ship alive for the past century; any errors are wholly my own.

Finally, I first conceived of this book while visiting the traveling exhibition of *Titanic* artifacts in New York City at the insistence of my friend and *Titanic*-o-phile Jennifer Heddle. On the day I found out we'd sold the book, I was visiting the exhibition again with my friend Naomi Novik. On the day I wrote the final page, I saw it a third time—now in Melbourne, Australia—with my hardworking Australian publicist, Jordan Weaver. Because I indulged Jen's passion for the subject, I got a great idea; because Naomi and Jordan indulged my newfound enthusiasm, I was able to soak up some wonderful details from the recovered artifacts and reconstructed rooms in the exhibit. So thanks are due to all three of them.

# IS BACK

Author of the *New York Times* bestseller STARGAZER

CLAUDIA GRAY

The Evernight story continues with a thrilling new chapter. When Balthazar agrees to help Skye Tierney, a human girl who once attended Evernight Academy, he has no idea how dangerous it will be. Skye's newfound psychic powers have caught the attention of Redgrave, the vampire responsible for murdering Balthazar and his family four centuries ago. Balthazar will do whatever it takes to stop Redgrave and exact long-awaited revenge against his killer.